Readers love
SEAN MICHAEL

Personal Best

"There is something almost magical about the relationship between an athlete and their coach… and Sean Michaels has managed to capture this special aspect of intensely close cooperation.…"
—Rainbow Book Reviews

"Definitely is a book for those who love the combination of sports and explicit sex with love in the air."
—Gay Book Reviews

The Eager Boy

"I love a good second chance book and having one crop up in a series I already enjoy was just a bonus."
—Love Bytes

Daddy, Daddy, and Me

"If you are looking for a light, fluffy, sweet romance that will leave a smile on your face… I definitely recommend this one!"
—Hearts on Fire Reviews

"Beautifully written, not too heavy…. Everything was written with a positive look… and it was good!"
—Diverse Reader

By Sean Michael

Add Love and Mix
Amnesia
Bases Loaded
Cupcakes
Daddy, Daddy, and Me
Daddy Needs a Date
Educating the Professor
First Steps
From the Get Go
Golden
Guarding January
Home and Heart
Inheritance
Just the Right Notes
Making a Splash
Of Love
Out of the Past
Perfect 10
Sports Pack Anthology
The Swag Man Delivers
Unlikely Hero
Unto Us the Time Has Come
X-Factor

DREAMSPUN BEYOND
THE SUPERS
#6 – The Supers
#29 – The Librarian's Ghost

DREAMSPUN DESIRES
THE TEDDY BEAR CLUB
#39 – The Teddy Bear Club

IRON EAGLE GYM
The New Boy
The Perfect Sub
The Luckiest Master
The Closet Boy
The Dom's Way
The Eager Boy
The Gentle Dom

PERSONAL BEST
Personal Best
Personal Best 2

Published by Dreamspinner Press
www.dreamspinnerpress.com

EDUCATING THE PROFESSOR

SEAN MICHAEL

Published by
DREAMSPINNER PRESS

5032 Capital Circle SW, Suite 2, PMB# 279, Tallahassee, FL 32305-7886 USA
www.dreamspinnerpress.com

This is a work of fiction. Names, characters, places, and incidents either are the product of author imagination or are used fictitiously, and any resemblance to actual persons, living or dead, business establishments, events, or locales is entirely coincidental.

Educating the Professor
© 2019 Sean Michael.

Cover Art
© 2019 L.C. Chase.
http://www.lcchase.com
Cover content is for illustrative purposes only and any person depicted on the cover is a model.

All rights reserved. This book is licensed to the original purchaser only. Duplication or distribution via any means is illegal and a violation of international copyright law, subject to criminal prosecution and upon conviction, fines, and/or imprisonment. Any eBook format cannot be legally loaned or given to others. No part of this book may be reproduced or transmitted in any form or by any means, electronic or mechanical, including photocopying, recording, or by any information storage and retrieval system, without the written permission of the Publisher, except where permitted by law. To request permission and all other inquiries, contact Dreamspinner Press, 5032 Capital Circle SW, Suite 2, PMB# 279, Tallahassee, FL 32305-7886, USA, or www.dreamspinnerpress.com.

Trade Paperback ISBN: 978-1-64080-897-3
Digital ISBN: 978-1-64080-896-6
Library of Congress Control Number: 2018944255
Trade Paperback published February 2019
v. 1.0

Printed in the United States of America

This paper meets the requirements of
ANSI/NISO Z39.48-1992 (Permanence of Paper).

Chapter One

"Kenneth? Kenn? Dr. Brannigan!"

Kenn turned on his heel. He'd been crossing the courtyard, entirely focused on his emails. He had to work on the syllabi for next semester's courses, make sure he remembered to grade the papers on post-Civil War industrialism for his 201 class, and write up this semester's midterms.

His office mate and oft-times drinking buddy, Timothy, came jogging up. "You're going to fall in a hole one day, texting while walking."

"I wasn't texting! I was reading."

Timothy chuckled. "Like there's a difference. You know they give you a huge ticket if they catch you doing that while driving."

"Good thing I don't own a car." He'd made it out of Bram's life with not much more than his laptop, his clothes, and his books. "And unless something has changed in the last day, neither do you, so I don't have to worry about borrowing and texting either, butthead."

Timothy's laugh filled the air, making everyone in the crowded courtyard turn and look. That was one of the reasons they'd become friends. Tim's joy was infectious.

"You coming to the Rainbow Mixer tonight?" Tim asked, walking along with Kenn toward the office. "The new student population is yummy, and I'm hoping to see a lot of them at the mixer."

"I have things to do." He could wash his hair, trim his toenails.

"No way." Tim shook his head and grabbed his hand, stopping them just short of the heavy wooden doors to the Wilde Building. "You didn't go last year, but I'm not letting you weasel out of it this year. I'm not asking you to hook up or meet the love of your life or anything. But you need to make more friends, get out, see and be seen."

"You know how I feel about parties, honey." He wasn't damaged or anything, just… not ready to put himself through the meat market again.

"It's a mixer. Show up. Have one drink. Let the kids see you in case some little freshman is nervous about coming out to you, and then we'll go have a slice of cheesecake and a coffee at Alice's."

"Oh...." Alice's apple cinnamon cheesecake was to die for. He'd have to do a hundred extra laps in the pool, but it was worth it.

Tim looked triumphant. "We can even go at eight o'clock—they're never that busy right off the bat. That way by the time it starts getting crowded, we'll be on our way out." Tim opened the door and ushered him in.

"You're a tempter," Kenn said. He shook his head. "You should be ashamed."

"Uh-huh. Fuck off."

They made their way up to their shared office, and Tim turned the sign they'd made for its door to The Professors Are In before they settled in at their respective desks. They worked silently for a while, each focused on what they were doing. Kenn's spreadsheets weren't exactly fascinating, but they had to be done.

"You should wear that bright blue shirt with the baby blue sweater on top of your skinny jeans," Tim suggested out of nowhere.

"I can't just go in this?" *This* was a retro Nine Inch Nails T-shirt and a pair of khakis with boat shoes. He knew he'd have to change, but it was totally worth the tease.

Tim looked appropriately horrified. "Don't make me come home with you and physically dress you."

"I don't think two people would fit in our studios, Tim."

It was a constant joke between them—the house where they both lived right off campus had been broken up into six tiny studio apartments. Thank God Tim lived next door. The pair of TAs who lived in two of the downstairs units slept in one apartment and made the second into a living room.

"Dude, we need to find bigger places." Tim grinned. "Just remember I know where you live, and I'm not letting you weasel out of tonight."

"And you remember that you promised me cheesecake, butthead."

"There will be cheesecake. And I'm going home to start primping. Don't stay here too long because you *are* changing, and you *are* coming."

"Uh-huh. I have a few more spreadsheets and a couple of—"

"I will text you at six thirty, dude."

"Uh-huh."

"I mean it!"

"Okay, okay." Kenn made shooing motions.

Tim's laughter echoed back to him from down the hallway. He'd show up, but it was only for the cheesecake. That was it. Only for the cheesecake and to shut Tim up.

Chapter Two

Dave grabbed his beer and took a sip before wandering away from the bar. He had to give it to the Queer Alliance—they really knew how to decorate for a Rainbow Mixer. It totally looked like a unicorn had barfed all over the place.

His newly self-appointed best friend, Anita, sidled up next to him. "Looks great, doesn't it?"

Given that she was on the event committee, he knew she'd had a hand in the decorations.

"Very colorful," he told her, hoping she didn't press him. He didn't like lying, but he didn't want to hurt her feelings either. He was generally more of a black leather and silver buckle sort of man, but this was… impossible to ignore.

She was happy with his answer, bouncing and kissing his cheek.

He was new to the campus, coming to the university to do his masters, and had found a room with five other TAs who lived in a great big old house—frat style, really. And honestly, he was grateful Anita had latched on to him. She knew everyone and everything about the school. She'd been the one to insist that the mixer was the best way to meet people.

It was certainly well-attended—undergrads and graduate students, along with professors, some of whom had the confident joviality of tenured faculty while others appeared more anxious to please. Impressive.

Anita took hold of his arm and began dragging him around, introducing him to everyone. It was a good thing he had a knack for putting together self-reminders for names and faces because he must have met a hundred people in less than an hour. His beer was long gone, and Anita seemed determined to ensure he met absolutely everyone before letting him go get another.

"Have you met Drs. Brannigan and Parker? They're from the history department."

"My first history profs," he joked. He shook their hands, giving the slender blond a longer smile. Pretty. Very pretty.

"I'm Tim, this is Kenneth." The redhead was bouncy, all kinetic energy. "Anita, you have outdone yourself."

Dave wondered for one brief moment what it would take to tame that vivacity. A little bondage? No, a lot of bondage. But most of his attention remained on the much quieter Kenneth. With this man the trick would be to make him lose control. It could be a delicious challenge.

"Thank you, Dr. Parker," Anita said. "I appreciate it. Do you mind if I leave David here with you? I have to check on the snacks."

"Of course. We'll make sure he doesn't get lost." Tim had a quick smile. "Oh look, Kenn! There's a reporter. Let's go talk to him."

"Go ahead, Tim. I'm not interested in publicity, huh?"

"Oh. Right. I got it. I'll just go and see what's what."

Dave chuckled as the redhead bebopped his way over to the reporter. "If we could bottle that energy...."

"Yes indeed. We all say that twelve times a day."

"I'm sure. So Anita said history. What's your focus? Is that what they call it? Or would specialty make more sense?"

"My focus is North American history, specifically post-industrial and LGBT studies. I also teach western civ."

"Cool. I'm archaeology. I'll be doing my first TA work this year." He was actually a little nervous. It was a sensation he wasn't that used to.

"Ah, I remember those days. I'm sure you'll do fine. Who are you working under? Dr. Jonas?"

"Yeah. She's one of the big reasons why I decided to do my masters here."

"Welcome to campus. It's a good place."

"Thanks." Dave liked Kenneth's quiet voice, and he wanted to engage him in conversation. "You have to tell me where the best pizza joint is. That's always the first place I try to discover."

"Do you like thick or thin?"

The temptation to ask if they were still talking about pizza was huge. Dave went for something not quite as suggestive, but he did let his eyes slowly climb from Kenneth's feet to his face. "I guess it depends what I'm in the mood for."

"If you like thin, then Oscar's is the place. If you like thick crust, Davidos is great."

"Davidos? You know I'm going to have to give a place that's nearly my namesake a try. Especially if they're thick...." He let the sentence trail off, his unspoken "Like me" lingering in the air.

Kenneth's gaze flickered away. "It's decadent. Try the sausage, if that's your thing. It's better than sex."

Interesting. Kenneth had gotten it, Dave thought, but wasn't sure what to do with it. Still, Kenneth had brought up sex, so Dave would run with it. "I love sausage—pun definitely intended. And nothing is better than sex. Of course if you need empirical evidence...."

Kenneth chuckled softly. "I'm not in the market for anything more involved than pizza."

"But you are in the market for pizza. You should come with me to Davidos. Better yet, we'll have one from each back at my place and compare them, see which one is better."

"Did you manage to find an apartment? I know that's the biggest concern around here."

"I'm rooming with a bunch of folks—it's how I met Anita. You'd like it. I'm serious, come see it and eat pizza with me and tell me outrageous stories about the academy." What he really wanted to know more about was Kenneth.

"Oh, I have papers to grade...." Those green eyes were fastened on Dave, though, the interest clear.

"Already? You're a hard taskmaster. On yourself as well as the students." He nudged Kenneth's shoulder. "Come on. Play hooky with me tomorrow evening."

"How about we meet at Davidos for supper? I don't have any evening classes."

Cautious. Dave wondered if there was a story there.

"Sure thing. Six?"

"Six thirty?"

A little pushy too. He kind of liked it. "Six fifteen." They could meet in the middle.

"I can manage that. Uh. Do you have a phone number if I have to cancel or something?"

"I was just thinking we should exchange deets." He pulled out his phone and handed it over.

Kenneth typed in his information. "There you go. Would... would you like another beer or something? Tim and I are supposed to get cheesecake after this, but I can tell he's not ready to go."

"Yeah, sounds good. You want my digits in your phone too?"

"Please." Kenneth handed his phone over, careful not to make contact.

Dave typed in his info and handed it back, knocking their fingers together as he did, absolutely unsurprised at the jolt of electricity that passed between them.

Kenneth was a keeper.

He smiled, letting the phone go. "How about that drink?"

"The bar is over here." Kenneth eased through the crowd, confident but not aggressive.

Dave dropped a step behind so he could check out what he was sure was a lovely ass. Sure enough, that bubble butt was perfectly encased in a tight pair of blue jeans. Yummy. He caught back up by the time they hit the bar. "So what's your poison?"

"I'll have a glass of white, I think."

"One glass of white and a beer, please." He passed over a twenty.

"I can pay for my own."

"You can buy me cheesecake later, and we'll call it even." He could be aggressive too. In fact he was very good at it.

"I... okay. That's fair."

Excellent. This way he could spend more time with the lovely professor. The bartender handed over the drinks, and he passed Kenneth's to him.

Once again, electricity sparked when their fingers touched, and he enjoyed the way Kenneth's nostrils flared. It was definitely not one-sided.

"Thank you. Are you a David or a Dave? And archaeology? What's your area of study?"

"North American studies. And Dave or David. Whatever turns you on. Just not Davie." He wasn't a kid anymore.

"No, you don't read as a Davie." Kenneth sipped his drink, and suddenly David could see Kenneth as Kenny, red bottomed and standing in a corner, kneeling in front of him, bound, head in his lap. Oh, those were pretty thoughts.

His prick took an interest, so he let his thoughts veer elsewhere. He didn't want a raging hard-on, not anywhere as public as where they currently were. "You're a potential Kenny, though."

"No one calls me that. I'm a Kenn."

"Is that what your students call you?" He couldn't see Kenny as anything but Professor Brannigan to the kids.

"Dr. B, for the most part."

"Oh, I like that. Dr. B." He let his tongue roll over it, made it sexy. That was a totally acceptable public name. Kenny could be utterly, perfectly private.

They moved out of the way of the bar, and a young kid—had to be a freshman—came over, looking like he'd gathered up all his courage to approach them.

"Hi. Hi. I'm Wilson."

"Hello, Wilson. I'm Dr. Brannigan. Pleased to meet you." Kenn held one hand out to shake.

The kid took Kenn's hand and shook it, then held on to it. "I'm in three of your classes this semester. You're like, my hero."

Now that was adorable.

"Western civ, North American 101 and…?"

"LGBT studies. I sit in the front every class. Remember me?"

Huh. This had the potential to be something other than adorable.

"Ah, yes. I'm teaching totally new material in that one, and I'm obviously into my notes." Kenn smiled. "This is David. He's teaching archaeology."

Dave shook the guy's hand, squeezing a little harder than necessary. *Back off, kid. You're a baby, and this one's mine.*

Okay, maybe not *his*, but he sure intended to try for it.

"It's my first year here too. Though I'm going for my masters, doing TA work. Seems like a friendly campus, doesn't it? I bet you make a lot of friends, if not here at the mixer, then at the club meetings."

"I hope so. I really do. I…." Wilson looked around. "Have you been to the meetings yet?"

"Nope. Have you, Dr. B?"

"I have not. However, I know some of the board, and they're very nice."

"There you go, kid. Attend the meetings. Meet people, and make sure you have breakfast every day. Most important meal of the day."

Wilson rolled his eyes. "Thanks, Mom."

Dave grinned. *That's right, kid. Nothing here for you—just us old folks.*

"I'll see you in class tomorrow," Kenn said.

Dave waited for Wilson to leave, then asked, "You teach five days a week?"

"I'm teaching three three-times-a-week classes this year, all mornings."

"Busy, busy." He had a hunch Kenn liked to keep himself that way.

"Yes. It's an income. Tenure is getting harder and harder to come by."

"Don't tell me things like that—I'm supposed to be full of hope, still," Dave teased.

"Ah, right. Teaching is lucrative and rewarding, and I don't live in the tiniest place on earth."

"And you have cheesecake on occasion with hot archaeology TAs."

"And nutso history professors that specialize in Tudor—"

The wild redhead in question came running up. "So. Cheesecake? Later? Please? Hot off-duty cop expressing interest."

Kenn chuckled. "Text me so I know you're safe, huh?"

"Best best friend ever. I swear I will bring you bagels between your nine and ten o'clock class." With that Tim gave Kenn a kiss on the cheek and was gone.

"I guess it's just you and me." And Dave couldn't see anything bad in that.

"I suppose, yes. I was going to head over to Alice's Diner. Do you know it?"

"Nope. I haven't had that pleasure yet." He started moving toward the doors.

"It's a few blocks away. I'm surprised you haven't been. It's an institution." Kenn smiled, the expression lighting up his face. "They have an apple cinnamon cheesecake to die for."

"I haven't been in town long enough, I guess. To die for, eh?"

"It's why I'm here. Tim promised to buy me cheesecake."

"And then he bailed on you? Does he do that often?" They went out the door into the night.

"We're neighbors, office mates, and close friends, but we're not lovers. He is totally on the market."

"But he promised you cheesecake."

"He did, and if I'd fussed, he would have changed his plans."

"Well, his loss is my gain."

"If nothing else, I'll introduce you to Alice's."

"Yeah, show me this miracle cheesecake. I need miracle cheesecake in my life." He offered Kenn his arm.

"Oh." That little surprised look made his balls ache. "Thank you. How gallant."

"I like the sound of that. Gallant. Very old-fashioned. It suits you."

"Thank you. I suppose I am."

"The historic history professor. Has a ring to it." He walked along with Kenn, enjoying the evening.

It was cool, but not cold yet in Ontario, and the campus was lovely, classic, like a picture. Dave loved this kind of thing, this ideal-looking slice of life. He loved knowing that all manner of mysteries hid beneath it. That it was never as clean and perfect as it seemed.

Kenneth seemed happy to walk along quietly. They turned down behind the math and engineering building, coming upon a well-lit fifties-style diner with a neon sign blinking Alice's. The place was surprisingly busy, given they were well past the dinner hour.

He opened the door for Kenn and ushered him in. As soon as they crossed the threshold, they were hit by warmth, by the smell of food.

"Dr. B!" A group of young ladies waved at him. "You want to join us? We're sharing the mammoth sundae!"

Mammoth indeed. The vast dessert came with plastic paddles.

"Not this time. You guys have at."

"You're a very popular professor," Dave commented. "I'm going to have to fight for time with you once the semester truly starts."

"You'll find a group of admirers and be busier than you think."

"I'm hoping for one admirer in particular, as it happens."

"Oh?" He was interrupted as the hostess walked up. "Table for two, please."

"Right this way." They followed her to a small booth about halfway down the row next to the window.

Dave sat across from Kenn. The guy really was good-looking.

"They have a huge menu—they're known for breakfasts and desserts."

"But you have a favorite that I need to try." He was totally a believer in recommendations.

"I'm going for the apple cinnamon cheesecake and a cup of coffee."

"That sounds delightful. I'll have coffee with mine too." He liked cheesecake okay; most of all he wanted to taste the thing that Kenn was excited about.

"Good deal." Kenn ordered for them when the waitress came over, then leaned back in the booth. "So this is Alice's. Open 24/7. Incredibly popular. You'll find RPGs, study sessions, bullshit sessions, and love affairs beginning and ending here at all hours."

"I love it. It's been here forever, right? As long as the university's been open?"

"It's been around since the twenties, believe it or not."

"I do. I'll have to look up the history of it. Maybe I'll make it my thesis." He let his foot touch Kenn's.

"I'm not sure that qualifies as old enough for archaeology." Kenn blinked at him, then shifted in his seat.

He slid his foot forward until he reached Kenn's foot again. "That would be part of my thesis—why it does."

"I.... Fascinating." Those eyes were so green.

He held Kenn's gaze. "I hope so. If I can turn the thesis into a book...." He grinned. "I'd be a modern day Indy. Not that he had anything to do with my wanting to become an archaeologist. Not at all...." He'd adored Indiana Jones from the moment he'd seen the beginning of the first movie.

"Yes? Not *Jurassic Park?*"

"Well, technically *Jurassic Park* would be paleontology not archeology. Besides, the first time I saw that movie it scared the shit out of me." He laughed, remembering his older sister being such a shit. "The movie was helped along by some realistic sounding dinosaur noises and hot breath right behind me."

"Have you seen the newest one?" Kenn began to relax visibly as they talked.

"God yes. Owen was the hottest fucking alpha I have ever seen." He might have rewound and watched those parts of the movie over and over. And over.

"I loved it when he said he was the alpha. Too sexy."

"Oh yeah." So Kenn had noticed how hot that was. Excellent. Dave was an alpha himself, and it was always nice to get confirmation that the guy he was with responded well to an alpha.

They chatted about movies, music, and work, and then the cheesecake was there—thick and creamy and decadent.

"Damn." Looking at it made Dave drool, and he was pleased he hadn't finished that second beer—it left more room for this cinnamony dessert. "Well, if it tastes half as good as it looks, it's going to be epic."

"It's going to be epic." Kenn waited for him to take a bite—and he'd have to explore that instinct later—then smiled at his moan.

The cheesecake itself was light and creamy, rather than heavy. The crust was just enough to support it and added cinnamon flavor with the smallest crunch. The caramelized apples on top were the slightest bit tart, which kept the caramel from making the dessert too sweet. Dave savored the bite for a long moment before nodding. He couldn't help but tease a little, though. "Not bad."

"If you don't like it, I'll take it home for breakfast." Looked like Kenneth could tease right back.

"No, no, I think I'll suffer through it." Grinning, he took another forkful. He watched Kenn closely, though. He wanted to see how Kenn looked enjoying something.

Kenn took a bite and closed his eyes, the look purely sexual and deliciously sensual.

Fuck yes. He would take one of those, please. And he didn't mean the cheesecake.

He continued to watch, and when Kenn opened his eyes, Dave smiled right at him, nice and slowly.

"It's good. I indulge myself once a month."

"Nice willpower, keeping it to that." Of course the damn thing had to have about five-million-and-a-half calories in it. "My weakness is poutine." He could eat fries with cheese curds and gravy like it was on the endangered list.

"Mmm. Yes, I can handle some of that, and it's fewer laps in the pool to work off."

"I should have known you were a swimmer. You have the body for it—broad shoulders, lean muscles. I bet you have a hell of a washboard for abs." And Dave wanted to see them. He wanted to do more than see them—he wanted to touch, to caress and stroke.

"I try. I was a competitive swimmer once upon a time."

"Oh, rock on! Did you ever get to the Olympics?" Those guys were amazing. The dedication had to be huge to get to that level.

"God no, but I was on the swim team all through my studies."

"Very nice. I've never really been a sports guy. I mean, I did phys ed all through high school but never went out for the teams. I prefer, uh… more private activities." One didn't just come out and say, "Hi, I'm a Dom. Wanna be my sub?"

"It was more for the scholarship and exercise than a love for the competition. I like to eat, so I need to exercise."

"That takes good discipline. I admire that in a man." That and a whole lot more. Dave touched his foot to Kenn's again, rubbed them together for a moment.

"Thanks. I take it you are one of those lucky bastards who are naturally attractive?"

"I work out to keep my shape, but attractive is about more than just muscles. You, for instance, are very good-looking, and I'm guessing it's not anything you've specifically done." Kenn was a handsome guy, and it had very little to do with how many laps he did on a daily basis.

"I keep myself in shape. Hell, I'm not even available, but I like to be ready."

"You're not?" Dave worked to not show it, and he was pretty sure he was successful, but that took all the wind out of his sails. He liked Kenn, a lot, and there was a ton of potential there.

"No. I—I had a difficult breakup, and I'm not quite ready for the scene yet. For the first year, I didn't even want to make friends, you know?"

For the first year? How long had it been? "I'm sorry to hear that. When did it happen?"

"Three years ago last June."

Three years? Someone needed some damn help getting over his ex. "He must have been a hell of a guy."

"He was…. Let's just say it was brutal and leave it at that, hmm?"

Brutal. That mixed with three years and not ready yet had Dave's mind imagining all sorts of abuse. On impulse, he grabbed Kenn's hand and squeezed. "I really am sorry. If you ever need to talk…."

"Thanks. I'm not suicidal or anything. Just cautious." Kenn didn't pull away from him, though. No. The sweet man held on the tiniest bit too long.

Dave conjectured Kenn was more ready than he realized. He didn't think it was wishful thinking, either. Still, he would go fairly slow and not try to parlay cheesecake at Alice's into sex in his bed. Not this time anyway.

"So, what do you do in your free time, David?"

"I'm a big reader actually. Mostly nonfiction, but I'll go on a tear on various subjects."

"I'd pretend to be surprised, but I'm not."

"Yeah? Most people are." He had the whole "workout alpha male" thing going for him, and not everyone looked past that.

"We're academics. We read."

Dave chuckled and nodded. "Yeah, I can't deny that. What about you? What do you do when you're not teaching or eating cheesecake?"

"I swim, I read, I play a lot of Sudoku."

"Now I know you're smarter than me. I suspected it, but there's the proof." Math had been the bane of his existence. Okay, maybe it hadn't been that bad, but it certainly wasn't something he did for fun.

"It's just to quiet my mind. I'm a bit of a worrywart."

He had a few ideas on how Kenn could quiet his mind. Dave knew better than to suggest it yet to this man who was three years into mourning his breakup.

Kenn's phone jingled, and he glanced down at it. "Tim's okay. Spending the night with the cop he met."

"Good for him, getting lucky." While Dave wished he was going to be getting lucky with the lovely Kenn, at the same time he was pleased at the slower pace. He would need to woo Kenn, earn his attention.

"Indeed." Kenn was only about a third of the way through his dessert. Maybe he wanted to linger as well.

"I bet you have some stories about crazy stunts your students have pulled." He thought the kid who'd all but drooled over Kenn at the mixer gave proof of that.

"The biggest thing you have to watch for is the plagiarism. They find things on the internet and think there's no way you can know."

"I'm planning to run student papers through one of the plagiarism programs online." It was his biggest worry, actually, not catching something.

"That's good. You'll learn too. They all have styles. You'll begin to catch them."

"I never could figure out why people cheated. If someone else writes the paper, you didn't get to learn about the subject. You really only cheat yourself."

"It's all about the grade for a lot of these guys."

"If you do the work...." He chuckled. "Sorry, I don't mean to preach to the choir."

"I know it's hard to understand when you're excited about teaching the subject, but...." Kenn shrugged. "It happens."

"So do you have a regular get-together with other profs to blow off steam over a beer or something?" Dave would bet not. Which worked for him—he wanted that standing date with Kenn. Just the two of them, though.

"Not really, no. I mean, other than Tim. We got to be friends because we share space."

Dave loved the little, barely visible flutter. Loved it. "Well, I think I'm going to need a debrief now and then. I was thinking Friday nights would be good. All I need is someone to debrief with."

"Do you...? I would be willing to until you found someone in your department."

"That would be great. Thank you very much. So can we start tomorrow night?" After all he wanted to see Kenn again, and he had a hunch the guy wasn't going to go out on an actual date with him.

"Well, we are meeting for pizza, so yes." Those green eyes were laughing at him.

"Right, right. But we're going to make it a regular thing, aren't we? You, me, beer, pizza, or some other comestible every Friday?"

"With the understanding that I'll be fine if you change your mind, hmm?"

"I won't, but it's very sweet of you." He supposed it would have been nice to make the same offer, but to be frank, he didn't want to give Kenn the idea this might not be permanent or that Kenn might one day not want to spend time with him.

"Would you like to take a walk after our dessert?"

"I think that would be great." He loved that Kenn wanted to spend more time with him too.

"Cool." Kenn lifted his cup, wordlessly asking the waitress for more coffee.

Dave had the last few bites of his cheesecake and sat back with a satisfied sigh.

"See? You'll be back now. Alice's sucks everyone in."

"What's the dinner here like?" He liked to have an alternative to pizza.

"I like the meatloaf a lot, and the patty melt. Also, the chili is to die for."

"Good to know it's more than just the dessert that rocks." The waitress refilled their cups, and he asked for some water. He'd had enough coffee really. One was enough for him or he'd be awake all night. Besides, the company was more than stimulating enough.

They continued to discuss a variety of topics, talking like they could go all night. Finally Kenn finished his cheesecake and sighed. "We should give them their table and walk off a few calories before bed."

"It's a plan." Dave glanced around. The place was crowded, but there were a few tables free and nobody was waiting, so at least they hadn't held anyone up. Frankly, the place could have been packed to the gills, with two to a chair, and he wouldn't have noticed since he was so wrapped up in his conversation with Kenn.

He left a couple of bills on the table and got up, offering Kenn his hand.

"I said I would pay, David."

"Force of habit." He picked the bills back up. "I'm getting our pizzas tomorrow, though."

"You are?" Kenn paid the tab and left a generous tip, which Dave was pleased to see.

"Yep. You got tonight, and you're doing me a favor by introducing me to pizza tomorrow." They left the restaurant, the air outside cool, refreshing.

"I suppose. What a lovely night."

"Yeah. I was thinking the same thing. So are you gonna show me around the campus?"

"You haven't explored?"

"A little, but I want to know what you think is worth seeing." He offered Kenn his arm, and, to his surprise, Kenn took it.

Smiling wide, he let Kenn guide their steps.

They found the duck pond, the student union, the pool hall right off campus that was just a dive.

The Wilde Building where Dave shared a cramped office with three other TAs. "My so-called office is in this one."

Kenn looked over at him and grinned. "Really? Me too. I'm on the third floor."

So they were close. He liked that. "I'm on the fifth. I'm pretty sure they've put all us bottom-of-the-ladder TAs on the fifth floor so the actual professors don't have to climb so many stairs." There was an elevator, but it looked like it was from the Dark Ages, and he'd yet to see it without an Out of Order sign on it.

"Could be. In fact, I think that's probably completely right."

"I knew the profs got all the perks," he teased, bumping their shoulders together.

"The ones on the tenure track. I'm just a glorified TA."

"You're on the third floor, though. So maybe halfway between TA and tenured prof. Can I see your office?" He bet it would tell him something about Kenn.

"Sure, come on up." Kenn pulled out his keys, unlocked the heavy door, and ushered Dave into the building and up the stairs to the third floor. He unlocked the door to his office and flicked on the lights.

Dave looked around, taking it all in. The room was marginally bigger than the one he shared, though the two big desks that backed each other made it seem smaller. Kenn's chair looked comfortable, the two that sat next to his desk, no doubt for students, far less so. The desk was neat and tidy, almost fastidious, but the shelf with books behind it was crammed full.

The other desk was pure chaos. Papers stacked wildly, coffee cups and pencils and sticky notes everywhere. He didn't have to guess which desk was which.

"Does it drive you nuts having an office mate who's so chaotic?"

"Not at all. We have an agreement. He never interferes with my space; I don't clean his." Kenn smiled at him and sat in his chair, spinning idly. "He's a mess, but he's one hell of a teacher, and he's a good friend."

"That's great. My desk is a cross between yours and his."

"We're all different, huh? My mom would say that's what makes us special."

"Yeah? I like that attitude."

"Have a seat if you want. Or if it's creepy, we can go back outside." Kenn looked so at home sitting in his chair, so in control.

Dave liked the dichotomy—knowing that Kenn was a sub by nature but seeing him in the alpha role of a teacher. "It's not creepy. I was enjoying our walk, though."

"Well, then, let's go. My hours are posted if you need me in here, but my phone is the way to get me normally." Kenn stood up and led him out, then locked the door behind them.

Dave grabbed Kenn's hand, linking their fingers together. Kenn gave him a shocked look but didn't pull away.

Smiling, he led them outside, not letting go. Kenn's hand felt damn good in his.

"So, we're getting close to my place, believe it or not." Kenn pointed to this huge, weird rambling house.

"You said it was tiny!" This wasn't anywhere near small.

"What?" Kenn looked utterly confused.

"Your place. You said it was small. This is, like, the polar opposite."

"Ah." Kenn began to chuckle softly. "Come inside, and all will be revealed."

He was being invited in. Score. "Cool."

Kenn unlocked the front door, and suddenly he got it. There were six mailboxes, a long hall, and stairs leading up. "Oh God. Six apartments?"

"Six apartments."

"Now it makes sense." He followed Kenn up a staircase that had clearly been a grand thing when the house was just a house.

"I'm up here to the left. I didn't know I'd have company, so excuse the mess."

The mess? The apartment was neat as a pin, books stacked floor to ceiling, the bed made. The only thing out of place was the coffee cup on the table.

"It's adorable. Really." He could see Kenn being comfortable here, happy. His bolt-hole, his safe place. David was honored to have been allowed in.

"Thank you. Have a seat, and I'll turn on some lights. Would you like something to drink?" Kenn motioned to an amazing overstuffed armchair upholstered in this insane rainbow fabric.

"Some water would be nice." He sat, the chair so comfortable. "I bet you sleep in this a lot." He could totally picture Kenn curled up, dozing over a book.

"I do. It's a great chair."

The light in the kitchen came on, and he got a glimpse of the room—clean and neat but tiny, with a half-sized refrigerator.

The studio was small, compact, but it totally suited Kenn. "I like it. The whole place."

"Thanks. It's miniscule, but you can't beat the location. Tim lives next door."

"I assume his place is just as tiny?" He was trying to decide if he would rather live in such a small place or share like he did.

"They're all exactly the same, really. Except I have a balcony, and he has a washer and dryer."

"So you guys share." He didn't need Kenn's nod to confirm it—he just knew.

Kenn brought over the water, and he deliberately slid their fingers together as he accepted the glass, biting back his moan at the tingling sensations. Kenn licked his lips, eyes moving over him, drinking him in.

Dave didn't vamp or lick his own lips or anything. He was himself, knowing that was what was going to win Kenn over, and he was proved right when Kenn shook himself and turned to sit on one of the two dining chairs.

"There might be enough room for us to share this chair. Then you'd be on a comfortable seat." He gave Kenn his best innocent look, but he bet Kenn knew as well as he did that innocent was the last thing he was.

"It's not that big, but thanks for the offer."

"Anytime." He meant it too. His lap would love to double as a chair for Kenn. The thought had him grinning, beaming at Kenn.

"I think you're the first guy I've had in here who wasn't Tim. We tend to have any parties in the common room downstairs."

"You'd kind of have to have them somewhere else. It feels cozy with the two of us—too many more and it would feel crowded." He loved knowing that he was the only other person aside from Kenn's best friend who'd seen the place, who'd had the privilege.

"Exactly. Two isn't too bad, but a dinner party is excessive. The common room is nice, and so far all the tenants have been exceptional."

"Are you all part of the queer community?" Dave imagined that would make getting along easier.

"It's not a requirement, of course, but yes." Kenn leaned back, stretching tall. "There are six apartments and the common area. Tim is next door. Jean and Beth are downstairs—they have two apartments, and they sleep in one and use the other as a living room. Doug lives downstairs too. He's the owner. Sweet kid who inherited the property. The other upstairs unit is empty."

Interesting. Especially if it turned out he needed the privacy that the setup where he was didn't afford.

"Is it as big as this one?" he teased. He wanted to know, though, how big it was. Just in case.

"Bigger, actually. It's got two rooms. I would have rented it, but it was occupied when I moved in, and now...." Kenn shrugged, eyes lit up and dancing. "Look at all these books. Who would want to move them?"

"They'd definitely be a pain in the ass, but I bet you'd find people willing to help. For the right incentive." He looked around again, taking it all in. "This suits you, though. Feels like you belong here."

Kenn nodded, and the sweet smile grew. "I like it. I'm happy here, and that's something to hold on to."

"Absolutely. Have you got a TV?" Dave looked around. He loved snuggling in front of the television.

"I don't. I watch everything on my laptop or my iPad. I keep talking about buying a smart TV, but I don't know where I'd put it."

"We have a huge shared one at the house. But I have a decent-sized one in the bedroom. I like being able to laze while I watch." He could picture him and Kenn nestled together in front of some show or other. It was kind of a test—if he could cuddle and watch with someone, they were good.

"So how does your situation work?" Kenn asked.

"There's four bedrooms upstairs along with a bathroom that we share. There's a master bath too, in Jenny's room. If we're in a bind, she's pretty good about letting us pop in. Then downstairs is a huge kitchen and a living room, along with two small rooms that are set up as offices so we can study or work or whatever. We share rent and utilities and stuff."

"Very cool. I'm afraid that I'm too much of an introvert for that situation. It sounds fun, though."

"It was the most room for the money. I saw a few apartments that were smaller than this for more money than the house was. I mean, I want more than a fridge and a hotpot and a bathroom I can't even stand up in."

"I can understand that, David. I'm a bit of a privacy whore."

What an interesting way to put it.

"And you've let me invade your privacy. Thank you." The truth was, he'd spent the whole evening with Kenn, and now he wanted to invade a lot more than the man's privacy.

Still, Kenn seemed different, special enough to take his time with. He didn't want to leave yet, though. He wanted to stay and spend more time with this intriguing guy.

"What's your favorite thing about teaching?"

"Seeing someone figure out that history isn't just dates and names that you have to recite back. That it's vitally important to see the patterns in what we do, in who we are as a society. History isn't a dead thing, but a living energy, and we must learn or we're doomed to repeat it."

Oh, he could see how students would enjoy taking one of Dr. B's classes. Look at that sudden, wonderful passion.

"You make me want to audit," he admitted. He was a bit of a history buff anyway—it went hand in hand with archaeology. "Our subjects make good bedfellows."

"They do. What about you? What's your passion?"

"My mom would tell you I just love digging in the dirt. She wouldn't really be wrong, either. I find it fascinating how the stuff we leave behind tells a story. I love knowing that it isn't the whole story, either, that any picture I might make from the things I find could be totally wrong."

"History is written by the victor, isn't it?"

"I like to think those of us who dig pieces of it up get a say too." He loved talking with Kenn, loved having real conversations that had nothing to do with a ball game or the latest video-game craze.

They began debating everything on earth—mummies and carpetbaggers, child labor and Aztec rituals. At some point Kenn removed his shoes and his sweater, moving to sit on the bed.

Dave got himself another glass of water, pouring one for Kenn as well, and they got right back to it. His ass was happily planted, and he couldn't remember being in better company.

It was the light creeping in through the window that alerted him to the time, and he looked at his watch. "Shit. It's morning." The last time he'd been awake all night he'd been cramming for exams.

"Lord. I have a nine o'clock and a ten o'clock to teach."

"And I've got office hours at eight!" That seemed like a stupid idea now. "Hopefully I'll have time to shower when I get home." He laughed. "You're something else, Kenn."

"You'll have to have a long nap this afternoon, huh? At least it's Friday...."

"Yeah. And I will have a long nap this afternoon. I want to be bright and fresh tonight."

"If you decide to cancel, I'll understand. It'll be a disappointment, but I'll totally understand."

Knowing that Kenn would be disappointed if they didn't meet up tonight made him happy deep inside. He grinned. "I won't cancel."

He wanted to give Kenn a kiss goodbye, but with him standing and Kenn on the bed....

"I'll see you tonight, then." Kenn unfolded himself from the bed.

"Yeah. I'm looking forward to it." He cupped Kenn's cheek and pressed their lips together, but he kept the kiss quick before turning to go. "Meet you at Davidos at six fifteen."

"I'll be there. Have a good day, David."

"You too. Mine's gonna be great. Started out that way anyway." He headed out, grinning like the proverbial fool. He couldn't have wiped the smile of his face if he'd tried, and he didn't have any desire to try.

Chapter Three

"You spent the night with him?" Tim's eyes were wide. "He's just a baby!"

"One, we're of an age. Two, we talked all night, that's all. Three, why are you in my apartment again?"

"Because I covered office hours for you while you slept, dude. Talk!"

"He's nice. We have a lot in common. That's all." Kenn rubbed his eyes, still feeling a little drugged after his sleepless night. He'd faked his way through two classes, thank God. Tim had covered for him when he'd napped away his office hours, and now he had to get ready for his date. No, not a date. They were going to sample pizza—that was it.

"Oh, please, up all night? And all I get is 'he's nice and we have a lot in common'?"

"Tell me about the cop."

"Married with children." Tim rolled his eyes.

"Oh God." Tim had the worst luck.

"He was a good lay until he started panicking about getting home and making sure he didn't stink of 'manlove.' His words, not mine. Maybe I should start going for the last guy in the room I normally would. Maybe that'll turn things around."

"I'm sorry, honey. Seriously. That really sucks." He scooted to the edge of the bed, reaching out for his best friend.

"Oh, he wasn't all that good in bed anyway." Tim grinned at him. "The handcuffs were fun, though."

"Tim!" He cracked up, stood and went to the refrigerator. "You want a Coke?"

"Don't you have a date to get to?" Tim asked, nonetheless holding out his hand for the aforementioned soft drink.

"I have an hour. Do you want to come?"

"On your date? Three's a crowd, honey. Especially with someone who you spent the whole night with." Tim opened the can Kenn had handed over and sucked half of it down. "I'm not heartbroken about last night, honey. I got an orgasm that wasn't by my own hand. How about you?"

"Tim, don't be crass." He shook his head.

"Maybe if you play your cards right tonight, you'll get laid too. It's crazy how past due you are."

"Shut up, Tim. I'm fine."

"You're a monk! It's not natural." Tim drank the rest of his Coke and bounced up, began wandering around Kenn's little place.

"I'm looking for friendship, Tim. That's it."

"I'm not trying to be an asshole, but isn't that lonely?"

"Sometimes." But that was okay. Lonely was better than miserable.

Tim came over to him and wrapped him in a tight hug.

Kenn leaned in, rested for a second. "Why couldn't we be a love match, honey?"

"You wouldn't believe me if I told you."

"What?" He laughed. "What is that supposed to mean?"

"What are you wearing?"

"Huh?"

"On your date. What are you wearing?"

He shrugged. "Jeans? It's just pizza." It wasn't really a date anyway. It was two guys with a lot in common trying out pizza joints.

"At least wear something bright and wonderful on top." Tim began going through his clothes. "God, you have some great shirts."

"I like the unusual ones."

"Oh, this one will bring out your eyes." Tim handed him an emerald-green number from Bali.

"It's not too much?" He tugged it on, the soft fabric making him feel oddly sensual.

"It's perfect." Tim stood back, admiring.

"You're sure?"

"Positive." Tim walked around behind him. "You're lovely. Now, do you want me to walk you there?"

"Sure, absolutely. Come on."

"You are not wearing those awful sandals. Wear the deck shoes."

"Those 'awful' sandals happen to be the most comfortable shoes I own."

Tim crossed his arms and stared Kenn down.

"You're so queer, Tim."

"You think, butthead?" Tim pointed. "Put the Dockers on and let's go."

Kenn checked his hair, put in an emerald stud earring to match his shirt, and splashed on some cologne. "Ready."

"You're still wearing the wrong footwear. So much for ready. Change them."

"You—"

"Do it."

Tim was the most stubborn man. And his best friend, always looking to help him.

"Why do I put up with your ass?" He changed shoes and grabbed his keys and his wallet.

"Because you love me." Tim put his hands in his pockets, rocked back on his heels, and headed out.

"I adore you. What are you up to this weekend?"

Tim shrugged as they headed down the stairs. "I was thinking about checking out that new gay bar, the Rainbow Cup."

"Looking to get laid again so soon?"

"I keep hoping one of them's going to be good for more than one night."

He chuckled, but he worried. "Be safe, huh? Seriously."

"I'll call you every night at ten, Mom."

"Okay." As much as they teased, Kenn knew Tim loved having someone there for him.

"You're the one who should call me tonight. Let me know that you're okay. Hopefully let me know that you're getting laid." Tim was starting to sound like a broken record.

"You're obsessed with my sex life."

"You do know it stops working if you stop using it, right?"

He had to laugh. Had to. "Just because I'm not getting laid doesn't mean I'm not using it."

"Nope. Choking your own chicken doesn't count."

"It does too! An orgasm is an orgasm." Wasn't it?

"Nope. Solos are not the same as getting laid."

"Are we really debating this?"

Tim laughed. "It seems like we are."

The conversation had taken them to the corner nearest the pizza place and David, who was waiting there. "What are you debating?" he asked as he joined them, walking beside them.

"Whether or not solo orgasms count as much as getting laid," Tim said.

Kenn glared. "Tim!"

David chuckled as they reached Davidos. "Pleasure is pleasure, right?"

"There you go. Goodbye, Tim. Call me tonight and check in." Butthole.

"Ditto!" Tim gave him a shit-eating grin and mouthed, *He's hot!* before splitting off and heading toward town.

"David, hi. Did you get some rest?" He hoped so. He sure had crashed and burned.

"Yeah, I went home after my office hours and slept until about ten minutes ago." David laughed, holding the door to the pizzeria open for him.

"Excellent. Tim took my office hours so I could rest." He'd have to work this weekend, but it would be worth it.

Once he went in, he let David take the lead and followed in his wake. It afforded him the opportunity to admire the guy. A fair bit taller than he was, David's muscles were nicely shown off in a tight blue T-shirt that made his eyes seem even bluer. The short brown hair had that just-out-of-bed quality.

"This okay?" David asked, choosing a table by the windows in the corner.

"Perfect." Kenn sat, inhaling the spicy scent that filled the air. He hadn't even known he was hungry until then.

"Now I'm glad I didn't get anything to eat all day." David looked around, checking the place out. "You have any recommendations?"

"I like the sausage and onion."

"Cool." David glanced at the menu. "I'm going to get the fully loaded baked-potato pizza, minus the bacon."

"You don't eat bacon?"

"No, I don't. I'm vegetarian, actually."

"Oh? Good to know." So, no sausage breath for him. That just seemed rude.

"I'm not preachy about it, though. I don't push it down anyone's throat, and I have no problem with you eating meat."

"Cool." Still. He'd have a… well, he'd just have a cheese pizza, he guessed.

"So how were your classes?" David asked. "Did you manage to be coherent?"

"I have no idea. I sure hope so." He'd been a total zombie.

David chuckled softly. "Well, you look great tonight." His gaze was warm as it swept over Kenn.

"Thanks. Tim picked the shirt."

"But you're the one wearing it so well. It makes your eyes pop."

Kenn chuckled, telling himself that a little harmless flirting was just that. A little harmless flirting. "Thank you."

"No, thank *you*. Everyone is jealous of me." There was no guile in David's voice—he clearly meant what he said.

"I seriously doubt that, but I appreciate the thought." Lord, he was falling for these lines? Honestly?

David shrugged. "You don't have to believe it, but I do. Hey, I wanted to thank you again for last night—or should I say this morning? Both?" David laughed, the sound charming. "I had the best time talking with you."

"I did too. Seriously. Time simply disappeared." And his time was precious.

"I know!" David's face lit up. "I liked it."

A waiter came to their table. "Hey, welcome to Davidos Pizzeria. Can I get you something to drink?"

David looked over at him, clearly letting him go first. It was very chivalrous.

"I'll take a Coke, please."

"Yeah, me too. And we'd like to share the garlic cheese bread, please." David shot him a grin. "If I'm having something garlicky, you need to join me."

"Do I? That way we can both have dragon breath?" David was adorable, honestly, and Kenn found himself nodding. "Sounds good."

"Dragon breath?" David laughed. "I've never heard it called that before—I like it."

The waiter chuckled. "So do you know what else you want, or should I just put the drinks and app in?"

"I think we both know. I'm having the loaded potato without the bacon, please."

"I'll go with two slices of cheese pizza." He'd never tried the plain cheese, and if he didn't like it, he could order himself something else tonight.

"Okay. I'll get your order in. The garlic bread and drinks'll be right up."

"Thanks." David was polite, but clearly his attention was on Kenn and not the waiter. "So, plain cheese? I don't know why, but I saw you having something spicier."

"Just a whim." He had been a little blindsided by the vegetarian thing, so he'd panicked and ordered the only thing he could think of.

A dull headache started up between his eyes, mostly from lack of sleep, he'd bet.

"You're not avoiding meat because of me, are you?"

"I don't want to make you uncomfortable. I love cheese."

"That's really sweet of you, but being vegetarian is totally my choice. If you want to give it a go, cool, and I'd be happy to help you out, but it's totally not necessary for us to keep seeing each other."

"Well, I would hope not." He was being polite more than anything. Maybe… maybe he was pondering a good-night kiss.

"Okay. I just wanted to make sure you knew that. What with the cheese pizza and all." David gave him a wry grin. "Food was an issue when I was growing up. My mother showed her love by feeding us, but my father accused all of us of being fat slobs most of our younger years, and my sister wound up bulimic. Part of my going veggie was to support her in a more positive way to control her eating. It worked too. She came back from seventy-eight pounds to a hundred and twenty-three."

"Good for her! Recovery is hard work."

"It is. You sound like you're speaking from experience…."

Kenn smiled but didn't respond. He wasn't going to talk about that—about his childhood or about his last relationship. Neither of them had been easy, and they were both over. Hell, he and his mom did fine these days.

Luckily the drinks came, along with the bread.

"Oh, this smells amazing." David grabbed a piece of cheesy garlic bread. It crunched as he bit into it.

Kenn took a bite, humming at the buttery goodness. Okay. Yummy.

"I have to tell you, this is a positive sign for how good the rest of the food is going to be." David took another bite.

"It's delicious. Nice and hearty."

"And garlic forward without hitting that burny, too-garlicky point." David licked one of his fingers, then sucked it into his mouth. He pulled it out with a pop.

Don't look. Don't. Wow. Damn.

"I do love a good garlic bread." David grabbed another piece, munching happily.

"I can tell." Kenn laughed and finished his piece, allowing David to have the lion's share.

"Sorry, I've had most of this. I didn't mean to pig out—it's just so good."

"No worries. I have pizza coming." He loved watching David eat, weirdly enough.

"Me too, only I have a whole personal pie coming. I didn't realize you could just get a couple pieces." Dave shrugged. "I'll probably have no problem eating the whole thing, though. Hey, maybe you can introduce me to your pool and I can join you working it off."

"Sure. I use the campus pool. You can get access. I'll have to try a bite of your pizza, see how it is."

"You can have a whole piece. It sounds yummy, doesn't it?"

"It does, yes." It would probably be better with bacon, though....

As if on cue, their pizzas arrived, and they looked even better than he remembered. David rubbed his hands together, looking eager.

Kenn added an ample amount of red pepper flakes to make up for the spice the sausage would have added and dug in. The pizza wasn't bad—it wasn't what he was used to, but it wasn't bad.

David examined his pizza, sniffed it, checked the bottom. When he caught Kenn watching, he grinned. "If I'm comparing with the other place, I need to make sure I check out every aspect of it."

"You're very thorough."

David tilted his head, then smiled and nodded. "Yeah, I totally am. It's mostly a good thing."

"Mostly?" he teased.

"It can be a bit of a monkey on my back now and then. Projects, papers, and exams for example." David licked his lips and took his first bite. "Oh. Oh yeah." He hummed and chewed at the same time, looking so pleased.

"You are a sensual man." No one had ever accused Kenn of that, for sure. No one at all.

"Me? Yeah, I suppose." David met his eyes. "I think everyone is, given a chance."

"You think so? I think it's fairly rare."

"Maybe it's a matter of making the effort to engage all your senses?" David shrugged. "I don't know—I'm not a psych major."

"Me either. I'm a dry, dusty history professor." He laughed at himself and took another bite.

"You don't seem dry or dusty to me, Kenn. Not one bit."

"Good. That's good to hear. Honestly."

"Trust me, I wouldn't have lost track of time and spent the entire night talking with you. I find you… fascinating."

Him? No one felt that way about someone like him.

Still smiling and watching him, David began to eat his slice in earnest. He grabbed one of the slices from his pie and put it on Kenn's plate.

"Are you sure?"

"Absolutely. I want to share it with you because it's pretty amazing."

"Well, thank you." He picked up the piece, surprised to find that the bite was flavorful, savory, almost rich.

David had stopped eating in favor of watching him try the slice, and he beamed at Kenn's reaction. "See? Delicious!"

"It's not bad at all." He went for playful and teasing.

"A master of understatement," David noted.

"Now that has been said about me before."

"I'm not surprised." David touched his foot like he had the night before.

They ate and chatted, laughing at each other's bad jokes. It was easy to be with David. Easy and a little bit exciting. Kenn felt awake, alive. Which, given his sleepless night, was amazing.

After they'd finished their pizzas, David gave him a wink. "So is dessert worth it here?"

"I've never tried it. I always go take a walk and get ice cream."

"That sounds delicious. It really does." David pulled his wallet out and set some bills on the table.

"Good. I'll buy dessert, then."

"Works for me. But you need to agree to take me to the other pizza place tomorrow night." David gave him a winning smile.

"You don't have other plans? An attractive guy like you?" He found that hard to believe.

"I have plans with you."

Oh. Oh, okay. That was the sweetest thing anyone had said to him in an eon.

David leaned in and kissed the corner of his mouth. "Come on. Take me for ice cream."

"It would be my pleasure." They walked down the road. It was a busy area—bars and coffee shops, bookstores and internet cafes.

"I do love a university town," David noted, grabbing Kenn's hand and twining their fingers together.

"Yes. It's so alive, isn't it?"

"It is. I bet summers are pretty quiet, though." David moved to the left and tugged him out of the way of a skateboarder.

"Thank you! And yes, it's like heaven." He forced himself not to snarl about the skateboarder. He didn't want to come off as old and stodgy.

David moved him to the other side of the sidewalk and grabbed his other hand, putting him on the building side. The simple act warmed him all the way to his bones.

They didn't say much as they walked, although every now and then one of them would point out a decoration in one of the storefronts or the way lights twinkled around a restaurant patio. It was always a pleasant walk, but with David, it was even better. Kenn kept reminding himself not to be too involved, to keep his distance. This was a friendship, not a love match.

If it continued as it was going, though, it would be an epic friendship.

They got to the little ice cream shop, a tiny wooden house-shaped building crammed between a restaurant and a bakery. The guys who ran it made the ice cream themselves, and it never once disappointed.

"Oh, this is cute." David went right up to the board to check out the flavors listed there.

"It is. Hey, James. Mike. How's it going?"

Mike grinned over. "Super busy. Yay Friday! You want cherry nut?"

"Please."

"And your friend?" Mike asked.

"This is David, he's an archaeology TA, and he's new to town, so I'm showing him around."

Mike beamed. "And Two Scoops of Cream is on your tour—that's awesome."

"Nice to meet you." David pointed at the board. "I'd like the key lime on a plain cone, please."

"You got it."

Kenn grabbed a bottle of water and paid for the drink and the sweets. "Ice cream always makes me thirsty."

David nodded. "All sweet things make me thirsty. I think that's why coffee or tea go so well with cakes."

They sat at one of the little tables for two scattered in front of the ice cream stall, David dragging his chair around to sit next to Kenn instead of across from him.

They ate their ice cream, lapping the creamy sweet. He'd not considered how weirdly erotic it was—licking, watching David lick.

"This is really good." David ran his tongue all around the bottom of the scoop, catching drips.

"They do a good job." Christ. Stop being a perv.

"Yeah, they do." David smiled at him, the look in his eyes warm as David watched him.

"You want a bite of mine?"

"Only if you'll have a bite of mine too." David held his cone up to Kenn's lips. "It tastes just like a key lime pie."

"Interesting…." He opened up, dragging his tongue through the bright treat.

David groaned and leaned in. "God, you're sexy."

He looked up, meeting David's sky blue eyes. David held his gaze until their lips touched.

Kenn gasped, caught for a moment between jerking back and pressing closer.

David hummed softly, his eyes closing before he pressed their lips together with more intent. Kenn's lips tingled, a light buzz zipping along his skin where it touched David's. He moaned, and that was the sound that had him drawing back, breaking the contact.

David's eyes fluttered open, and he took a deep breath. "Okay. Wow." Then David touched Kenn's lower lip, another of those jolts of electricity sparking between them. David's eyes went wider.

"I...." He wasn't interested in dating. He wasn't ready for another relationship.

"Shh. It was just a kiss." Even as David said it, the look in his eyes belied it.

"Right. It didn't mean...." Well, he couldn't say it meant "nothing," because that was crass.

"It meant more than either of us expected." David didn't try to kiss him again, though. "I don't expect you to put out just because I bought you a couple slices of pizza. You're already too good a friend, and besides, that's not the kind of guy I am."

"And I don't put out, so you would be disappointed."

"But I'm not expecting anything, so I won't be." David took another lick of his ice cream, tongue lingering on the sweet treat.

"Fair enough." Kenn nibbled on a cherry from his cone. David was watching him, the gaze heavy now that they'd kissed. "So, what are you up to this weekend?" Small talk. Small talk was good.

"Well, we're supposed to check out the other pizza joint tomorrow evening, right? And if you'd be willing to show me the ropes at the pool, I'd love to get a few laps in."

"I am, sure. Absolutely. I go every Saturday at 6:00 a.m. I know it's early, but I don't want to interfere with the swim team."

"Okay, six it is. No up all night talking for us tonight. Unless we go from talking to swimming and then sleep the day away."

"That was fun, wasn't it? I didn't even know all that time was passing."

"It was great. I love being able to sink into a discussion with someone and not worry that they're going to think I'm attacking them if we happen to disagree on anything. It was a great night."

"It was. Honestly." He nodded, then jumped as melted ice cream spilled over his fingers. "Dammit!"

"I could lick them clean for you," David offered.

"Be good, you turkey," he answered.

"Turkey!" David cackled and handed him a couple of paper napkins.

"Thank you." God, he hadn't had so much fun in ages.

David began to gobble. Loudly.

Kenn cracked up, the sound tickling the fuck out of him.

David looked pleased—and utterly unconcerned that everyone had heard him. It spoke to David's confidence, how secure he was, how easy in his skin.

David settled back into his chair and licked at his cone again, working to get all the drippy places that had melted while he'd been doing things other than eating ice cream.

"Dr. B? Hey, how's it going?" One of the young ladies Kenn had taught last year was passing by with friends. She waved, then stopped, grinning at him, and he hoped he could fake not knowing her name.

"Good. Good. Busy as always. You?"

"Starting to get into the swing of it, yeah. I wish I was in one of yours this semester."

"I'll be teaching some 300 levels next year. Look for them."

"That's great. You're hard, but fair, and your courses are fascinating."

"I appreciate it. You ladies have a good evening, hmm?" Go on. Shoo.

"You too, Dr. B." She looked over at David, gave him a warm smile, and she and her friends continued on their way.

"You totally don't remember her name."

"Huh?" He went for innocent.

"That girl—you might recognize her from one of your classes, but you haven't a clue beyond that who she is."

Don't blush. Don't blush. "Nonsense. I'm sure she has a name."

David chuckled. "Uh-huh."

"Shut up. I'm terrible with names. Always."

"I'm just teasing you. How many kids do you see a semester?"

"Tons. The freshman classes are huge, you know?"

"I know. You can't be expected to remember thousands of names every year. Not unless they're noteworthy." David waggled his eyebrows up and down suggestively.

"Or if they're a friend's name, not a student's."

"You gonna remember all the Davids this year?"

"I'll remember you." He had no doubt about that.

"I sure hope so!" David looked affronted, but a smile broke through the mask. "I'm not easy to forget."

"No. No, you aren't. I imagine you'll be so busy soon that I'll hardly ever get on your social calendar."

"I will make room for you, Kenn. No matter how crazy marking gets, or midterms or whatever, I'm going to make time for you."

Oh. His heart fluttered. Genuinely fluttered. "Thank you."

"I've never met anyone like you before, and I know to hold on to a good thing when I find it."

"I...." Kenn didn't know how to respond. He didn't know what to say.

"You wanna get out of here? I could show you my room, since you showed me yours."

He shouldn't. He should beg off and go home. It was the most logical decision. "Sounds good to me."

"Good. The place should be pretty quiet tonight. It's Friday, after all." David stood and held out a hand to hm.

"Do your roommates like to party?" He took the hand, hauled himself up.

Their bodies came close, and he could feel the warmth pouring from David.

"Some of them are party people, yeah. But the rule is no parties at home, so they have to go out for any shenanigans."

"That's nice for you if you need to study, huh?"

"Yeah. It's a pretty old house, and I think the owner wants to make sure the place doesn't get trashed."

The walked along, David still holding his hand.

"How did you find it?"

"Kijiji."

"Ki-what?"

"Kijiji—the place to list things. Like craigslist?"

"Ah." Sometimes he felt like he was getting old.

"You can find anything on there. Even jobs. It's kind of crazy."

"Rock on." Did people still say that?

They walked along, turning into the residential area to the east of the campus. The houses here were old and large and converted into apartments like his own. Quite a few were still one dwelling, though.

David turned up a path to an old, dilapidated house that was all the more charming for its need of repairs. It had character.

"This is fabulous." He would love to take a big old house like this and renovate it one day.

"Isn't it? You've got to see the interior." They went in, and the place was warm inside. Warm—that was the best way to describe it. The wood might be worn instead of polished, but it looked lived-in rather than shabby. The furniture looked like it belonged too. Eclectic but solid.

"So down here is all common area. The rooms are upstairs. Did you want anything out of the kitchen, a drink or something before we go up?"

"No. No, I'm fine, thank you."

"Okay. I've got a tiny fridge with drinks in case you get thirsty." David led him up an amazing staircase. About four feet wide, it wound its way upstairs, the wood handrail gleaming.

They went into the second door on the right. It was about two-thirds the size of Kenn's entire apartment, with a large bed against the back wall and a cushioned window seat that looked like the perfect perch for reading. Speaking of reading, there were stacks of books everywhere. The place wasn't a disaster, but it wasn't neat, either.

Someone needed a maid. He chuckled. Not everyone was a neat freak.

"Why don't we sit on the bed? That's not a come-on. It's the most comfortable place to sit."

"I'd love to." Kenn sat gingerly, trying not to be self-conscious.

David put a couple of pillows against the headboard and leaned against them. He put two more pillows on the other side and patted the space beside him. "Come sit back—you can't be comfortable perched on the edge like that."

"Are you sure?" He moved up and settled next to David, finding it surprisingly cozy.

"See?" David grinned at him, looking at ease and happy. Looking hot, really.

"Yes, I see." He probably looked like a monkey, smiling back like he didn't have a thought in his head.

David leaned in but stopped shy of pressing their lips together. "I want to kiss you again."

"Do you? Is that wise?" He wanted it too.

"Honestly? I don't care if it is or not." David closed the last scant inch between them, and his lips were warm and soft as they moved gently against Kenn's.

He reached out and let his hand rest on David's thigh, finding it muscled, solid. David hummed in response, lips continuing to glide against his, making his skin tingle. Kenn sighed and relaxed, letting himself enjoy it for a moment.

David closed his eyes, pressing their lips together a little bit harder. There was a promise in those kisses. A promise of more, of pleasure and joy.

You don't have love affairs, Kenneth. He had to remind himself of that. He was too needy, too apt to cling, and no one wanted that.

David brought his hand up, cupped his cheek. It was so warm, the touch so gentle. Oh. Oh, he leaned into those fingers and moaned.

At the sound, David slid his tongue along Kenn's lips, the touch almost ghostlike. Kenn's lips parted like they had a mind of their own, the slick caress near perfect.

David didn't try to shove his tongue deep or make gross noises or anything. The delicate caress of David's mouth was just enough to cause more tingles, to feel super intimate.

To show Kenn that David cared.

David pulled back slowly, eyes opening, gaze finding Kenn's. Smiling, David rubbed their noses together. "I could become addicted to kissing you."

"That would be dangerous, wouldn't it?" He wasn't going to fall in love, wasn't going to lose himself.

"Dangerous?" David frowned, tilted his head. "Kissing you? I don't think so at all."

"No? I think kissing *you* might be."

"Nonsense." David leaned in and kissed him again.

This time he opened up when David begged entrance. David slipped his tongue in, sweeping gently through his mouth before touching Kenn's tongue, sliding along it.

Kenn inhaled, his eyes crossing as heat began to build inside him. David nibbled on his lower lip, teeth not scraping, not hurting, only making him feel. His nipples tightened, along with his ball sac, and he told himself to relax, to let it go and chill.

More kisses followed, each one different except for how they all made him feel like he was the center of David's world.

A voice inside him insisted that this was a terrible idea, that he shouldn't do this, but he ignored it. For now. For a few more kisses.

David didn't try to do anything else, didn't draw him closer or roll on top of him. It was simply the kisses. Of course, simple was a misnomer. They were amazing and wonderful. Arousing. Not simple at all.

Together they sank onto the sheets, sliding down until they were lying flat, face-to-face, exchanging kisses. It felt like they could do this all night long.

The lamplight drew fascinating shapes on David's face, making him look like an otherworldly being. His long lashes rested on his cheeks, the closed eyes making it seem like David was concentrating 100 percent on Kenn.

He smiled, tracing David's jawline with one finger. David hummed, the sound pushing into his mouth and filling him.

"I should go. I'm sure it's getting late." He didn't want to, though.

"It's the weekend, right? We can stay up as late as we want."

"You make a good argument."

"I'm extremely motivated." David gave him another kiss, and it was sweet, delicious even, and he let it go. He wanted this, badly. More than coffee on a Monday morning.

David didn't say anything else, just continued to kiss him. Kenn lost track of time, of everything around them. All that existed were the kisses David kept pressing on him.

His cock was hard, but he wasn't moved to anything more. He could stay right here.

David seemed to be in the same mind frame, not trying anything with him. The focus was on the kisses. Totally on them.

By the time they pulled apart, Kenn's lips felt swollen and heated. David smiled at him, eyes warm, aroused, but still David didn't push him or try for more.

"Wow." Very articulate, Dr. Brannigan.

David didn't seem to mind, grinning at him and rubbing their noses together. "I totally agree."

"Good, because otherwise…."

"It would suck." David slid his fingers through Kenn's hair.

"Exactly." That made his toes curl.

"Well, it doesn't suck. Although I do." David's eyes twinkled.

"David!" Oh damn. His body burned.

Chuckling, David rubbed their noses together. "What? It's the truth."

"Is it? I… I have to admit, I've been known to as well."

"Oh yeah? That's wonderful. I'm rather fond of being sucked."

Could he do this? Kenn wondered. Just have a meaningless thing where he didn't get involved? Even as his body said yes, his heart wasn't so sure. David had already become his friend.

"What are you thinking, Kenn?"

"I'm wondering whether I could have a meaningless fling with someone I'm already friends with."

"What's wrong with a meaningful fling?" David asked, still playing with his hair.

"Nothing. Nothing at all."

"Then I vote for that, because anything I do with you now wouldn't be meaningless at all." David held his gaze, refusing to let him look away as they spoke.

"I've sworn off relationships," he whispered.

"But we're in a relationship now, aren't we? We're friends. Good friends, I'd like to think."

"I think we are. Good friends." He didn't kiss men he didn't like.

"Then we're already in a relationship," David informed him. "So you can't say you don't do them." David kissed him before he could rebut or question the logic.

He groaned, the sound shocking him with its volume. David deepened the kiss, like that had been a signal to do so, tongue sliding along his again. This time, though, David drew him close, rocking them together, nudging their erections against one another.

He wasn't the only one reacting to what was happening between them. David was clearly as affected, and it made him feel sensual, sexual.

He explored David's spine, tugging at his shirt idly. David shifted for him, and the shirt slid up as the end came out of David's jeans. This was a mistake. A terrible, wonderful mistake.

He touched the smooth, warm skin of David's lower back, drew a lazy circle. Groaning, David pushed closer, and their erections pressed against each other, hardness to hardness.

He was in so much trouble. So much wonderful trouble.

David caught hold of his tongue and began sucking gently. He could feel each pull deep inside him, settling in his balls. Each tug made him whimper, made his hips roll.

"Wanna take our shirts off?" David asked, wriggling out of his own, offering him a great chest to touch. David's pecs were firm, his abs washboard. So... inviting.

He reached out, flattened his hands on David's chest. David's moan made the skin beneath his touch vibrate.

"Your turn, Kenn. Let me see you."

He moaned, slowly unbuttoning his shirt. David leaned in, kissing his skin as it was revealed by the unbuttoning. His nipples drew up, the little promises of pleasure making him ache.

When he got enough buttons undone that they were exposed, David groaned. "Waiting for me."

Kenn shook his head, but it was true. He played with his nips when he jacked off. He loved nipple play.

"You want me to take it slow?" David leaned in and blew on his right nipple, air warm with a barely there touch.

He moaned softly, his toes curling.

"You've got sensitive ones, eh?" David blew again, harder this time so there was more air, but the touch was still gentle as hell.

"Yes, I guess so." He brought David's face up, took another kiss.

David smiled into the kiss, tongue slipping out to touch his lips. As it did, David slid his fingers over Kenn's left nipple, making it zing.

More. He thought the plea, then made himself relax, made himself breathe.

David rubbed his thumb across the same bit of flesh. "I want to taste them."

"I...." He swallowed hard, but he wanted it. At least a hint.

David held his gaze for a moment, but must have read it in his face because he bent and whipped his tongue across Kenn's right nipple.

Kenn whined softly, hips rolling up instinctively.

David touched the tip of flesh with his tongue again, then wrapped his lips around it and began to pull. Kenn's mouth opened, his eyes going wide with the rhythmic pulling. Every now and then David would flick his tongue across the tip of his nipple, marrying the two amazing sensations.

Kenn moaned, the sound refusing to stay caught inside him. David made a noise just like it, low and needy.

"I…. This is getting intense."

"It is." David raised his head, sharing the pillow with him again and smiling. "Nothing below the belt. Not tonight."

"Nothing below the belt." That was fair.

"Not tonight." David kissed him again, and it was as good now as it had been earlier. Better, maybe, the throb of his nipple adding a little something extra to each kiss.

He held on, sharing one kiss after another, becoming more and more dazed. The touch to his left nipple made him gasp like he'd been pinched. He hadn't, though, David's fingers super gentle, almost featherlight. He held on to David's shoulders, steadying himself.

David was intoxicating, honestly. Kenn was drunk without a drop of alcohol passing his lips.

He moaned and rocked into David, licking into David's lips. David focused on sliding their tongues together and teasing his nipples with those gentle, crazy-making touches. God, when he masturbated, he'd squeeze hard, tug them, make them ache. That made it hyperreal, though—this wasn't his own hand, and he wasn't on his own. It was David who was touching him, making him feel good.

His cock was hard as nails, but he kept his hips still, kept his erection away from David.

Groaning, David wrapped his fingers around Kenn's nipple and tugged, still gentle. At first anyway.

"Driving me a little crazy, you know?"

"You need more?" David pinched, and he felt the little sting down to his toes. "I'm trying to go slowly as I don't have a complete canvas to work with."

"I… a complete canvas?"

"Just above the belt, right?" David slid his fingers down across Kenn's belly, stopping at his waistband and teasing his fingers back and forth along that line.

"Uh. Uh-huh…." His belly rippled.

"Oh God, that was pretty." David continued to stroke, eyes on Kenn's stomach.

"Lots of laps."

"This kind of lap?" David asked, scooting partway down the bed and licking at Kenn's belly.

"Oh...." He arched like the world's biggest slut, pushing into David's lips.

David tugged a bit of skin from next to his navel between his lips, sucking hard enough to leave a mark.

Fuck, that burn was sweet, and he had to muffle his moan in his fist.

When David was finished with drawing it up, he pulled back and licked, then blew across Kenn's wet skin.

"I.... You're making it difficult to resist you."

"Am I supposed to be sorry about that? Because I'm not."

"No?" He chuckled and stretched, trying to relax, chill the fuck out.

"I like you, Kenn. I haven't gotten along with anyone as well as I have with you in forever. So I'm going to take it slow, and I'm going to enjoy every second in your company. But I'm also going to hope for more."

"I've sworn off relationships—romantic entanglements. I'm not..." Capable. Able. Functional. "...ready."

"I know. But eventually you will be, right?" David didn't let him answer, kissing him again. God, would that ever not be distracting?

He let the kisses carry him away, make him float into a world of pure sensation. David began touching again too: soft flicks to his nipples, harder rubbing of one finger around the areola, pressing into his skin, and the occasional, shocking because it was rare, pinch and tug.

He began to moan, and he told himself to stop, to breathe. David wasn't helping, though, continuing to touch him, to turn him on. He finally had to pull away, curl into himself, breathe.

"Kenn?" David's hand was warm on his shoulder.

"I need to get hold of myself."

"You're allowed to have emotions," David murmured.

No. No, he wasn't.

David rubbed his back, hand warm on his bare skin. "Talk to me."

"I just...." No. No, you can't fuck yourself. "I'm sorry. I needed to breathe."

David stroked his cheek, then slid his hand over Kenn's head. God, the man was warm. Kenn wanted to sink against David and let the guy hold him. He didn't, though.

"You think maybe what's going on between us is trying to tell you that you're ready?"

"I think that… I have fucked everything up with lovers. Everything."

"It takes two to fuck things up, Kenn."

"That's the rumor." It wasn't true, though.

"Then it wasn't just your fault," David insisted.

"You don't understand. I have a problem with… with being too demanding." He wanted to be taken. He wanted to be made to scream. He wanted to…. He shook his head. Stop it.

"Too demanding? You might have to be more specific."

"I ask too much from my lovers. Really, it doesn't matter."

"Then you've had the wrong lovers. And of course it matters."

"Shh. You don't…." He turned and offered David his mouth again.

David accepted the distraction, humming softly as he slid his tongue into Kenn's mouth. The kiss was still good, still amazing, even with the weight of his worries hiding behind it.

David held the back of his head, rocking him, cradling him, and it was so good. Tugging Kenn up against his solid body, David deepened their kisses further.

He stopped stressing about things—for a second, he told himself. For a minute.

David rolled onto his back, bringing Kenn with him. That put Kenn half on top of David, their skin sliding together. Humming, David slid his hands along Kenn's back. He slipped one of his legs between David's, bringing his balls against one hard thigh.

David arched, rubbing them together, but only the once; then he focused back on the kisses and the gentle touches, leaving tingles along Kenn's spine. He let himself lean, so slowly that David wouldn't notice, putting sweet pressure on his balls.

David explored, his fingers sliding all over Kenn's exposed skin, but not wandering below his waist for even a moment. Every touch made the ache a little bit better, a little bit deeper.

Their kisses were noisy, and the sounds joined the clamor of their breath gasping from them, filling the room with a sexual symphony. Insane. Wonderful and utterly insane.

Kenn had no idea how long for the kissing lasted. It seemed like it went on forever, but also like they'd only been doing it a few minutes.

His skin was on fire, each touch seeming more than the last, the kisses only serving to make it all even better.

"Driving me out of my mind, David."

"Okay. I'd drive you home later, too, but I don't have a car." Then David brought their mouths back together again.

Did that even make sense? Seriously? He didn't think so. Still, David's touches and kisses really were intoxicating, and he didn't care if what David had said made sense or not. He was busy.

He began to rock against David's leg, moving in slow, steady waves. He almost missed it when David slid a hand onto his ass, cupping it and guiding his movements. He groaned his agreement, his hands holding David's cheeks.

David began meeting his movements, too, flexing his leg and pushing up every time Kenn rocked down. It increased the pressure on his balls and against his cock. God yes. Yes. That was what he needed. That and more.

He was totally throwing caution to the winds, but he couldn't quite remember why he needed to be careful—David's warm hands and hot mouth conspired to make him lose his mind.

He found himself dragging his fingers up and down David's sides, sliding them along the warm skin over and over. David began to feed low moans into his mouth, each one making his insides vibrate.

"I don't want to cream my jeans." He wasn't a kid anymore.

David pulled back and looked at him, eyes somewhat glazed over. He blinked a couple of times. "Um… okay. You want to take them off or stop? I vote for take them off. I can get rid of mine too."

"We've gone a long way to stop…."

"God knows I don't want to, but if that's what you need, we will."

"I need to touch you." He reached for David's slacks.

David helped, sucking in while Kenn worked open the button and the zipper, then lifting his hips so Kenn could tug the jeans down off David's lean hips.

Pretty. God, he wanted to get his lips around that cock.

Moaning, David bucked, thick cock bouncing toward him for a moment.

He dared to lean down, drag his tongue across the tip. Salt burst over his taste buds, and he moaned deep in his chest.

"Oh fuck! Kenn... please." David's hands moved to his head, opening and closing but not tugging or pushing.

"Yes." He groaned and dropped over the fat prick, took what he so desperately needed.

"Kenn!" David's cry echoed around the room, the strong legs spreading wider. He took David in to the root, swallowing hard around the tip. His cheek rubbed against David's fuzzy belly, and the scent of healthy man filled his nose.

"Oh my God! Kenn!" David closed his hands over the back of Kenn's head, clinging to him.

He groaned and nodded, head bobbing, mouth stretching at the corners.

David babbled—nonsense words, praise raining down on him—and Kenn groaned, reaching down to tug his cock.

"Don't stop. Please, don't stop."

He didn't intend to stop until David shot, filled his mouth with spunk. He swallowed hard, pushing David's balls with his free hand.

"Gonna," David warned, hips jerking.

He tightened his lips, demanding David's orgasm.

"Kenn!" His name echoed around the room as David came, shooting hard and filling his mouth, flooding his throat.

He drank it down, lapping at the tip of David's cock to clean it. A shudder went through David, and he began to pet Kenn's head, sliding his fingers through Kenn's hair.

The touch made him shiver, and he closed his eyes against the rush of emotions he felt.

"Come up here and let me say thank you properly."

"Yeah?" He could handle that, maybe.

"Uh-huh." David grabbed his arms and tugged him up, closed their mouths together, and Kenn gave himself over, telling himself that he could take this, accept this for now.

Sliding his hand down Kenn's body, David found his cock and wrapped around him. David took long, slow strokes.

"Oh...." Kenn's eyes went wide as lightning shot up his spine.

David didn't say anything; he just kept stroking, the pleasure expanding.

"Please." Kenn needed to come so badly.

David tightened his hand, squeezing him, and he arched up, the pressure enough to make his eyes cross.

"God, you're pretty," David told him.

"I need." He felt like his eyes were burning, like he was on fire as he drove into David's fingers.

"Tell me what you need. I'll make it happen."

He wished. "We're good. You're good."

"You got it." David kissed him again, fingers working his cock, making him feel like heaven.

He reached down and pushed on his slit a bit, enough to make it burn.

"I can do that." David did, too, thumb worrying the slit, fingernail catching every now and then.

"Oh fuck." Kenn groaned, lightning slamming through him. "Soon."

"Yeah, do it. Come for me, Kenn."

"Yes." God yes. He groaned as David rubbed his slit again, his balls drawing up as he shot.

David groaned. "God, you smell good."

He would have thanked David, but he had no words.

David took a kiss, and that sort of said it all anyway. He pushed all the grateful emotions he had into that kiss.

David wrapped his arms around Kenn and kept him close, warm.

"Do you want me to go?"

"No. I mean, I'm comfortable and warm, and if you'll stay, I'll pull up the comforter."

"I'll stay." He wanted to stay.

"Score!" David laughed as he said it and hugged Kenn tight, then kissed him. "I might be pleased about your decision." Shifting and moving, David got a comforter up over them, cocooning them together.

"Thank you, man." He was blinking, a little dazed from his orgasm.

"Ditto." David dragged his fingers up and down Kenn's spine.

Sleep. He was going to sleep with someone he'd just shared orgasms with.

How… unusual.

Chapter Four

DAVE WAS a morning person, but when he was curled up around a hot body, well, he didn't want to get up any more than the next person. He kept his eyes closed and tugged Kenn closer.

Kenn moaned and cuddled in, parted lips brushing his collarbone. He tilted his head back, offering Kenn his neck. The gentle kisses went on and on—lazy, sloppy, wonderful.

He started rocking his hips, sliding his cock along Kenn's belly. Kenn's hardening shaft knocked up against his. Oh, someone was interested, eager, and sweet as pie.

He slid his hands along Kenn's back. His fingers did seem to love the smooth skin. God, he wanted to explore every inch of Kenn's body.

Although right this second, he was pretty happy to be the one being explored, Kenn's lips and tongue making his skin tingle.

"Mmm. I really should go home, I guess…." He didn't sound very sure.

"I think you should stay. I think what we're doing is the best way to start the morning. I'll even make you breakfast after." He could make Kenn an omelet. Or pancakes. Oatmeal. Scrambled eggs. Bacon. Whatever Kenn wanted.

"I'm willing." Two of his favorite words.

"Perfect." He pulled Kenn closer so their skin rubbed more firmly. The extra friction felt fantastic.

"Been a while since I woke up naked with someone."

"It's a glorious way to wake up, isn't it?" David was warm and turned on and happy. It rocked.

"It is. I've missed it."

"We're here, together, now." He tilted Kenn's head up and brought their mouths together, taking a kiss.

He didn't want Kenn thinking about any other lovers. Especially whoever had hurt Kenn so badly he was three years into self-enforced singlehood and celibacy.

He deepened the kiss, sending one hand to Kenn's ass and wrapping around it so he could keep rocking them together.

They found a rhythm—slow and steady and sure, one that made Dave's mouth dry. He moaned into the kiss, his hips bucking on their own, driving harder against Kenn. He leaked onto Kenn, his morning hard-on aching as he bounced against Kenn's belly.

Dave was raring to go, so eager he was going to be quick off the mark. He needed to make sure Kenn was right there with him. He pushed his free hand between them, finding Kenn's nipple and rubbing his thumb against it.

It hadn't escaped his attention how Kenn had responded to a little hard play, a touch of sting. He rubbed a moment longer before taking it between two fingers and pinching.

Kenn groaned, face buried in his throat.

He did it again, bucking hard against Kenn's body. Their cocks bumped solidly, and a shiver went through him.

"Damn. Do that again!"

He obliged, bucking up against Kenn and moaning as their cocks collided again. Kenn reached down and gathered their cocks together, squeezing them in his fingers.

"Oh yeah, don't stop. Don't."

"I won't." Kenn stroked them, tugging them good and hard.

"Mmm. Good morning to us."

"Yes. Yes, a very good morning." Kenn's laughter was a joyous thing.

Dave pressed their mouths together, taking the sound of Kenn's joy into himself. It warmed him inside and out, and he deepened the kiss. He loved this, the way Kenn was letting him in.

He wanted to roll Kenn onto his back and drive them together, but he thought it would be better received some other time. Besides, he appreciated the fact that Kenn was taking the lead, was participating fully and eagerly.

The last thing Dave wanted was to frighten his new lover.

He ran his hands up and down Kenn's back, long sweeping touches as he kept kissing.

He let himself fantasize as Kenn kissed him, imagining the amazing things he would do with that gorgeous swimmer's body. He ached to play and play hard. Patience, he told himself. Patience. After all, it had won him a most amazing blow job and a night with Kenn already.

He slid his tongue with Kenn's, participating without taking over the kiss. He had to let Kenn take the lead for now.

Kenn found his cock, stroking him, petting him gently, base to tip. He groaned, Kenn's touch almost magical. He thought because they were going slow, because he wasn't rushing, even these simple touches felt amazing. Kenn seemed so focused on his pleasure, on making him ache.

He reached for Kenn's cock, eager to make this sweet man feel good too.

It fit so well in his hand. He could imagine it, pierced and ringed, Kenn bound to his will.

Groaning, he tightened his fingers and stroked, working his hand up and down along Kenn's hot flesh. He loved how it made Kenn's fingers clench, how it made Kenn squeeze.

"You feel good," he whispered into Kenn's ear. He played with Kenn's slit, rubbing his fingers along it one after the other.

Oh. Oh, listen to Kenn's breath hitch. He was going to make it his main project to learn all of Kenn's noises, what drew them out, what they each meant.

"Sensitive there?" he asked.

Kenn nodded. "Sorry."

"You do not need to apologize for your body. Besides, I happen to think being sensitive is a wonderful thing."

"Really?" Kenn stopped the conversation with a kiss.

The kiss couldn't stop his thoughts, though. Couldn't stop him from wondering why Kenn would think that it was bad to be sensitive. Then Kenn twisted his wrist on an upstroke, hitting Dave's glans on the way, and his focus was suddenly right there. He bucked, his body demanding more.

Kenn did the twisting trick again, and Dave moaned, his eyes crossing. He was going to have to try that himself. He did it to Kenn, adding a little slide of his thumb along that sensitive slit.

One of Kenn's legs drew up, like he'd pushed a button. That was amazing. He slid his tongue through Kenn's mouth, caressing his tongue at the same time as he rubbed Kenn's slit again, keeping that touch gentle. He bet Kenn would totally get off on being slit-fucked.

He let himself imagine as Kenn jacked him. That swimmer's body bound, knees pulled back and spread, the sounds and lube spread out between them.

"Kenn!" He bucked as his orgasm took him, his spunk shooting up over Kenn's hand. Damn. Damn, that would be incredible, and he really wanted to get a chance to do it with Kenn.

"Mmm… good morning."

"It really is." He focused back on the task of jacking Kenn off. "Your turn now."

"Oh, you don't have…." Kenn's eyes crossed.

"I want to." Clearly Kenn's ex was a total asshole if Kenn was saying it was okay if he didn't reciprocate in the orgasm department. "There's nothing I want more."

Kenn moaned deep in his chest.

He wanted to hear more of those noises. He wanted to make Kenn orgasm in a million different ways. Right now, this would do. He continued stroking, moving his hand from base to head, making sure to work the tip every time.

Kenn was moving for him, hips rocking the long prick along his palm. He pinched a little bit, taking hard, hungry kisses as he went.

Kenn cried out into his mouth, and heat poured over his hand as Kenn came. Oh, good boy. So good. The praise wanted out.

"That's a great smell," he said instead. "So good."

"Thank you. That was a wonderful way to wake up."

"I agree." He pushed Kenn's hair out of his face and took another kiss, bringing their lips together.

"We missed our swim time."

"We did. I'm trying to be upset about it, but I'm not managing very well."

Kenn's laughter was soft, muffled.

Dave grinned and rubbed their noses together. "I really like you, Kenneth Brannigan."

"Thank you. I-I think you're the nicest friend I've made in a long time."

"That's one of the best compliments I've ever gotten."

Kenn pinked for him, the expression so damn pretty.

He cuddled with Kenn, enjoying holding him, sharing warmth, Kenn's skin against his. So sweet. So dear.

"So I know you're having supper with me at the other pizza place—what are you doing with the rest of your weekend?" He was hoping to talk Kenn into spending it with him.

"I have no idea. I'm sure I have work to do, but…."

"But I might be able to talk you into spending the day with me?"

"You might. I seem to like it."

"You're not alone in that. I like it too."

Kenn blushed deeper and buried his face in Dave's shoulder.

He kept his arm around Kenn shoulders, stroking the warm, smooth skin. Someone craved sensation, connection. That worked for him. He could connect with Kenn all day long.

Chapter Five

Kenn couldn't believe he was sitting here in a pair of borrowed shorts, leaning against an equally nearly naked man as they read. He was devouring an old Dean Koontz book; David was reading Clive Cussler.

It was lovely.

He couldn't remember ever feeling this comfortable with a lover. How many men would be happy with you both being in your own world even while you were together?

Not a lover, he reminded himself. He didn't have lovers. Just a friend.

A very good friend.

"How's your book?" Dave asked.

"Good. There's something about horror from this era. It was the best. You?"

"It's great." Dave kissed the top of his head. "Are you hungry? We could hunt up food."

"Sure. Let me find my clothes." He wasn't going to be with other people half-nude.

"You're okay as you are," Dave noted, folding over the page of his book and setting it down.

"You have roommates…."

"You can wear my robe or a T-shirt." Dave stretched, his belly rippling enticingly.

He smiled, but he wasn't sure. That seemed so… intimate.

Dave got up and went to his dresser. "T-shirt or button-down? They're both clean." Dave held both out.

"Are you sure?" The T-shirt looked comfy.

"I totally don't mind." Dave tossed both to him.

The T-shirt was crazy soft, light blue with a sloth riding a unicorn and the words My Spirit Animal across the bottom.

Okay, that was adorable. He slid it on, humming at the soft slide.

"Looks good on you." Dave pulled on another T-shirt from his drawer. This one red with three penguins on it, doing hear no evil, see no evil, speak no evil.

"It's comfortable." Kenn stroked his belly, his nipples.

He looked up to find Dave watching him, eyes on Kenn's hands, tongue sliding along his lower lip. He dropped his hands immediately, cheeks heating.

Dave held out his hand. "Come on, let's go find something to eat."

"Sure." He slid his fingers into Dave's, tangling them together.

It was electric, where their hands met. Dave smiled down at him. "What do you like to eat for breakfast?"

"Coffee."

Dave laughed. "Well, I'm sure there's coffee. You want anything with it? Eggs? I'm pretty sure we've got those. Toast of some sort. I can't promise you more than that. Hell, I'm not sure I can promise you that."

"We can manage. I'm easy."

"I promise not to take that the wrong way." Dave led him out of the bedroom to the stairs.

Kenn rolled his eyes, but solely at himself. He wasn't sure there was a wrong way to take it. He'd certainly proved himself to be easy enough for Dave.

Dave held his hand all the way to the kitchen. They didn't run into anyone, and even the kitchen was quiet, though the coffee pot was a third full, proving someone had started the machine and drunk some.

"It's pretty quiet around here Saturday and Sunday mornings. I think folks are mostly nursing hangovers and recovering from being out late." Dave let go of his hand to open the fridge and inspect its contents.

It was surprisingly full—eggs and veggies, bacon and milk. "Do you all share?"

"Sort of. We all put some money in the pot once every two weeks, and Annie shops for basics with that. We all buy any extras that we want. How about veggie omelets? We've got asparagus, onions, garlic, peppers, mushrooms, and broccoli. Sound good?"

"Sounds amazing. What can I do?"

"You any good at chopping? Let's start with the onions—get them in first, then we can add the other stuff. If you'd like meat in with your omelet, I can do them separately."

"No. No, I wouldn't do that to you."

Dave gave him a warm smile. "I appreciate you being willing to eat veggie with me. I promise not to be offended if you feel the need for meat, though."

"No big. I'll satisfy my craving for sausage with Timothy."

Dave's mouth dropped open; then he giggled. "You can totally eat my sausage any time you'd like."

"Nom, nom, nom." Kenn could tease too. Friends teased.

"We're going to have to call yours something other than sausage, seeing as I'm vegetarian. I'd hate for it to be off the menu. Carrot? Parsnip? Daikon radishes are pretty long and thick...." Dave's eyes danced merrily, twinkling at him.

"I'm not sure calling it a carrot is sexy, but whatever gets you through the night...."

"Calling it a sausage isn't really that sexy, either, is it? It's one of those things people do." Dave finished taking things out of the fridge, then grabbed a couple of knives and cutting boards. "Let's slice some veg."

"Sure. What are you looking for—chunky or tiny?"

"Whatever makes you happy." Dave grabbed a large frying pan and set it on the stove, then joined him at the counter.

Kenn started chopping, going for fairly small because it went inside eggs. Dave worked next to him, humming to some song that was playing in his head. They worked together comfortably, easily. He couldn't believe he was doing this, that he was happy. He glanced over at Dave, who looked back and grinned, then went back chopping.

"Help yourself to some coffee," Dave suggested when they were done.

"Is it good coffee?" He was a little picky.

"It depends on who made it and how long it's been sitting there. I usually pick one up on my way to work," Dave admitted. "You want orange juice instead?"

"I think so. You?" He might go pick up coffee here in a bit.

"Yeah, that would be good. I'm pretty sure I have some left." Dave put the onions in the pan, then checked the fridge. He pulled out a box of orange juice and grabbed two glasses from the cupboard. When it turned out there was only three-quarters of a glass left, he gave that to Kenn and filled the other glass with water from the tap.

"I'll go get dressed and grab coffees for us if you want?"

"The food's going to be ready in about five minutes—how about we get coffees after we eat?" Dave stirred the onions then added the garlic.

"Sounds perfect." Lazy and luscious and easy.

A woman dressed only in boxers and a spaghetti-strap T-shirt came in and grabbed a mug, went over to fill it with coffee.

Dave turned toward her. "Good morning."

She grunted and buried her nose in her mug.

Dave chuckled. "This is my friend Kenn. Kenn, this is Annie."

She swallowed a few times, then lowered the cup and gave him a smile. "Hey, Kenn. Nice to meet you."

"Good morning." He felt like his cheeks were going to catch on fire.

"Annie's not a morning person," Dave pointed out.

"God no, I'm not." Annie downed the rest of her mug of coffee, then refilled it with the last from the pot. She took another sip and made a face. "This is the worst coffee ever." She opened the fridge and added a bunch of milk to her mug.

Good to know. "Dave warned me, thank goodness."

"This one is worse than usual. But I have to be at the library in twenty minutes and actually contribute to the group, so…." She shrugged, added a bunch of sugar to her cup, then shuffled her way out.

"Oh, I hate Saturday meetings," Kenn commented. "I never schedule them."

"Yeah. I'll probably have to do grading and studying on the weekends, but ick. Plus this group she's working with are idiots." Dave poured the eggs into the pan.

"I read a lot on Saturday. Sunday is for brunch and preparing lectures."

"Well, I've certainly enjoyed spending this morning reading with you."

"Yes. It's been… the loveliest Saturday in recent memory."

Dave beamed at him, then turned back to the pan and flipped the omelet before sliding it onto a plate. Dave placed it in front of him. "Ta-da."

He applauded, giving credit where it was due. "It looks amazing."

"Thanks. I like having an omelet on the weekend, but brunch on the weekends is surprisingly expensive, so I learned how to do my favorites." Dave plated his own and set it down on the table before sitting next to Kenn.

"God, don't I know. I splurge every Sunday. It's an indulgence, but...." He liked pretending he was still someone's husband, like he wasn't living in a tiny apartment and walking everywhere.

"Yeah? Where do you go? Is there somewhere special here?" Dave drank some of his water, then dug into his omelet, but Kenn was aware he had Dave's full attention.

"There's a little restaurant that does the whole shebang—mimosas, rashers of bacon, pancakes, eggs Benedict, cantaloupe."

"I love cantaloupe. It's like a sweet little palate cleanser. And who can resist a mimosa?"

"I've always loved Sunday brunch." Always.

"So maybe tomorrow you can show me your brunch place." Dave grinned. "It could be a continuation of the culinary tour you've been taking me on."

"I could." It would be worth it, this once. "We could toast one another."

"I'd like that." Dave put another bite of omelet on his fork and nodded at Kenn's plate. "Don't let it get cold."

"Right. Sorry." He needed to relax. This was a weekend out of time.

"If you don't like it, you can tell me. I promise not to get upset or anything." Dave was so nice.

"Nonsense. What's not to like? I was caught in my brain. It happens."

"Cool. And not nonsense. I don't want you to think you can't tell me how you feel about food. Well, about anything, really. I'm all about communication."

Kenn smiled and nodded, but focused on eating, on the now. He could process everything later.

"We were talking about getting coffee after we'd eaten. How about turning it into a walk with coffee, since we missed out on swimming? That way we still get some exercise in. It looks like a lovely day out there."

"I'd love that. We can have a wander, and I'll show you around." Kenn grinned, waving his fork. "We could go on a used bookstore crawl."

Dave's face lit up. "Yes!" Then he laughed. "Now that I've revealed that I really am the world's biggest dork...."

"We can share the title. I don't mind."

"You don't seem like a dork to me." Dave speared the last bit of his omelet. "You seem like a really nice, smart guy who's got great interests and is fascinating."

He shook his head. No. He was merely a professor and a decent friend. "Just a dude."

"Well, you're a dude I like an awful lot." Dave finished his omelet and drank the rest of his water, then took his dishes over to the sink. "Bring yours over when you're done. I'm just going to wash what dishes we used. It's amazing how quickly the counters get disgusting when you've got five different people living under one roof. I always make sure I'm not contributing to any funkitude."

"I can only imagine. The space is nice." He ate noodles and frozen dinners every night he didn't go out.

Dave made short work of their dishes, doing Kenn's, too, when he was done. "There we go. Like we were never here. You wanna share a shower before we get dressed and go out?"

"Lord, I haven't done that since...." Bram. "A long time ago."

Dave's grin got wicked. "Then it's about time you did it again. Come on. Before anyone else is up so we have lots of hot water."

"I like the way you think." He grabbed Dave's hand. "Let's go."

They raced upstairs, laughing as they went, and Dave tugged him into the bathroom a few doors down from his bedroom. "I think I've got clean cloths in the cupboard." Dave checked and pulled down a couple of dark blue bath towels. "Bingo!"

"Woo!" His cheeks were burning, heated, and his body was beginning to respond.

Dave set the towels down on the counter and moved to turn on the water, bending over the tub, butt in the air, tempting him.

He reached down, unable to resist, and squeezed.

Dave hooted, the sound surprised, and shot up straight. He turned, laughing, and hugged Kenn. "You surprised me."

"You stuck it out there, didn't you?"

"I guess I did at that. Although I was doing what I always do. But next time I'll do it on purpose and be expecting it."

Next time. Oh, that sounded... amazing.

Dave tested the water with his hand, then switched it so it came out of the shower. He yelped and pulled the shower curtain closed. "Someone left it pointing out of the tub. Butthead." Dave was laughing, though.

Kenn wasn't sure he could share a bathroom with a roommate, but he respected the hell out of Dave for it.

Dave went over and locked the door, then stripped. He held the curtain open for Kenn. "After you."

He shucked his clothes and bowed. "Thank you, sir."

Dave hummed softly at his words, followed him into the shower, and slid one hand along his spine. Oh, that was nice. There was something about Dave's hands, about the lovely touch.

The water fell around them, and Dave stepped up close, smiling down at him, before bringing their mouths together.

Kenn tried to remind himself that he wasn't into this, but... who was he kidding?

He sank against Dave, who supported him, holding him close as they kissed. Dave's hands moved over his skin, petting him, encouraging him to melt.

"Want to make you feel good, Kenn. I want to make you come."

"Again?" Oh God.

"That was hours ago—of course again." Dave grinned and nibbled at his lips. "I want to give you all the orgasms."

"I... thank you." That was the correct response, right?

"Mmm, you're welcome." Dave cupped his balls, arm against his cock, putting pressure on it. His eyelids went heavy, and the urge to press down was so hard to resist.

"You want to fuck my hand?" Dave asked. "You're allowed." Dave's grip tightened, and Kenn moaned deep in his throat. "Or you can have a little ache."

"Please... I don't...." He couldn't face that about himself again. Never again.

"Don't what, baby?" Dave squeezed his balls again.

He didn't answer—he was caught between pleasure and panic.

Dave let go, nuzzling his face, hands moving to wrap around his waist. "You want me to stop and I will, Kenn."

"I'm sorry. I.... God." He shut himself up with a kiss. Shut up, you idiot.

Dave groaned, mouth opening and letting him in. He kept kissing, making sure Dave knew he wanted this. No talking. No secrets. Just fun, easy sex.

Dave leaned back against the tile, bringing him along so he could lean against all that warm skin. Dave grabbed his ass and squeezed.

He chuckled and wrapped his arms around Dave's middle and held on. Dave kept holding his ass with one hand while the other slid up along his spine to his head. Cupping his skull, Dave tilted his head and deepened the kiss.

That eased the tension again, allowing him to breathe. Whether Dave noticed it or not, that was the time he chose to turn them, putting him up against the tile and pressing against him. His cock pressed against Dave's thigh and Dave's heated belly, burning against his skin.

He began to rock, hips arching to give Dave more.

"Oh yeah. God, you're sexy, Kenn. Feels so… weak, saying that. It's not nearly good enough."

"I want you." He wanted not to fuck this up.

"Lucky me." Dave smiled into his eyes. "I want you to want me." Dave took another kiss, moving against him.

He opened up and let Dave in, soft moans shared between them. Dave rocked against him, dragging their skin together in an age-old rhythm. It was easier like this, not thinking.

Dave wrapped a hand around his cock, fingers exploring, pinching the tip and rubbing his slit.

He arched, his heels leaving the tub. Oh fuck. Please.

Groaning, Dave tightened his hold, and every time his hand slid up around the head of Kenn's cock, Dave rubbed his slit. Again and again.

He humped, world spinning madly around him. The water splashed down around them, and nothing else existed but him and Dave.

Dave's kisses covered his face, soothing him as that touch made him fly. He could only hope Dave was with him as they humped together, like they were trying to meld their bodies into one.

"Fuck," he groaned. "Dave. Soon."

"Yeah. Do it. Wanna smell your come."

His eyes went wide, and he gasped, spunk spraying from him, leaving him weak-kneed. Dave's hand stayed on his ass, holding him in place as Dave continued to hump against him. Then Dave's face went lax, and he came as well.

"Better." God, so much better. "Thank you."

"Mmm, thank you too." Dave's kiss was sloppy this time, full of a goofy smile. "Being with you makes me happy."

"You make me...." He shook his head. No talking.

"I'm going to assume you were about to say happy too. So if it was something else, you'll have to tell me." Still wearing his goofy grin, Dave grabbed the soap and ran it over Kenn's body.

"I'm trying to remember that I don't have love affairs, Dave."

"That's the saddest thing I've ever heard." Dave stroked his cheek. Then he grinned. "Besides, we're not having a love affair. We're having a friend affair."

"Right. We're having a lovely new friendship with orgasms."

"Exactly! We can call it anything we want. We make our own rules, Kenn."

"Thank you." He was so grateful that Dave understood him, heard him.

"We'll have to have another one where that came from later. Maybe between our walk and pizza." Dave tugged him properly into the spray of water, hands sliding on his skin, helping the water wash away the soap.

His balls were never going to recover.

Ever.

Dave washed himself next, making quick work of it. Then he turned off the water. "I like that look on you. The boneless, melted, you just had a great orgasm look."

"You bring it out of me." No question.

"I hope so." Dave kissed his nose, then wrapped him in a towel, drying him gently, like he was precious.

He tried to return the favor, but he was clumsy and fuck-addled. Dave didn't seem to care, more focused on him. When they were done, he peeked out the door, then held out his hand.

"If we're quick, we can run for it."

"Come on, then." They could cuddle a minute before coffee, right?

They held hands, running down the hall wearing only their towels. Dave was laughing by the time they shut his bedroom door behind them.

He pulled Dave onto the bed, wrapping the covers around them both, hiding them away. Dave shared kisses with him, rubbing their noses and cheeks together. "You're something else, Kenn."

"Thank you. This has been.... Thank you."

"Yeah, it has been great, hasn't it?" Dave pushed his hair off his face. "I'm having the best weekend ever. So thank you."

Kenn answered with a hard kiss. It wouldn't last, but… he wanted to enjoy this for as long as he had it.

Chapter Six

DAVE WHISTLED as he headed out of the class he TA'd on Wednesday afternoons. He'd had to stay an extra twenty minutes to deal with questions from students, but now his time was his own. He sent a text off to Kenn.

Hey Prof—wanna get supper?

They'd had a wonderful weekend, making love, wandering, eating, reading together. They'd even managed to go swimming on Sunday morning.

Kenn had been busy when he'd texted and asked to get together on Monday, so Dave had been good and not asked yesterday. But he honestly missed Kenn's company. It was more than sex he enjoyed with Kenn.

I'm already home & in a shit mood.
I could bring you something and me to cheer you up.
It took a full minute before Kenn returned with, *I'd like that.*
See you soon.

He pocketed his phone and headed for Annie's. He was pretty sure the diner had takeout. He didn't know what Kenn's favorite was, aside from the apple cinnamon cheesecake. He ordered a slice of that and a slice of the plain apple pie, along with the vegetarian burrito and the meatloaf special.

In a surprisingly short time, he was on his way to Kenn's with two bags of food.

He headed up to Kenn's room and kicked at the door. He was surprised when Tim answered the door.

"Hey. I was bringing him some Tylenol. He's in a mood."

"Hopefully some food will cheer him up and help get rid of his headache." He went in. "Kenn?"

"Hey, come on in. I'm sorry." Kenn looked like he'd been crying, maybe, or sick.

"I'll leave you guys alone," Tim said. "Feel better, Kenn."

"Thanks, Tim."

Tim left, and Dave put the food down on the little table and went over to where Kenn lay in bed. "Oh, dude. Are you sick?" He put his hand across Kenn's forehead.

"No. No, just a rough day."

"That sucks." He pressed a soft kiss to Kenn's lips. "I brought the meatloaf special. And if you don't like it, you can share my veggie burrito with me. And better than that, I may have picked up a certain dessert too."

"You're so dear. Thank you. How were your classes?"

"Eh. I was thinking about you," he admitted. In compromising positions.

"Oh...." Kenn's cheeks went a deep, dark red.

He stroked one, fingers lingering on the heated skin. "Lovely man. You want to eat in bed or at the table?"

"We should probably get up, but...."

"But you can stay right where you are, and I'll feed you. I think that I'm going to enjoy that."

He kicked off his shoes before curling up in the bed with Kenn, stroking his cheeks, kissing him gently. He fed Kenn one kiss after another, thinking maybe Kenn needed this more than the food.

"I missed you," Kenn whispered.

"Yeah, I missed you too." Crazy because it had only been a couple of days, but Kenn made him happy simply by being there.

Kenn closed his eyes, and they were bruised, unhappy. Dave kissed one eyelid and then the other.

"What's wrong, honey?"

"I can't... it's just... nothing. It's nothing."

"It doesn't look like nothing."

Kenn shook his head but wouldn't meet his eyes.

"You can talk to me, Kenn." In fact, it was rather important.

"Not about this. I'm sorry. It's complicated."

He felt a stab of hurt that Kenn wasn't willing to trust him. "How about that food, then?" he suggested.

"Yes. Yeah, I.... Yes. Sounds good."

He got up and grabbed the bags and some cutlery, then returned to Kenn's side. "So, do you like the meatloaf from Annie's?"

"I do. It won't upset you?"

"I wouldn't have picked it up for you if it did." He didn't believe in pushing his food choices on others.

"I worry about you." Kenn took the container with the meatloaf, peppering it liberally.

"You do?" That had him feeling good again. "Why do you worry about me?"

"Because I don't want to offend you and because… because I'm going to have to be careful about seeing you."

He frowned. "Well, I'm not offended. But what do you mean you have to be careful about seeing me?"

"I have an ex. He's not a nice man."

Well now he was worried about Kenn. "Is he stalking you?"

"I can't talk about it. It's complicated, and… I like you. A lot."

"You're scaring me, Kenn." He took Kenn's hand in his. "If he's hurting you or threatening to hurt you or anyone you're seeing, then he has to be stopped. That's not right."

"It's not right. None of it is."

"I wish you'd tell me. I'm really worried about you now."

"You'll think I'm awful. I don't want to be awful in your eyes."

"I'm not going to think that." How could anything Kenn had done be awful?

"You will."

"Did you kill anyone?"

"No!"

"Well, then, I'm failing to think of anything that you've done that's so bad I'm going to think you're awful." He pushed a strand of hair off Kenn's face. "Tell me."

"I… I'm bad about wanting things, and I was married. He didn't approve, and he… I…. It was…." Kenn stopped, breathed.

Dave tried to parse what Kenn meant out of the words he'd actually said. "You had an affair?"

"No. I had been looking at things online, and he caught me. He was very angry. We had a fight and afterward, after I woke up, I ran away, got a divorce. He said I was a deviant. He leaves me alone, but he saw us together and…."

Whoa, that was a lot of information in one breath. But it also confirmed his feelings about Kenn, that his instincts that said he could turn

Kenn over his knee and then turn him inside out were good. Then there was the second half, which confirmed that his ex was stalking Kenn.

"Okay. Looking at things online doesn't make you a deviant. If things turn you on that don't turn everybody on, that only means you like different things. I guess he couldn't give you what you wanted, and that made him mad. That was on him, not you. And I want to talk to you about that because I look at things online too. I like to do things that aren't usual for everybody. But first I want to know what you mean by saying he saw us together. Does he live here? Did he randomly see us together and say something to you? Or is he watching you?"

"He has a private investigator. I'm so sorry."

"No, that's not for you to apologize for. You aren't doing this—he is." Dave shook his head. It was all kinds of wrong. "Have you spoken to the police?"

"It's not illegal to have a PI. It's not illegal to take pictures in public."

"But then he spoke to you after he saw us together. Said something to you."

Kenn handed over an envelope. It was filled with pictures of them together. They'd seen each other for a weekend!

"This is creepy, Kenn. I think you should tell the police. Establish a pattern. Because I was wrong—this is more than creepy, it's crazy." And he was worried it was going to escalate. "Did he just send pictures, or did he include a note or call you or something?"

"Just the note, but he wants me to know he's watching. I don't look online anymore, I swear. You'll get a note next, I'm sure, warning that I'm... nasty. It was just.... God, how embarrassing...."

He leaned in and kissed Kenn, hard and quick, hoping to ease him a little. "What did the note say?" He looked through the pictures, trying to find it.

"Little pervert, fucking with students."

"Okay. First of all, I'm not your student. I'm not an undergrad. And we're almost the same age. So that's crap." He took a deep breath. "Why don't you tell me what it is that you've looked at online that's so terrible? I promise I won't react badly." No matter what it was.

"Can't we just eat? Please? My head is killing me."

"Sure. I just wanted you to tell me so that you can stop worrying about him telling me. If I already know, then it takes away his power."

And he thought it might ease Kenn's mind, to know that he wasn't judging Kenn the same way the ex had.

"I watched BDSM videos, kink—all sorts of things that weren't appropriate for Bram's husband. It was curiosity. I didn't do anything."

Yes! He'd known Kenn was a kindred spirit. "I happen to watch BDSM videos myself. I'm a Dom. And I *have* done stuff. So I'm not going to freak out when your asshole ex decides to 'warn' me." He hugged Kenn tight. "It's okay. I'm not shocked or upset or angry."

"I want to eat, okay? I'm stressed out."

"I know. I'm trying to help you unstress, but food is definitely a good not-stressful thing." He gave Kenn another hug, needing to offer comfort. Then he gave Kenn his fork and opened his own container. The burrito was pretty unimaginative—onions, peppers, salsa, guacamole, and cheese, but it was hearty enough, and he took a big bite.

Kenn ate about half his meatloaf and then pushed the food away and curled onto his side. Dave wrapped his arm around Kenn's shoulders. When he finished his meal, he put his container on the floor.

"So you know I went to Annie's for our dinner, right?" He waited for Kenn's nod. "I brought dessert. Three guesses what I got you, and the first two don't count."

"You spoil me." Kenn lifted his face for a kiss.

He gave it, lips lingering on Kenn's. One kiss became two and that became three. God, kissing Kenn felt good. "Treating you right isn't spoiling you—it's just treating you right."

"I'm sorry about all this. I was hoping…." Kenn shrugged. "I should have known better."

"This isn't on you—it's his fault. You guys aren't together anymore, and you shouldn't have to worry about how what you do affects him." He grabbed their desserts.

"He told me when I left that I'd never have another lover."

"Seriously? What kind of asshole does that?" He shook his head. "I'm sorry, but this guy doesn't sound right. Do you mind if I ask how you wound up with him?" Although Dave assumed even the biggest asshole could play nice for a while—be charming, romantic, and say all the right things.

"Grad school. He was powerful, strong, wealthy. He seemed to be perfect, but… he wanted someone to host his parties and show off to his friends. That was all." Kenn sighed. "I was an idiot."

"A trophy husband, huh?" He rubbed Kenn's arm. "So if you weren't the right guy and you obviously had irreconcilable differences, why is he so hot on making sure you don't meet anyone else?"

"No one defies Bram. No one."

"That's insane, honey. What is he, the head of a mafia or something?" He opened the dessert containers and offered Kenn the apple cinnamon cheesecake, along with a clean fork.

"A big conglomerate in Toronto. He's the CEO. He… he gets what he wants, and one of the things he wants is for me to be alone."

"Well, that's not going to cut it with me. We like each other, Kenn. And just because you were married to him once doesn't mean he owns you. He didn't then, and he doesn't now." He leaned in and gave Kenn a quick kiss. "Eat your dessert."

"I appreciate you not being angry. It's a shit situation."

"Uh-huh. And one you're not in control of. I'm pissed at him. I think he's a shit human being, and I feel bad you had—have—to deal with him. But I'm not angry with you at all. You're just trying to live your life, and you deserve to."

"Yes." Kenn took a shaky bite of dessert, then the second one that was stronger, hungrier.

It was good to see, but Dave was still worried about Kenn, both for his mental state and for him physically. He'd make some inquiries about what recourses Kenn had with the cops.

"Do you want a bite?"

"Absolutely." He gave Kenn an eager grin, then opened his mouth and leaned in.

The bite wasn't as sweet as the man offering it.

He closed his mouth over the fork and slowly pulled way, watching Kenn the whole time. Kenn blushed, teeth sinking into his bottom lip.

"Mmm. Tastes good." He held Kenn's gaze a moment longer before grinning.

"Uh-huh. It does."

"Not as good as you, of course." He leaned in and licked along Kenn's lower lip. "Oh yeah, so much better."

"You don't have to. You have to know that."

"I don't have to what? Kiss you? I know that. And you don't have to either. For my part—I want to kiss you. I like touching you, Kenn. I like making love to you. I like just spending time with you. It's one of my favorite things."

"Thank you." Kenn kissed him back, then pushed into his arms.

He hauled Kenn to the end of the bed, leaving the desserts up near the other end. Then he brought their mouths together and focused on making Kenn feel good. He wrapped one hand around Kenn's hip, the other around the back of his neck.

Moaning, Kenn rubbed against him, body so wonderfully eager. Kenn wanted him, wanted this. He wanted it too, and they were both grown men. No one else had the right to make decisions for them.

And God, the possibilities that were before them.... His Kenn was kinky. He was kinky. It was a match made in heaven.

He lay on his back, pulling Kenn on top of him so they could feel each other's bodies.

Kenn cuddled immediately, easily, like there was no one he'd rather be with. Dave hummed and slid his hand into Kenn's hair to cup his scalp and tip his head so their kisses got deeper. He wanted to help Kenn relax, to melt, to forget.

To enjoy himself.

He slid his free hand along Kenn's back, down to that sweet ass. There were too many clothes happening, but he'd get to that eventually. Right now he simply wanted to touch. "Pretty baby...."

"Shh." Kenn sucked his bottom lip in.

It was going to take more than that to shut him up, but he went with it for now, enjoying Kenn's kisses, his touches, and the heat of Kenn's body against his.

Kenn was growing erect against him.

"I want you too, Kenn. I want to be naked with you. I want to feel your body next to mine."

"Still? Even now that you know?"

"What part of what you told me do you think would send me running?"

Kenn's cheeks went pink. "I—"

"The fact that you're into kink?"

"I'm not! I looked at some videos!"

"Does that mean you'll want to stop seeing me since I told you I'm into BDSM? That I'm a Dom?"

"N-no. No. Of course.... Look, I'm sorry. I can't cope with all this."

He stroked Kenn's back, trying to soothe him. "Easy, honey, easy. You were afraid I'd be turned off by your desires, but I'm not. Just the opposite. This should be a good thing."

"I'm so ashamed."

"What are you ashamed of, Kenn?" He couldn't see what Kenn had to be ashamed of.

"I'm just... it was just curiosity, okay? I wouldn't try anything."

"That's a shame." It really was. Especially as he believed Kenn would not only enjoy it but get a lot out of it.

"I know." Kenn sighed softly. "Maybe I should go take a shower."

"Or we could stop talking and make love."

Kenn latched on to that. "We could."

He wasn't into making Kenn stressed or upset. They could revisit the non-vanilla sex issue some other time. He cupped Kenn's head again and kissed Kenn thoroughly. Kenn moaned for him, opening right up.

He slid his hands down Kenn's back, then tugged his T-shirt out of his jeans, fingers sliding along Kenn's skin as he dragged the shirt up Kenn's torso.

Kenn lifted his arms with a moan, letting Dave have his way. He got the T-shirt partway off, up to where their mouths stopped it, and he laughed as he tugged the material between their lips, forcing them to stop kissing for a moment. As soon as Kenn's shirt was out of the way, he licked at Kenn's lips. Kenn was relaxing, melting against him, moaning deep and low.

Up and down Kenn's back he ran his fingers. His own cock was hard now, pressing against Kenn's belly as he caressed the silky skin.

"Mmm...." Kenn grabbed his cock, stroked up and down.

"Open our jeans and do them together," he ordered softly.

"Yes. Oh yes." Kenn fumbled with Dave's zipper, then his own until he managed to get them pressed together.

"Oh God. Just like that." He bucked, sliding both their cocks in Kenn's grip, and it felt so good that he did it again and again. He shoved one hand into Kenn's jeans, grabbed Kenn's ass, and pressed it down to bring them tighter together, trapping Kenn's hand between them.

Kenn's forehead rested against his, both of them breathing hard.

He slid his fingers over so they rested in Kenn's crack, his little finger resting on Kenn's hole.

He loved how Kenn's pupils flared for him.

Would Kenn agree to penetrative sex? He teased Kenn's hole with his finger, pushing against it but not going in.

Kenn moaned softly, body rocking against his touch. Maybe not today, but he would have Kenn back to his place, with his bigger bed, and he would make love to his sweet boy.

Bringing their mouths together, he rocked up into Kenn's body, finding a happy rhythm.

"Soon." Kenn offered him a hard, hungry kiss.

"Yeah, come on, let's do this." He bit at Kenn's lower lip, offering hard for hard.

Kenn gasped, arching into him, fingers squeezing tight. Dave nodded. More. He wanted more.

He finally said it out loud. "More." Then he pushed a hand between them and knocked the tips of their cocks with his fingers.

Seed sprayed over his hand, Kenn offering himself right over. Dave breathed in deeply, trying to pull back off the edge.

Kenn moaned for him, hand still working. Dave groaned, tumbling right over, giving it up for Kenn.

"So pretty," Kenn whispered.

He smiled. "Thank you, Kenn." He kissed Kenn's nose.

"Thank you for coming over. Seriously. Can you… can you stay?"

"Yep." He could totally duck out early the next morning to take a shower before he started the day. "I will stay. Let's rescue your cheesecake."

"We can watch a movie, relax, hold each other." Sweet, needy baby.

"Works for me. As long as you share a few bites of your cheesecake with me."

"As much as you'd like. I just want to be with you a little bit longer."

"You've got me all evening and all night long, because there is nowhere I would rather be." It was cliché, maybe, but it was simply the truth.

Kenn held on to him, and he thought maybe there were tears as they cuddled. He didn't make a thing of it, though. Kenn needed a safe place to be right now, and he was very much down with being that safe place.

He kissed the top of Kenn's head and held on to him. Time would help Kenn to trust him enough to share his deeper desires. Until then, he was perfectly happy being with this lovely, fascinating man.

Chapter Seven

Kenn went to class, taught, did his office hours, stole whatever nights he could with Dave, and hid otherwise.

Guilt and shame haunted him, and whenever he wasn't sleeping with David, he had terrible nightmares of the night Bram beat him, thrashed him until he couldn't stand up.

He curled up on his bed with a book, fighting sleep, fighting the urge to call David.

His phone beeped with a text despite the fact that it was almost three in the morning. It couldn't be Bram, could it? No. No, he didn't have this number. Right? He wasn't supposed to anyway.

He almost didn't look, but in the end took a very quick glance at the sender. Better to know if he was going to have to get another new number.

Dave. It was from David.

Woke up thinking about you. You up?

Yes. And he was going to lose his mind.

Would you be pissed at me if I asked to come over for a booty call? R u lonely 2? I'll unlock the door.

Yes! B there in 10.

Dave was thinking about him too. That thought warmed him.

He straightened up, unlocked the door, stripped down, and slipped back into bed, waiting like a virgin on his wedding night.

The knock came at the nine-minute mark. Dave must have really hustled to get here.

"Come on in. Door's open."

Dave slipped in and closed the door behind him, locking it before coming to the bed. He pulled off his hoodie and T-shirt. "You want me to turn out the light?"

"Yes, please. Come to bed." He lifted the blanket, exposing his naked body.

Dave's smile was warm and eager. He turned the light out, then came back to bed, stopping for a moment before slipping in with him. He'd obviously stopped to take off his jeans because he was naked when he pressed against Kenn.

"Sorry if I'm a little cold."

Kenn snuggled in, offering his warmth. "Hey."

"Mmm, hey." Dave put an arm around him and kissed him softly. "I'm glad I texted. Would have been silly for us both to be awake and not together."

"I was having terrible dreams, so I got up to read."

"That sucks. You wanna tell me about them?" Dave pulled him in tighter, cuddling him in the dark, the covers pulled up close all around them.

"No. No, I'm fine. It was silly. Awful, but silly. Why were you awake?"

Dave shrugged against him. "I don't know. All of a sudden, I was wide-awake and thinking of you. I really needed to talk to you, but I didn't want to wake you, you know? I figured a text was a good compromise."

"It was perfect. Thank you for… reaching out."

"I'm glad you were up. This is much better than lying in bed worrying about you." Dave laid kisses over his face.

"Much better." Kenn moaned, chasing those kisses with his lips.

"Mmm, yeah." Dave licked his lower lip, then his nose, making him giggle. While he was laughing, Dave closed their mouths together. Kenn's entire body woke up, his cock filling in a rush.

Dave groaned and cradled his head with one hand, the other sliding down his spine toward his ass, the move familiar, comforting, and exciting. He wrapped one leg around Dave, drawing them together. Perfect.

Dave's kiss was slow and easy, and so were their movements, the gentle rocking sliding their cocks together. It built a slow fire between them, and all Kenn could do was moan and rock, loving it.

"I could do this day in and day out. I hate leaving you here all alone for even a night."

"Is this normal? This immediate attraction?"

"I think it is if you find the right person. Besides, it's been what? Two weeks?" Dave smiled against his lips. "Two weeks is a long time." Of course the attraction had started two weeks ago.

"Maybe two and a half."

"Well there you go—it's been forever." Dave licked his lips. "So I don't think it's outrageous at all."

"Oh good. I feel like a teenager, like I'll want you 24/7."

"Me too. It's fun, isn't it?" Dave grabbed his ass with both hands, squeezing.

"Yes. Yes, it… mmm…." He arched into Dave's hands.

Dave laughed softly, the sound happy, sexy, and they rubbed faster together. "I want to make love to you, Kenn. Not right now, but maybe Saturday night? We'll do dinner. We'll have candles. We'll make a wonderful night of it."

Oh, how sweet. "I'd love that. I haven't… in a long time."

"It's been a while for me too. We'll take our time." Dave kissed him again, their bodies still moving together.

"I'm not frightened." He leaned up, lips near Dave's ear. "I like it, making love, having pressure inside me."

Groaning, Dave rocked harder, sliding their bellies and cocks together. Ramping things up. "What else do you like, baby?"

"Mmm… touching."

"Oh yeah. Touching is the best. What kind of touching do you like best?"

It was easier to whisper to each other in the dark. "What kind? You mean, like yours?"

"Oh, that's a good answer." He could feel Dave's smile. "But beyond that, do you like barely there touches? What about deeper touches? How about stronger touches? Something more? Something else?"

"I like deep. A lot."

"Yeah? Like this?" Dave squeezed his ass, fingers digging in.

He gasped, the ache making his toes curl. "I—"

"Shh, it's okay. We're good. You can have anything you want."

"I like it. Your deep touch."

"Me too. I like touching you too. Like this. Deeper. I like touching you all over. God, you're so sexy, so necessary."

"Yes." He began to scoot down, heading for Dave's cock. He wanted to taste.

"Oh God, baby. I love it when you do that. That is a very good touch. Very good."

"Love the way you taste." Loved the heady words pouring down over him too.

"I'm glad. Would suck otherwise. Instead, you suck." Dave laughed, the sound dark and throaty.

Kenn began to chuckle, tickled pink.

"That was bad," Dave admitted. "It wasn't even on purpose." He laughed again, petting the top of Kenn's head.

"It was. Funny, but bad." He nudged the tip of Dave's prick.

Dave groaned for him and slid his hand through Kenn's hair.

Feeling daring, he whispered, "Please talk to me." Then he took Dave in, all the way to the root.

"Oh God. Fuck. Okay. Okay. Love your mouth. Love the way you take me in. You suck so fucking good. Fucking is good. I'm gonna do you so well on Saturday." Dave moaned. "I can't wait to feel you, tight and hot around me."

Kenn grunted, hands under Dave's ass to tug him closer.

That earned him another moan. "I can't wait to touch you deep. For you to beg me for more. So much more."

God yes. Please. Kenn swallowed, head bobbing as he worked his ass off.

Dave's words began to hitch. "You want my hand. I'm going to give it to you. Gonna make you come so hard. Want to love on you."

Kenn humped the sheets, sucking furiously as Dave tempted him.

"Don't come," Dave told him. "I want to make you come myself. So don't come. Hold back. I know you can."

He cried out softly, but he nodded, nudging Dave's balls gently. Dave groaned, the sound drawn out. It wasn't going to be long before he made Dave come.

Thank God, because he wasn't going to hold off much longer.

"Kenn!" Dave curled around his head and shot, filling his mouth. He held Dave in, swallowing over and over until he was dizzy.

Dave stroked his cheek. "So good, baby. So good. Come up here now. Let me help you out."

He climbed back up Dave's body, his balls aching.

Dave pressed his thigh between Kenn's legs, nudging up against his balls and giving him something solid to rub on.

Kenn's head fell back, and he rocked, his eyes crossing with the pressure.

"God you're sexy like that." Dave's hand landed on his ass, herding him harder against Dave's body and encouraging his movements. He humped, fighting to find his pleasure.

One of Dave's fingers slid to his hole and tapped it a few times as Dave sucked on his tongue. He twisted and sobbed, driving himself toward his orgasm.

"That's it, baby. Let me see your face as you come. I want to smell you too."

"Dave!" His gasp was loud in the darkness.

"Uh-huh. That's me, baby. Come on. Shoot for me." Dave squeezed his ass again, finger pushing against his hole.

He came hard, his balls throbbing painfully as he shot.

"Mmm. God, that's hot—you're hot." Dave kissed his face, one sweet touch of his lips after another. Kenn melted against Dave, raw inside.

"I've got you, baby." Dave kissed him again. "I don't want to let go either."

"Oh good. I was aching for you."

"You could have called me, you know." Dave wrapped his arms around Kenn.

"I didn't want to seem needy, clingy."

"I don't think you're clingy at all. And I happen to like needy. Hell, I feel needy myself."

"Really?" Oh, that was a comfort.

Dave grabbed his hand and shook it. "Hi there. You might have met me? I'm Dave, the guy who texted you in the middle of the night."

"Hi, Dave. I'm the guy who's incredibly grateful you did."

Dave chuckled and drew him in closer, wrapping around him. "I'm really glad you were awake too. Is it okay if I stay?"

"Please. As long as you'd like." Please.

"Thank you." Dave relaxed, stroking him idly.

He cuddled in, curling into Dave's arms.

"Sleep, baby. I'll still be here in the morning." Dave kissed the top of his head.

"Thank you. Good night. No dreams."

"No, I don't need them. I have you in my arms."

Oh. Oh, sweet. Yes.

Neither of them needed to dream.

Chapter Eight

Dave spent the morning grading. Then he went shopping and picked up everything he needed for the evening. Food, decorations, lube, and condoms. Then he grabbed a sweet bouquet from the florist, the flowers all white and green, striking.

He headed over to Kenn's, carrying enough bags that when he got there, he had to knock with his foot.

"Coming!" Kenn opened the door, eyes going wide. "Oh my goodness! Come in."

He leaned in and grabbed a quick kiss. "I have everything we need for a romantic meal." He was wooing Kenn tonight.

"You spoil me. Wow." Kenn looked amazing—lean and relaxed in soft, loose cotton pants and an open button-down shirt.

"It's one of my favorite things." Spoiling Kenn, making him feel good, those things made him super happy.

Kenn kissed him, then took the flowers to put them in a vase.

Dave took the food out of the bags and immediately put on the potatoes to get them parboiled. Then he set the table, refusing to let Kenn help. "It's my gift to you."

"Would you like some music?"

"That would be lovely. Something to help set the mood." He grabbed the candles from his bag and set them on the table before finding his lighter and getting them burning.

Kenn came toward him, drawn to him. He held out an arm, holding Kenn close when he immediately came over. He leaned and swayed with Kenn, closing his eyes for a moment. They danced, cheek to cheek. So dear.

Dave hummed along to the music, thinking he should have danced with Kenn sooner—this was wonderful. Kenn surprised him, moving like a dream.

"I missed you today," Dave murmured, speaking softly to not break the atmosphere they were creating.

"Mmm. I was anticipating you all day."

"Me too. I could hardly concentrate on my grading." He kept drifting off, thinking about this evening. He had it bad for Kenn. He thought that was a good thing.

"I should ask how your classes are going, hmm?"

"They're going fine. I should ask how yours are going too."

"I have this down. I love teaching these classes."

"Yeah? That is awesome." He was glad Kenn had something he loved. Something that he enjoyed filling his days with.

"I was born to teach." Kenn cuddled in closer.

"You were born for other things, too, I'm sure." Like being with him. Like kinky stuff where he got to love on Kenn in the best and most intense ways.

"Mmm. Like slow dancing?"

"No. Like slow dancing with me." He smiled against the top of Kenn's head.

"Yes. Like you. Full stop."

"Oh, I like the way you think. I like that you're on the same page as me." He dipped Kenn playfully, and he loved how Kenn trusted him completely.

He stole a kiss while Kenn was draped over his arm, then brought him back up, laughing softly as he turned them in a circle.

"Mmm.... That was lovely." Kenn's eyes were warm, smiling for him.

"I should probably rescue the potatoes." He didn't want to let go of Kenn, though.

"Okay. I like potatoes." Kenn wasn't pulling away.

He danced them to the stove and checked the potatoes. They could use a few minutes more.

Kenn was so oral—nuzzling his jaw, nibbling on his earlobe.

"You hungry, baby?" he asked, grinning.

"Um-hum. I could eat you up."

"Oh, it's like that, is it? I could let you."

"Here?" Kenn slid down his body, nuzzling along the way. Fuck, he was a lucky man.

"Uh. Uh-huh." He could go for that. He so could. He watched as Kenn went to his knees, his cock going hard.

"I love having you in my mouth, sucking you off." Kenn opened his slacks, cheek smooth as he rubbed.

That touch resonated all through Dave's body, and he moaned, running his fingers through Kenn's hair. "You shaved for me."

"Um-hum." Kenn freed his cock.

"Sweet baby." He groaned as Kenn rubbed his cock again, hot lips teasing his cockhead. He stared down, soaking up the sight of his boy on his knees.

"I love how you look on your knees in front of me. It makes me hard. You make me so hard." Kenn was beautiful. He shone.

He stroked Kenn's forehead, then pressed his thumb between Kenn's lips. His balls ached harder as Kenn immediately began to suck, pulling on his finger like it was his cock.

Dave's knees wanted to buckle. "God, I love your mouth, baby. You suck me like it's your mission in life."

"Mmm…." Kenn sucked harder, fellating his finger, eyes closed in bliss.

He watched Kenn's face. How could anyone not know what a treasure they had in this man when he sucked like that? When he took such pleasure and comfort from it? Dave wasn't stupid like Kenn's ex. He was going to be incredibly grateful for this gift. Every damn day.

Everything else faded, his focus tightening to Kenn. His balls got tighter and tighter, and finally he pulled his finger out of Kenn's mouth. Immediately Kenn went for his cock, sucking him fiercely.

"Fuck!" He bucked, and curled his fingers around Kenn's head, unable to stop himself. He worked on staying still and letting Kenn set the pace.

Kenn swallowed him down, working his balls, stroking him, petting him.

"Baby, so damn good. Gonna make me come so fast." Like boom, he was fighting it already, knowing it was a losing battle.

Kenn's hum vibrated through him like someone had hit a tuning fork.

He nearly choked on his own tongue it was so good, and he opened his mouth, though no sound came out, as he came, spunk pouring from him, his entire body shuddering.

Kenn groaned and drank him down, hand moving in his lap. The urge to order Kenn not to touch himself was huge, and the words were out before he could hold them back. He blamed the orgasm.

"Stop that. I'll make you come."

Kenn's cry was sweet, raw, and needy.

Fuck, yes. That's what he thought. He hooked his hands beneath Kenn's arms and tugged him upward, dragging the slender body all along his own. Kenn arched against him, hips driving against his thighs.

"Easy. I'm in charge of this orgasm. I get to decide how quickly you get off." He pushed his hand into Kenn's pants, finding the hard cock damp at the tip. Kenn's hips rolled, driving up toward his fingers.

"So eager. Love how much sucking my cock makes you need." It was a wonderful quality in a sexual partner, and Dave appreciated it a lot. He thought it went a long way toward proving Kenn was a natural sub.

"You feel so good. Taste so good."

"So glad. It would suck otherwise. Instead of you sucking." He groaned at himself. "God, that was bad, but you have me kind of brainless, you know?"

"Orgasms. I get it. Totally. Me next?"

"Working on it." He rubbed their noses together. "Relax and let me get you there."

"Relax. Yes. I ache for you. I need you."

He chuckled. "I don't expect you to actually relax. But I do want you to trust me to give you what you need."

"I do. I wouldn't let you in otherwise."

He took Kenn's mouth, kissing him thoroughly as he stroked the long cock. Oh, that was lovely, that heat.

He worked the tip with his thumb, letting it push hard, hoping to make it sting and feed Kenn's need for a little pain.

"Gonna make me stain my pants." What a shame.

"They're washable." He stroked harder, working the tip.

"Oh…." Kenn went up on tiptoe, driving toward him. Demanding baby.

"So needy. I love it." So much nicer than a lover who simply lay there. "Wait for me. Breathe."

"Trying…."

"You're doing great, baby. Love making you wait a little for it. Makes everything build." It turned them both on, him delaying Kenn's orgasms.

Kenn melted against him, encouraged by the praise.

"Soon, I promise. You're going to shoot all over me."

"I believe you."

"Good. Good." He kissed Kenn again, then squeezed the head of Kenn's cock and whispered, "Come for me now."

Kenn gasped softly, teeth sinking into his bottom lip. He pinched the tip of Kenn's cock, and his boy cried out, coming for him like a dream. Shooting right in his pants.

"Mmm. There we go, baby." He kissed the side of Kenn's eyebrow, making Kenn give him a warm, lazy smile. "Nice to have the edge off, isn't it?" He was going to have to let Kenn change into his robe or something. That might be fun, actually, to change into robes.

Oh. Potatoes. Save the potatoes.

He put Kenn on the bed and went over to the stove to grab the pot and drain the water. The potatoes were overdone, but he figured putting them in the oven to roast would crisp up the outside. The steak was the star anyway, right?

"Let me go change, and I'll help."

"You should just put your robe on. Nicely easy access."

"That sounds naughty." And Kenn was intrigued.

"That's what I thought." He waggled his eyebrows at Kenn.

"I'll go change." Kenn disappeared in his little bathroom.

Dave smiled, transferred the potatoes to a pan, and stuck them in the oven. Then he grabbed the frying pan, put some oil in it. He didn't turn it on yet—the meat wouldn't take that long. He oiled and salted and peppered the steak, letting it sit there and warm to room temperature. He basically did everything he had to get ready, so he could focus on Kenn when he got out of the bathroom.

"What do you need me to do?"

He turned around, curious to see if Kenn had indeed put the robe on and if so, how tightly he'd closed it.

Kenn was in a light robe, the belt barely holding on. Oh yes. Yes, please.

He held open his arms, and Kenn flew into them. Letting one hand slide beneath the robe, he wrapped it around Kenn and tugged him in close. There was something sexy about being fully dressed while Kenn was almost naked. He pressed their lips together, expressing his admiration through their kiss.

Kenn moaned for him, low and sweet, tongue sliding against his.

"I should probably get our supper cooking," he noted as their lips parted. "The potatoes'll be about ten more minutes, maybe fifteen. How do you like your steak?"

"Pink but not bloody, please."

"You got it. Mine's a portobello." He turned the stove on under the frying pan.

"I…. Let me cook the steak. I feel bad."

"Or I could do both portobellos I brought if you'd like to give it a try? I'm not trying to push you into veggie, but if you'd like to try…." He truly didn't mind if Kenn wanted the steak.

"Let's do that. I'll pop the steak in the freezer. I'd feel better that way. Honestly."

"If you're sure. Does this mean you're going to turn vegetarian whenever we're together?" He didn't want Kenn feeling bad whenever they had a meal together.

"Is that a problem?"

"Not for me. I don't want you to feel like you have to change your eating habits to please me or anything like that."

"I don't want you to have to kiss me with meat mouth."

"Oh, that is the sweetest thing anyone has ever said to me or done for me." He cupped Kenn's face and brought their mouths together. He kissed Kenn quite thoroughly. He'd never had someone who offered themselves so openly.

Did Kenn have any idea what a joy he was? Dave suspected not. "Okay. Let's get the portobellos in the pan, and we can keep dancing if we want. Or chatting or whatever."

"I bet we can manage both."

"I like the way you think." He gave Kenn another quick kiss, then moved to work on the main component of their meal. "You ever considered going vegetarian before?"

"No. I don't think about food much. I mean, I eat, but my thing is sweets."

"So if you wind up eating vegetarian all the time, you wouldn't be upset." That would make Kenn the first person he'd dated who didn't think him being vegetarian was a problem.

"I live on pizza, oatmeal, and pastries."

"We can probably do better than that." He could happily feed Kenn on a regular basis.

"Um-hum. Maybe. You're doing fine so far."

"I hope you like the portobellos. They really are meaty." He rubbed some oil and spices on the big mushrooms and put them in to slowly cook through. "It'll probably be about twenty minutes. Won't hurt them if it's longer."

"You want to cuddle on the bed for a while?"

"I do. We can cuddle and talk and anticipate our dinner and our after-dinner activities." He guided Kenn to the bed and started stripping. Cuddling was way more fun if you were both naked.

"Would you like a robe, or are you warm enough?"

"We are going to keep each other warm. Plus you've got covers."

"I do." Kenn slipped in and held the blankets open for him.

He followed Kenn down, snuggling in. They warmed the area quickly, and it felt good, felt right. He opened up Kenn's robe, hands on his lover's smooth body.

"Are you looking forward to later? When we make love."

"I am. I enjoy penetration. I miss it."

"God, you really are a wonder. I am the luckiest man in the world."

"How about you? Are you looking forward to it?"

"I am. I can't wait to watch your face as I push inside you." He curled their lower bodies together, tangling their legs. "I can't wait to feel you tight and hot around my cock."

Kenn's expression softened, and he moaned. "Oh God."

"I'm going to pound into you. Soft and easy at first, but then I'm going to go faster and harder."

"David!" Kenn pushed closer. "That's… that's hot."

"You want to hear about how I'm going to open you up?" He was getting off on how much Kenn liked to listen to him talk dirty.

"Please." Kenn's lips were soft on his ear.

"I know the standard thing is to start with a single finger. My favorite way however, is to start with my tongue."

Kenn's cry was the sweetest thing he'd ever heard.

"You like being rimmed, Kenn?" Which was a crazy question—who didn't like being rimmed? It was pretty damn amazing.

"I want to try," Kenn groaned.

"Have you never been rimmed before, Kenn? Oh man. It's going to blow your mind." How could it be that no one had ever given Kenn that pleasure? It was such a simple thing.

"No, never. I've done it, but…."

"Oh, that's not fair. Not fair at all. Turn around, baby. Let me take care of you."

"What? Now?"

"Yeah. I don't think you should go a moment longer without knowing how it feels to be rimmed. Shame on your other lovers for taking but not giving." He kissed Kenn really quickly, then wiggled his tongue as obscenely as possible.

"I.... Dave!" Kenn laughed, the sound husky, wanton.

He kissed Kenn's nose, then started turning him. "I mean it, baby. I want you to know what it's like." And there was nothing wrong with eating dinner all jazzed up from a rimming.

He slid down, dragging his lips down Kenn's spine. Kenn made the most wonderful noises. He was anticipating how much bigger they would be when he got to Kenn's ass.

"I can't believe.... Please."

"Take a breath." He pushed Kenn forward slightly, encouraged him to move one leg out so it opened that sweet ass to him. Then he blew air from the top of Kenn's crack to his hole. His lover shivered, and before that sensation had faded, Dave licked that tight little hole. Kenn whimpered, asscheeks clutching.

"Sweet baby." He licked again, then again, working on getting Kenn's hole wet.

He thought Kenn might be sobbing, the sounds muffled but wild.

He kept it up, flattening his tongue and sliding it back and forth over Kenn's hole. Then he pressed the tip of his tongue against the tiny ring of tight muscles.

"Fuck.... Killing me."

Uh-huh. And he was going to make it even better. He pressed harder, stabbing his tongue in hard enough to breach that sweet hole.

Kenn pushed back, begging for him, eager, wanton. Oh, his boy hadn't been lying about loving assplay. He still couldn't believe no one had done this for Kenn before. It was criminal.

He pushed his tongue in, breaching Kenn's hole and pressing in deeper.

"Oh God. I need you. I need you to take me. I've been so empty."

Oh, poor baby. He pushed his tongue in as deeply as he could and then began to fuck Kenn with it.

Kenn bucked back against him, humping hard.

Fuck it. He was going to turn the food off and take care of Kenn.

"Please. Please, Dave. Please. I need you. Now." Kenn begged so prettily, spreading for him, hips up and back.

He withdrew his tongue. "Let me go turn off the stove." He patted Kenn's ass before going over and making sure everything was turned off. He blew the candles out for good measure. Just in case. Then he grabbed the bag from the pharmacy, which had the lube and condoms in it, and returned to Kenn's side.

Kenn leaned toward him, body begging for him, for his touch.

"I'm going to take care of you, baby. I promise." Dave leaned in and licked at Kenn's hole again as he grabbed the lube out of the bag. He got it open and got his fingers wet.

He started with one, pushing it into Kenn without fanfare. Kenn didn't need to be teased. Kenn needed to be filled. Kenn pushed back toward him, accepting him into that perfect tight heat. He groaned, imagining how Kenn was going to feel around his cock.

"So hot and tight. You're going to feel perfect. I can't wait to be sinking my cock into you."

"Yes. I ache for it. For you, Dave."

He wished Kenn had voiced his need. Dave could have helped him out ages ago. Never mind—they were here now.

He pushed a second finger in with the first. "I hear you. I'm going to make it good."

Kenn was wild, bucking back against him, trying to get him in deeper.

"Easy. Easy. You want this to last longer than a few thrusts." He wanted Kenn to be able to revel in it, to enjoy every single second and for there to be a lot of seconds.

"Sorry. Sorry, overeager."

"Totally understandable. You're allowed, even. But a few deep breaths and we'll make it last." He continued to work Kenn with two fingers, twisting them together and pushing them deep, then spreading them wide and pulling them back out.

Kenn nodded, obviously forcing himself to relax, to gather his control.

"I'm not going to tease, baby. I promise." To that end, he added another finger, quickly stretching Kenn so that it wasn't such a shock to his lover's body when he pushed his cock in.

"I know. I've got this. I was…. You feel good."

"And you feel incredible. You're going to be magic around my cock." He fingerfucked Kenn a little longer. "You ever play with plugs?" Kenn would so get off on that.

Kenn shook his head, taking shaky breaths.

"We'll have to look together online and buy one. See if you like it." Kenn was going to love it, Dave knew. He pulled his fingers out and grabbed a condom, ripping the package open and sliding the latex over his erection. "Ready for it to be me now, Kenn?"

"I am." Kenn was still, quiet, waiting for him.

He took a breath, and then he stopped. "Wait. I want to see your face. Lie on your back for me."

"What?" Kenn blinked back over his shoulder.

He reached over and stroked Kenn's face, fingertips sliding across his lover's lips. "I want to be able to see your face, to look into your eyes."

Kenn kissed his fingers, moving slowly, turning over to face him.

He smiled down at Kenn. "There you are. My beautiful boy." He bent to kiss Kenn, then guided his cock to Kenn's hole. He pressed, already feeling the heat from Kenn's body with his cock only touching Kenn's hole. "I want to watch every second. I want to know you're with me."

Kenn keened softly, bucking up and trying to take him in. He stroked Kenn's lips, then pressed in, Kenn's hole spreading around his cock. So fucking good. So hot and tight.

He groaned as heat flooded him. Damn, he wanted.

He kept pressing in, filling Kenn slowly but surely, his gaze holding tight to Kenn's. He made a noise as his hips hit the backs of Kenn's thighs. He was inside Kenn, buried deep, and it felt amazing.

Kenn looked blissful, joyful, utterly at peace.

Damn. He had a new mission in life—make sure Kenn wore that expression as often as possible.

"So pretty, babe." He took a kiss, then another kiss. Then he began to move, pulling almost all the way out before pushing back in again. He matched kisses with thrusts, joining them at mouth and ass.

Oh. Oh, he could... forever. Forever. He pushed in deep, taking Kenn. A low groan came from Kenn, and he matched it. He continued to thrust, filling Kenn over and over. Kenn began to slam up, meeting his thrusts now.

"Fuck yes." He slammed in harder, giving Kenn his all as he wrapped one hand around Kenn's hip.

"Oh." Kenn gasped, eyes rolling back. "Fuck me. Yes."

"That's the idea." He rocked and rolled, finding his rhythm and plowing into Kenn.

Kenn took it and took it, sobbing softly, face a study in bliss.

Every now and then Dave would bend and bring their mouths together, kissing Kenn hard before he'd focus back on what their hips were doing. Every second was pure sensation, and his balls drew up against his body, his head pounding hard.

"Soon…." Kenn arched into him, legs wrapping around him and holding him tight.

He nodded. "Yeah. Soon as you're ready, you can come." He let go of Kenn's hip in favor of wrapping around Kenn's erection.

"You too. Us. Together. Please."

Oh fuck yes. Together.

"Yeah, babe. I'm ready. Right now." He flicked his thumb across the tip of Kenn's cock.

Kenn's lips popped open and he spent, body gripping him like a fist. Dave's eyes rolled back in his head at the amazing pressure, and he came, filling the condom. One day they'd go bareback. One day he'd trap his seed in that sweet ass.

He pressed kiss after kiss on Kenn, not wanting to come out, not wanting this to end yet. Kenn took everything, his kisses lazy, happy.

Finally, it was time to come out. He grabbed hold of the base of the condom and pulled out. He got rid of it, then lay down next to Kenn.

Kenn grabbed him, drew him in, and held him.

"You good?" He was pretty sure he was reading Kenn right, but it never hurt to be sure.

"Yes. Thank you. I've missed… I've missed that."

"I wish I'd known. I would have suggested we do it sooner."

"It doesn't come up in conversation, really. I like anal sex. Wanna?"

That had him laughing softly. "Yeah, I guess not. You needed bad, though. I'm not going to make you wait so long for the next time." He pressed a few kisses over Kenn's face. "In fact, I'm going to make sure you get everything you need."

They could use Kenn's laptop and get something shipped overnight. He couldn't believe Kenn had never used a plug. Never been rimmed, never plugged…. Poor lovely wanton.

"You're who I need right now, Dave."

"Ditto, Kenn." He held Kenn close, stroking his back. He trusted that his instincts were leading him right and Kenn needed him because he could give Kenn what he desired, knew how to make Kenn fly. For more than just sex.

They had what the other craved. They did. They just had a journey to get there. He had a hunch it was going to be a memorable one.

Chapter Nine

The mushrooms were delicious—rich and spicy, beefy and filling. Kenn could eat those any day. So far, being vegetarian with Dave hadn't been a problem at all.

Dave had refused to let him help with the dishes, instead insisting that he sit at the little table. Dave did the last dish, then came over and sat across from him. "I think we should do a little online shopping before we have dessert."

"Online shopping? For what?" He was willing, sure, but he didn't know what they needed.

"You need a plug. I can't believe you've never had one. Hell, I couldn't believe you hadn't been rimmed before either."

"My…. I shouldn't talk about him, huh?"

"You're allowed. I promise I won't be jealous. I know I won't be. He clearly wasn't what you needed."

"Bram was…. We had sex on Saturday nights." Blow job, a fuck, and then they read and watched TV.

Dave's eyebrows went up. "Was he a lot older than you?"

"Fifteen years, yes, but…." That wasn't that old.

"No, I meant like in his sixties. That's very… well, I didn't know him, but my God, you were starving for it."

"He wanted someone on his arm, not the messiness of sex."

"That's sounds really sad. I'm sorry."

"I'm sorry too. It was terrible at the end, but…."

"But it's over now, and you can be as sexual as you want."

"Yes. Yes, I suppose I can." Whatever that meant.

"So let's open your laptop and buy a plug." Dave said it like it was the most normal thing in the world.

"Just… buy one? Okay." No way.

"Yeah. I mean, we'll check them out first, see what you like. It won't be random." Dave opened Kenn's laptop and went to Google.

"Do you want coffee?" Kenn was all nerves, buzzing with a weird excitement.

Dave shook his head and pushed back from the table a little. "I want you to sit in my lap while we do this."

"In your lap?" He moved to Dave immediately, drawn in.

Dave nuzzled their cheeks together. "That's better, isn't it?"

"You make me feel things, you know?" Things that he probably shouldn't. Things that made him worry and ache.

"Good. I want you to feel so many things. I want to share everything with you." Dave typed something in Google, then clicked on the first link, the screen filling with a plethora of plugs.

Kenn's eyes went wide. "Good lord."

"I know, eh? So many choices. How are we going to narrow it down to just one?"

"Dave, I can't... I can't do that." It was naughty.

"You can't narrow it down to one? I'm more than willing to buy more than one. They aren't that expensive."

Kenn's cheeks were on fire. He couldn't do this. They were so... hot.

"How about we start with which one draws you in the most?" Dave dropped one hand down, rubbing Kenn's belly through his robe.

"They're obscene." And fascinating.

"I suppose. That's not a bad thing, though. I mean, we're getting one to put inside you." Dave was a little breathless as he spoke.

He hid his face in Dave's throat, his cock threatening to fill.

"You're going to be so sexy." Dave rubbed his cheek on the top of Kenn's head. "It's going to change the way you sit and the way you walk."

He moaned softly, legs trying to make room for his cock.

"Mmm. We'll make love again when we've made our purchase," Dave promised. "We can have dessert when we wake up in the middle of the night in each other's arms." Then he clicked on the laptop, and one of the plugs, bullet shaped and with a base, filled the page. "What do you think of this one?"

"I.... Oh God...." He wanted to... die. Hump Dave's leg. Beg.

"That's a yes, huh? Of course maybe that'd be your reaction to any of them?" Dave went back to the screen with all the plugs. "You point out one you want to take a closer look at."

"I can't."

"You can. Do it."

His heart began to pound so hard, shattering against his ribs. "David…."

Dave held him tight. "You can do this, babe. It's good and fun and absolutely wonderful."

"Yeah?" He managed to meet Dave's eyes.

"Absolutely. I know your ex made like it was dirty and wrong. But he also only wanted to have sex one night a week, so consider the source. There is nothing wrong about us looking at and buying plugs. There's nothing wrong with us using them. What we do—that's our business."

Kenn turned to the screen, his natural curiosity taking over. There were so many—different colors and materials, sizes and shapes. "There are all these options."

"Yeah. It's rather stunning. And you can have any one that you want. Or two. And then when we're tired of them, we'll buy another one."

"I like the metal ones." He whispered the words, but Dave heard him.

"Yeah? They're pretty sexy. If you had to narrow it down?"

He clicked around, coming back to a round one with a thin neck.

"Mmm. That's pretty. I can imagine using it on you. Can you imagine what it would feel like slipping into you?"

Kenn's hand fell into his lap, and he rubbed his cock. He could. He'd watched videos. He'd seen things. Dave settled his hand on top of Kenn's. "No touching without my permission."

His lips fell open, and his cock jerked hard. "What?"

"When I'm here with you, this is mine." Dave dropped his hand and moved to rest it on Kenn's cock. Dave squeezed. "Mine. If you want to touch, you can ask me."

His heart began to pound, and he licked his lips, torn between standing up and nodding.

"Do you understand?" Dave asked, gaze holding his.

The look in Dave's eyes was firm but not mean, just… masterful. Kind too. Dave wasn't being an asshole, he could tell.

"I hear you. I … I don't know what to do."

"Say 'yes, Sir,' and stop touching yourself." Dave leaned in and rubbed their noses together. "This is for fun, excitement to increase our pleasure."

"Yes…." Okay. Just a game, something for fun. "Yes, Sir."

"Mmm. Do you like the way it feels? Saying that, I mean." Dave rubbed his cock, the touch light, barely there.

Kenn's eyelids got heavy, that hand perfect against him. "I do...."

"I thought you might. I love hearing you say it." Dave laid his hand on Kenn's cock, resting it there now. "Let's buy a plug and set up delivery. Then we can continue touching."

"Oh, okay. Sounds good."

"So which was your favorite? This one?" Dave clicked on the one he'd been looking at, bringing it up on the screen.

"Yes. Yes, that one. God, I can't believe we're talking about this."

"Why? Because your ex said it was wrong? I'm not being an asshole. I'm honestly curious why."

"Because he called me filthy and hit me until I couldn't stand back up." Kenn was suddenly icy cold, and he stood. "Pardon me."

He made it to the bathroom and stood there on the tile, shaking like a leaf.

No one understood how ashamed he'd been, how badly he'd been hurt.

Dave knocked on the door, then slipped into the bathroom and wrapped around him. "Kenn... I didn't know. My God. God. I'm so sorry that happened to you."

"It doesn't matter. I just.... It doesn't matter."

"Of course it matters. He abused you. He should have been arrested. And you've spent how many years thinking your desires were wrong, when they aren't. You are not filthy. Not at all."

"I shouldn't have snarled. None of this is your fault. Not a bit. You've been good to me."

"No, don't do that. You're allowed to have feelings. You're allowed to be upset. I poked a sore spot. A very deservedly sore spot. You can apologize for snarling, but don't say you shouldn't have." Dave kept holding him, warming him through.

"I just... I'm really tired of worrying."

"You don't have to worry with me. I think it's amazing that you're excited by this kind of stuff. I am too. And there's nothing wrong with that at all." Dave rubbed his arm and his back. "Come back to bed where it's warm, hmm?"

Dave led him back to the bed and curled up around him. "You should have gone to the police when he did that to you."

"I did."

"And what happened?"

"I got a restraining order, but I knew it wouldn't do any good. He knows how to get around it, and he has friends in high places too."

Dave shook his head. Restraining orders were so nonspecific, and it was hard to prove they'd been violated. Dave squeezed Kenn tightly. "You deserve so much better than this."

"I'm okay. I got away. I left with next to nothing, but I got away."

"I wish there was something I could do."

"I know." Oh, this was the beginning of not seeing each other again, wasn't it?

"Well, I can't change what happened to you back then, but I can make sure you're treated right now."

"What?" Kenn blinked, surprised.

"I want to give you what you crave." Dave smiled at him. "You'll need to trust me, but if you do, it'll be amazing."

"I thought…." He'd thought for sure that Dave was going to break up with him.

"What did you think? I want to know." Dave stayed close, fingers warm as they ran up and down along his skin.

"That you would… that I'm just too much."

Dave held him tight. "I don't think you're too much at all. I'm eager to learn about all the things that excite you. I think we're going to have so much fun together."

"You do? We are?" Kenn cuddled right in with a deep sigh.

"I sure hope we are. I think we have the perfect recipe for it. Two guys interested in sensation and toys and having fun together. I'm planning to enjoy every second with you, Kenn." Dave smiled against his cheek. "I plan for you to enjoy it too."

"You're making my heart pound."

"In a good way, I hope." Dave placed a hand over Kenn's heart, palm flat, which teased his nipple.

"Yes. Yeah, in a good way." He took a deep breath, Dave's hand slipping on him a little.

"I want you to know you can say anything to me. You can tell me anything. I'm not going to run away or send you away. Or do anything awful to you. I promise."

"I don't know how to… come to terms with all this shame and need."

"Will it help if I tell you there's nothing to be ashamed of in your need? If I tell you over and over and over again until you believe it?" Dave's fingers went back to dancing over his skin, warming it.

"I know you can't understand, but... I feel so...." Dirty.

"Feel so what, babe? I want to understand. I do."

"Naughty. Wicked. Excited."

"Those all sound like good things to me," Dave admitted.

"Me too," he whispered.

Dave kissed him softly. "Then let's go with that, eh?"

"I'm going to try." He wanted to try.

"You need to talk to me, though, okay? If I do something you don't like or that scares you or that is really amazing. Or if there's something you want to try. You need to tell me. I can't read your mind, and I don't know everything you went through, though I hope what you told me was the worst of it."

"The guilt was the worst." It could be crippling—freezing him solid.

"I don't want you to feel guilty about the things you like. I understand that might not happen overnight. But if you share with me when you are, maybe I can help you change that. Sound good?"

"Why on earth are you interested? I have all this baggage." It seemed ridiculous. Insane.

"What kind of a person would I be if I said I wanted to see you, but only if you don't bring any of your baggage with you? I mean, seriously."

Kenn chuckled softly, tickled to death that he'd agreed to have cheesecake with Dave that first night.

"God, I like that sound." Dave nipped at his nose. "Upshot of everything I've said is communication is key. I don't care what your ex might have been like on this front. I like talking and trusting and loving."

Kenn nodded. He liked the idea of all those things too. He liked the idea of being... happy again. Not merely getting by but outright happy.

Dave hugged him tight. "I'm so glad you're taking a chance on us."

He hoped he wasn't doing something incredibly stupid, trusting Dave like this.

"Now, you want dessert, or do you want to make love again?"

"Can we sit together for a few minutes? Just be?"

"Absolutely." Dave pulled him in closer again, so warm, the fingers on his skin easy and gentle.

"Thank you." This was the best gift—this friendship.

"Oh, did you want to actually sit or is this good here in bed?"

"I like it here. It's—" *Safe.* "—comfortable."

"Cozy. Like a cocoon just for us." Dave rubbed their cheeks together. He was so sensual, so tactile. He leaned in, his fingers sliding over Dave's skin.

Dave hummed, the sound so happy, pleased. "Tell me more about your history studies. I like hearing you talk about the things you love."

"Only if you share the favor. You have some fascinating research." He'd loved that part of earning his doctorate—researching new things.

"I do," Dave agreed. "We'll take turns. Share, then kiss, then share, then kiss. The best of both worlds."

"That sounds like heaven." Kenn settled in. "We had a great conversation in class Wednesday…."

Chapter Ten

DAVE RUSHED home from his last class. He had to throw together a quick bag for the weekend at Kenn's. He needed a shower first. There was something wrong with the heating in his classroom, and it had been sweltering. His shirt was literally stuck to his back.

Still, he had the plug they'd ordered washed and in a baggie, two new books to share with Kenn, and the whole weekend ahead of him.

"Do you want to play, man?" George asked as he walked in the door. "We have a spare controller."

"Thanks, but not today. I have plans." Wonderful, fun, exciting, sexy plans with his special man. He was probably grinning like a fool, but he didn't care.

"Ooh. Again? Lucky duck!"

"Yeah. I am." He was the luckiest man in the world.

He checked the time on his phone. He needed to hustle harder; he didn't want to lose a moment of his time with Kenn.

His phone buzzed. *Bought us pizza for supper.*

He could feel his smile getting wider. *Perfect. Be there soon as I shower.*

cusoon <3

<3 2

He grabbed fresh clothes and went to the shower, making short work of cleaning himself and getting dressed. He did his teeth, then grabbed his toiletries and added them to his bag, along with clothes for a couple days, the plug, the books, and extra underwear.

Shouldering his bag, he headed out, eager to get to Kenn's. He waved at George as he left, his focus snapping to hotfooting it to Kenn's.

HE ROUNDED the street to Kenn's, meeting up with Timothy on the way, the man full of bounce.

"Hello there! You heading for the house? Kenn's home. Happy and singing like the world's largest weirdassed bird."

Good. Kenn was looking forward to this as much as he was.

"You mean the world's largest beautiful bird." His man was stunning, not weirdassed.

Timmy cackled. "Oh, I do like you. Kenn deserves that. Do you two want to go see a movie tonight? There's some good stuff playing."

"I think we'd planned to stay in, but if we change our minds, Kenn'll text you, 'kay?"

"Totally. I'm going at nine, so holler." Timmy grinned. "If not, have the best night. I'm glad you made him sing."

"Yeah, me too." He gave Timmy a wave and kept going, more eager than ever to see Kenn. Singing, eh? Go, Kenn.

He could hear the music playing through Kenn's door as he reached it but just barely, not enough to piss off the neighbors. He knocked loudly, wanting to make sure that Kenn heard it over the music and his own singing—if he still was.

"Coming!" Kenn opened the door, wearing a tiny pair of shorts and holding a feather duster.

Dave's jaw dropped. "Wow. You look great." Edible.

"I was cleaning up, that's all." Kenn pinked.

"You're still edible, no matter what you're doing."

"Come in. Come in. Hello." Kenn leaned in and kissed him.

He kept kissing Kenn back as he closed the door behind him. Then he dropped his bag and cupped Kenn's face in both hands. Kenn stepped right into him, cuddled in with a happy sound.

"Your skin feels amazing. You should always go around with very little clothing." He could get behind that.

"Flatterer." Kenn stole another kiss, lingering on it.

He shook his head when their lips had parted. "Truth."

Kenn smiled at him, kissed the corner of his lips.

"Have you ever played Truth or Dare?" It was all the rage among students. He used to do it all the time when he was an undergrad.

"Of course. It's been a while, but I have."

"You wanna play?" He waggled his eyebrows.

"You're serious?" Kenn laughed, the sound so warm. "Sure. I'm not lighting farts, though."

"Oh, I was thinking more along the lines of blow jobs and rimming, maybe dancing with a plug in—that kind of dare."

"Dave!"

He did love a handful of happy man.

He laughed and picked Kenn up, spinning him around. "You've got to admit, giving me a blow job is way better than lighting your farts."

"Giving you a blow job is a glorious thing." Kenn cupped his balls.

He groaned. "We probably shouldn't touch until there's a dare saying you can."

"That's no fun, is it?"

Wicked little man.

"Well, if you give me a blow job now, what'll I ask you to do for a dare?" He had plenty of ideas, actually.

"True. Okay. No touching. Truth or dare?"

He laughed softly. "I'm gonna start conservative and say truth."

"Mmm.... What's your favorite thing to eat?"

"You."

Kenn chuckled, shook his head, but accepted said the answer.

"Truth or dare?" Dave asked.

"Truth."

"What's your best memory?"

"I don't know... maybe.... I think my first professional article getting published. I was so proud."

"I love that." He loved that look of pride on Kenn's face too.

"It was cool. I was over the moon."

"Have the subsequent times lived up to the same feeling? Or is nothing quite like that first time?" He hadn't been published yet, and he could only imagine.

"First times are truly special, aren't they?"

"Yeah, they are." He smiled at Kenn, remembering their first time the weekend before. He slid a finger along Kenn's cheek. "They really are."

Kenn moaned, turning his head to kiss Dave's finger.

"Mmm." He hummed happily, fingers curling, stroking Kenn's skin. "Your turn to ask," he whispered.

"Um-hum... truth or dare?"

"I'm going to leap in and go for dare this time." He was curious as to what Kenn would start with.

"Kiss me." Kenn's grin proved that he'd been planning.

"Starting slowly, I see. I approve." He leaned in unhurriedly and rubbed Kenn's lips with his, then rested them together, breathing with

Kenn before turning it into a long, slow kiss. Kenn opened for him, giving it up to him.

He groaned, letting the kiss linger as long as he could. When their lips finally parted, he leaned their foreheads together. "Truth or dare?" he whispered.

"Dare." Kenn licked his lips.

"Make my nipples hard." Dave had been waiting for that too.

Kenn's fingers slid beneath Dave's T-shirt and up his belly, heading slowly and steadily for his nips. He held his breath as Kenn moved, so leisurely. He watched Kenn's hand move beneath his T-shirt and suddenly wanted to see Kenn at work. He quickly pulled off his shirt so he could watch.

Kenn chuckled softly. "I bet you're a visual learner."

"Yep." He took in a deep breath, his nipples already hardening, anticipating Kenn's touch.

"Hmm…." Kenn drew a circle around his nipple—first one and then the other.

"Oh God." He swallowed and let out a deep breath. "Such a sweet touch."

"Mmm…." Kenn kept circling, and Dave's nipples drew up tight.

He shivered. "I can't believe how quickly you made that happen."

"Visual learner."

He chuckled. "Ask the question, babe."

"Truth or dare." As he asked the question, Kenn pinched his nipple.

"Dare!" The word came out as a yelp.

"Did I hurt?" Kenn leaned down and kissed his nipple.

"God no. It was the surprise. The touch was great. You're great."

"Oh good." Kenn stepped closer. "I dare you to make me hard using…." He trailed off, blushing hard.

"Using what? My mouth, my hands, something else? You're going to have to actually tell me."

"I… I can't believe I'm doing this."

"You are. You're so sexy," he whispered into Kenn's ear. "Go ahead and say it. Tell me. You know you want it."

"Your voice. Just your voice."

He groaned. That was unexpected but totally hot. And doable. Hell, Kenn's cock was already awake from the kissing and touching they'd done so far.

"I can do that. I'm going to tell you about the plug we bought. It arrived yesterday. I have it in my bag, washed and ready to go. You remember what it looks like? It's got a base to keep it from going in and getting lost. It's got a tapered top that's rounded. It's going to feel so good hitting up against your gland."

Kenn's moan filled the air. Dave was going to have this dare in the bag.

"I'm going to take my time putting it in. I'm going to lube you up first with my fingers. Not too much, though. I want you to feel the stretch from the plug." He loved this, loved how his boy craved his words.

He resisted reaching for Kenn's cock. He'd bet it was already hard, but he had a few more things to say.

"At first you'll think it's not that big—the tip isn't after all. Then it gets wider. And wider. I'll stop when the widest part is holding you open, let you really feel the stretch for a while before I plunge the whole thing in."

Kenn cried out, pushed in and kissed him desperately. Dave kissed Kenn right back, grabbing Kenn's ass and tugging him closer. Oh yes. He'd made his boy hard.

Kenn rocked against him, rubbing hard.

Dave shifted his hips, moving them back. "Truth or dare, babe?" He wanted to keep playing, to draw the game out.

"Mmm... truth?" Kenn groaned softly.

"Tell me how you're feeling right now. Every little detail."

"I want you. I'm hard, and it feels good. I'm a little exposed."

"How does being exposed make you feel? Excited? Nervous?"

"I'm not nervous. I trust you. I've been naked with you—more naked than I've ever been, right?"

"Yeah." He slid his hand down to cup Kenn's ass again. "You're not quite naked enough at the moment. In my opinion, of course."

"No?" Kenn grinned, and Dave loved the way confidence looked on his boy. "Truth or dare?"

"Dare." He was done with talking and getting very aroused. Confident Kenn was hot.

"Get us naked, lover."

"I'm going to start easy." He slid his fingers to the edges of Kenn's tiny shorts, and slowly tugged them down, holding Kenn's gaze as he did.

Heat flared in his lover's eyes. Damn.

Once he'd pushed them down as far as he could reach, he slowly went to his knees to take them right off.

"Oh God…." Kenn moaned softly.

He rubbed his cheek along Kenn's hard cock. Then, after Kenn had stepped out of his shorts, Dave pressed a kiss on the tip. He hummed, licked quickly to take Kenn's taste into himself.

"Oh…. Please." Kenn arched toward him.

"That wasn't the dare, babe." He stood, making sure to drag his clothed body along Kenn's naked one as he went. Then he started stripping out of his own clothing.

Kenn touched him as he bared himself, fingers dancing on his skin.

"Making me hard." It so wasn't a complaint, though it seemed they weren't going to get a whole lot more game playing going on.

"Good." Kenn groaned, eyes searching his body.

"Uh-huh." He cleared his throat as he got the last of his clothing off. "Now, truth or dare?"

"Dare." Kenn came toward him, gravitating forward.

"I dare you to give me a blow job."

"Such a challenge." Kenn's smile was Cheshire cat wide. "I'd love to."

Then Kenn knelt down before him, lips parted.

Taking the base of his cock in hand, he pressed forward, pushing his cock into Kenn's mouth. His boy opened, easy as pie, eager for him.

His cock slid along Kenn's tongue, and Kenn closed his lips, surrounding him with heat. He groaned and rocked in, waiting to see Kenn's response. Kenn didn't tense; he let Dave in deep.

Dave let out another low moan and drew back slightly. Rocking forward again, he pushed his cock back along Kenn's tongue. Kenn groaned, tongue flashing over his shaft.

He rocked slowly, cock pushing in, taking Kenn's mouth, his throat.

Kenn's moan vibrated all through his body—beginning at his cock and emanating outward. He was a lucky bastard to have a cockhound for a boy.

Kenn's hands crept up and grabbed his ass, and he pushed back into the hold, then rocked forward again. Kenn squeezed, encouraging him to keep moving. So he did.

Swallowing around him, Kenn moaned deep in his throat.

"Damn." He shuddered, his balls drawing up against his body. Moving faster, he rocked into Kenn's throat time and again. Those warm eyes stared up at him, offering him everything.

He cupped Kenn's face in his hand and let Kenn have his come as it poured out of him. Kenn swallowed hard, drinking him in, hands cupping his ass and pulling.

Dave kept watching Kenn's face, taking in the happiness, the bliss. He would use this mouth as often as he could, fill that need in Kenn.

He cupped Kenn's jaw, rubbing in lazy circles.

"That was the best dare I've ever had. It was good for you too, hmm?" He was never going to make Kenn feel less than awesome for loving to suck.

"Um-hum." Kenn cleaned him off, the soft licks making his ass clench.

"Are you going to ask me?" Because those little licks were going to make him lose his mind and forget everything but making love to Kenn. Not that anything was wrong with that, not at all. But he wanted to play a little longer too.

"Truth or dare?" Kenn murmured against his shaft.

"Definitely dare. Definitely."

"Give me what I need." Oh, so many options.

"You realize that leaves me wide open." Of course, what Kenn needed was for him to decide what the next step was. That was why his boy hadn't asked for something specific.

"I do."

"Then it's time to get on the bed. Hands and knees. I want that sweet ass right here for me. Your little hole exposed."

Kenn whimpered softly but stood and climbed on the bed.

"Put your head on a pillow, I want you to hold your hole open for me."

"What?" The flush that covered Kenn's spine was so pretty.

"Put your head on the pillow and let your shoulders support you as you hold your hole open for me." He was pretty sure Kenn had actually heard him the first time, but repeating it would give Kenn a moment to get used to the idea, or figure out the words to say what he really meant.

"Oh God...."

He stroked Kenn's ass, waiting. He could be patient. He was exceptional at it, in fact.

It took a few endless minutes, but eventually Kenn leaned down for him.

"Such a good boy." He stroked Kenn's ass, then ran his finger along Kenn's crack. "Now all that's left is holding yourself open for me. Let me see this pretty little pink hole."

Kenn's moan was pure need, a low desperation, but he slid his hands back to hold his cheeks open.

"Look at you. So pretty. So sexy. You make me need, Kenn." He slid his finger along Kenn's crack again, this time lingering at Kenn's exposed hole.

Kenn clenched but didn't let go. He was trying so hard.

Grabbing the lube, Dave splurted some on his fingers. "I've got lube. It's going to be cool to start with." He spread a bunch along Kenn's crack. Then he pushed some right in. Kenn arched, but took him, body clenching around his touch.

"You're so hot inside. And so tight. It makes me want to take you, fill you and feel you around me." He pushed more lube into Kenn's hole. "But first we're going to play with the plug. I'm going to use it to open you up for me. I'm going to watch you walk around with it, sit with it."

"Dave...." He loved hearing the sound of his name like that.

"You're going to love every second of it. After all, it's what you need." And they both knew it. Both of them.

He pushed two fingers into Kenn's hole, turning them up and twisting them around inside Kenn. Then he tugged them out again.

"Let me get the plug. It's in my bag."

"Okay."

"Don't move, boy."

Kenn shivered, and he placed a kiss in the small of Kenn's back before getting up. Where did he leave his bag? It wasn't like the place was that big. Oh, there, right by the door.

He went and grabbed the plug out of his bag and returned quickly to Kenn's side. "Such a good boy, staying still, you deserve a reward."

Dave swooped down, licked Kenn's hole once, earning a sharp cry. So he did it again, then slid his tongue down to Kenn's balls. He took one in his mouth, sucking on it gently as he got the plug lubed up by feel.

Kenn rocked and whimpered, toes curled tight.

He let Kenn's ball slip out of his mouth. "Beautiful." Every time Kenn got what he truly needed, he glowed. It made Dave even more eager to do this for Kenn. To Kenn. With Kenn. Whatever. Together.

He needed to share this with Kenn, to explore their options.

"I've got the plug all ready now. Are you ready for it, babe? Ready to feel it pushing into you? Ready to be stretched open by it? Ready to have it fill you?" He touched his finger against Kenn's hole, pressing against it with every word.

"I don't know. I need...."

"It's okay that you don't know, because I do." Dave lined the tip of the plug up with Kenn's hole and pushed, only enough for Kenn to feel it.

Kenn stilled, panted, waiting for him.

"Can you feel the anticipation building?" He pressed a little harder, watching the very tip of the plug begin to open Kenn up. "Can you?"

"I feel you. God. I feel you." Kenn pushed back.

"That's the plug." He rubbed around Kenn's hole with his finger. "And that's me." Then he pushed the plug forward, meeting Kenn's motions so that a good inch of the plug went into Kenn's body. He knew it would be cool and unyielding. Foreign. Which would make it exciting. "I love watching you, watching your hole spread, go pink and swollen."

Kenn moaned for him, fingers digging into his own ass as they clenched.

"Stunning." He pressed the plug in a little deeper, spreading that tight hole a little wider. He loved the spread, finger tracing the ring of muscles, teasing Kenn.

Kenn's moans filled the air, his boy pushing back, begging for more. He offered it, pushing the plug in deeper still. Now the widest part of the plug was holding Kenn open. He moved with Kenn, keeping his boy spread as wide as possible.

"How does that feel? Right there?"

"Big. Hard. Full."

"Those are good words." He rubbed Kenn's ass with his free hand, testing the muscles.

That earned him a laugh. "Are they?"

He grinned. "They are." Then he slapped Kenn's right asscheek. Not hard, but enough to make a noise.

Kenn went still and then gasped, ass working the plug. Dave groaned, watching Kenn's hole flutter around the thick middle of the plug. Then he slapped Kenn's ass again.

"You shouldn't…."

"Shouldn't what?" he asked, watching as Kenn pushed back, ass searching for another swat. He imagined Kenn had no idea he was asking for it like that.

"Slap." Kenn moaned softly. "We shouldn't."

"Why not?" Would Kenn be able to vocalize it?

"It's… naughty."

"So? I mean, you and I enjoy some naughty things, don't we? And there's nothing wrong with naughty. We're not hurting anyone, and it's nobody else's business what we do."

It was important that Kenn understood that. They were adults.

"Naughty things excite us and get us off. We love being naughty together." Every time he said naughty, Kenn keened softly. "We can be wicked. Perverse. Filthy. We can be anything we want."

On the last word, he pressed the plug in the rest of the way so it nudged against Kenn's gland.

Kenn gasped, rocking forward on the bed as it was seated.

"Mmm. Nice. That feels so good, doesn't it? That and every naughty thing we've done, and every single thing you can imagine." He grabbed Kenn's ass and massaged, rubbing hard.

He kept massaging with one hand and drew the plug out with the other. He pushed it back in, making sure it went in fast.

"Oh! Dave!" Kenn tried to sit up, his expression blissful.

Dave stopped, the plug in deep, and massaged Kenn's ass again. "You let go of your asscheeks."

"Uh-huh." Kenn looked almost dizzy.

"Can you hold them open again?" It would make fucking Kenn with the plug easier, but if Kenn wasn't up to it, he could totally adapt.

"Uh-huh." Kenn fumbled back with a low moan.

"Good boy. So good. So strong." He stroked Kenn's asscheeks, so proud of his boy, of taking what he needed.

He waited until Kenn had spread his cheeks again; then he grabbed the base of the plug and tugged the metal out of Kenn before plunging it back in. Kenn's sounds were sweet, lovely, driving him to move faster, push harder.

"Please...." Kenn moaned.

"Please what? More? Faster? Stop?" He slowed the movements of his fingers.

"I don't know. Don't stop. Please don't stop."

"I won't stop. Not until you've come for me." He pushed the plug back in and drummed the fingers of his free hand across Kenn's buttcheeks.

"Uhn." Kenn humped up into his touch, eager and hungry.

"Harder, eh?" He slapped Kenn's right asscheek a few times, again timing it with thrusts of the plug.

Kenn gasped, body flushing a sweet rose. God, his boy made his mouth dry. He continued to swat Kenn, nothing harsh. He wanted to warm Kenn's ass, to give him a thrill from the naughtiness of spanking. Make him remember Dave every time he sat.

"Love your ass, Kenn. It's perfect." He kept swatting, loving the way Kenn's ass bounced back against him. "Sweet and pink, round."

"Dave...." Was that turned on or scandalized? Both?

"Use your words, Kenn. Tell me how it makes you feel." He twisted the plug, then settled it.

"I...." Kenn moaned, his body trembling. "I—I don't know. Hot."

"Hot is good." He was happy with that—it showed that Kenn recognized he was enjoying this. Loving it, even.

"Hot is good. I need more. Touch me."

"I am touching you." He swatted Kenn's ass again. If that wasn't a touch, he didn't know what was.

Kenn moaned and rocked back for him.

He went for a straightforward fucking with the plug then, using Kenn's own motions to push the plug in with strength. Meanwhile, he alternated cheeks, swatting one and then the other.

Kenn began to moan, harsh low groans escaping from him.

"You want to come for me, Kenn? You want to spill from the plug and my hand?"

Kenn cried out and began to move for him, faster, body begging.

He added more strength to his thrusts with the plug, giving it a little twist to give Kenn extra sensations. "You've got a hungry little hole, babe. You're beautiful like this."

Kenn arched, pushing back against him.

Dave thrust hard, banging the plug against Kenn's gland.

"Oh. Oh. Oh," Kenn cried out, humping up hard.

"That's it, Kenn. Come for me. Come."

"Yes!" Kenn threw his head back, hips jerking restlessly as he shot.

Dave left the plug seated in Kenn's body, then touched him, sliding his skin along Kenn's arms and legs, his back and torso. Kenn shivered, hiding in his folded arms.

"You don't have to hide from me, Kenn. I love how you look with pleasure wracking you. You are stunning. Beautiful. Sexy."

"I just…. Thank you. God, that was…."

"Pretty damn good, if I do say so myself." He patted Kenn's ass, hoping to make it burn.

"Uhn." Kenn curled into himself, moaning softly.

He pulled Kenn to him. "How did I do on my dare?"

"You win." Kenn whimpered against his throat.

"No, babe." He tapped Kenn's ass. "I think we both won."

Kenn gripped the plug, working at it. He loved that: Kenn reveling in this so-called naughty thing that he needed so badly. That he could have anytime he needed it, really.

Kenn held him, lips on his collarbone.

"I'm so glad I met you, Professor Kenneth Brannigan."

"Are you? I'm glad to have met you as well."

"Yeah, I truly am." He kissed the top of Kenn's head and settled, holding Kenn close. "We're going to have such a wonderfully naughty time together."

Chapter Eleven

Kenn couldn't believe he had the plug in.

Still.

They were having pizza. And it was still in. He was sitting on his kitchen chair, eating pizza like it was a normal, everyday thing.

With the plug in.

Every now and then, he'd glance at Dave and find his lover watching him, grinning at him.

He didn't know what to say. He felt like ants were all over his skin, like he wanted to wiggle and move constantly, but he had to sit perfectly still.

"How's the pizza?" Dave asked, eyes intense as they held him in their gaze.

"Good." He had no idea. None.

"Thanks for ordering the veggies and remembering that I don't like olives. I appreciate it. You're always thinking of me."

"Of course I am. I care for you."

"Yes, but you remember all the little details. It makes me feel very cared for."

Kenn dipped his chin, unaccountably pleased. "Good. Good, I'm glad."

Dave touched his leg with a foot, sliding it along his calf. "So how's that plug treating you?"

"Dave!" Dave had not said that. Out loud.

"What?" Dave looked totally at ease with their conversation. "It's not like there's anyone else here. You, me, and the plug in your ass. That's it."

He'd never once talked about sex with Bram. Never. Dave was so easy.

"Is there dessert?" Dave asked. "I mean, other than you, of course."

"I bought a chocolate cake and some doughnuts for the weekend."

"Oh, that sounds really good. Are you ready for dessert? We could have tea with it." Dave gave him a small laugh. "I want to watch you move with that plug inside you."

"I...." He tightened around the plug, making it shift in his channel. "T-tea?"

"Please. Something to go with the chocolate cake. And maybe we can enjoy both tea and cake in bed."

"Sure. You like milk, not lemon."

"See? All the little details that you've discovered in passing you remember. It's a wonderful quality." Dave took his arm and tugged him close, taking a soft kiss. "Thank you."

He leaned a bit and kissed Dave back, humming softly. Dave's hand slid along his spine, all the way down to his ass. Then Dave touched the base of the plug, pushing it in several times.

Kenn gasped, arching up. He wasn't sure if he was trying to get closer or get away.

Dave kissed him again, short and quick. "Okay, go ahead, let me watch you move."

His cheeks were on fire as he headed across the tiny kitchenette. He tried not to freeze up, mince.

"I love watching you walk with the plug in," Dave said again.

"Be good." Don't make it worse.

"I thought I was being very good."

"I'm making tea." He didn't need to get hard.

"And you're looking good—no, amazing—doing it."

Oh. Oh, that made him blush, but he nodded his thanks. "How much cake do you want?"

"Why don't you cut a little bit more than you want, and we'll feed each other from the same slice."

"Oh, that's a good idea." Sensual.

Dave smiled and continued to watch him. That gaze was almost a touch, it felt so heavy on him.

Kenn cut a large piece of cake, brought it to Dave, then went back to the kettle to pour the water for tea.

Dave didn't touch the plate of cake. He was still watching every move Kenn made. Every now and then he would hum, the sound making Kenn feel on display, but also lovely.

He carefully brought the tea; then he grabbed the milk. Dave poured the milk into his cup. He picked up both his tea and the cake and carried them over to the bedside table. Climbing into bed, Dave arranged the pillows so they were supporting him, then patted his legs. "Come sit with me."

Kenn headed over, taking Dave's hand when he reached out. Dave tugged him down onto his warm lap. It was a softer place to land with the plug in his ass than the chair had been.

He gasped softly, wiggling instinctively. Oh, that was sweet.

"Feels good, eh?" Dave slid warm fingers along his spine.

"Yes." He closed his eyes for a second. "Yes, it does."

It felt like he was flying a little bit.

"I'm glad. It's supposed to." Dave's tongue slid across his lips, then Dave kissed his eyelids, touches like feathers. He leaned toward his lover, hands sliding over his shoulders.

"Need to feed you cake," Dave murmured, dropping more kisses over his face.

"Uh-huh...." He wasn't really listening as he savored the kisses.

So it was a shock when Dave suddenly smeared chocolate over his lips. Less surprising was Dave licking at his lips afterward, feasting on the chocolate. He chuckled and pushed closer, rocking gently on Dave's lap.

Dave smeared chocolate on his own lips next. "There you go, babe. For you."

He leaned close, humming as he gathered the rich, dark sweetness. The flavor was intense on his tongue, but even better was the hint of salt, of Dave, beneath the chocolate. He pressed closer, searching for more, for Dave.

Groaning, Dave cupped his face and deepened their kiss, tongue pushing into his mouth. This was better than any dessert could ever be. He straddled Dave's thighs, rubbing and rocking as they devoured each other.

"So sweet." Dave muttered the words between nips to his lips. Then Dave tugged on his lower lip, teeth sinking into it.

He arched in a slow wave, his eyes crossing. The ache made him want more. Dave gave it to him, too, nibbling and biting as he encouraged Kenn to move. He sighed softly as the plug stirred inside him, rubbing him.

"The plug is amazing, isn't it?" Dave slid a hand between his thigh and Kenn's ass, finger pushing at the base of the plug.

He couldn't argue, not with the way he gasped.

"I love seeing you like this. Turned-on and wild and free. So sensual and sexy."

"I'm not used to hearing that about me."

"You're going to hear it a lot from now on, I promise. I won't be stingy with my praise, with letting you know that how you look turns me on."

"Oh...." God, that made him shiver, just the idea. Did that make him vain? Proud?

"You deserve to know and to hear it." Dave rubbed his arms and kissed his nose.

He shook his head. "I—I don't know."

"Why wouldn't you?" Dave asked, hands slowing, stilling.

"I don't know. I don't want to be vain."

"I don't think you need to worry about that. Because you do deserve it."

His cheeks lit afire, and he ducked his chin. "Thank you."

Dave kissed the top of his head, then tilted his chin, looking into his eyes. "You deserve as many good things as you can take."

He couldn't handle this. It made him feel dizzy, important, uncomfortable. Then Dave's mouth closed over his, tongue pushing into his mouth, and it didn't help the dizziness, but it did settle his stomach and light him up.

He melted, relaxing with a moan. Dave gathered him close, again sliding his hand to Kenn's ass to play with the plug.

He began to stiffen, but the urge to stay relaxed was too strong to deny.

"We don't have to do anything," Dave whispered. "We'll kiss and touch and feel good."

"Kiss and touch...." He could get into that. He flattened his hands over one of Dave's nipples.

"Mmm. I do love your touch. It makes me feel special."

Kenn smiled, moving to pluck the little hard nub, keeping his touch light, gentle. Dave took a deep breath, nipple pushing into his hand. He kept kissing, nuzzling as he caressed that sweet bud. He knew how good this felt, how intense.

Low, drawn-out moans filled the air, Dave clearly lost in the sensations.

Kenn loved those sounds, loved that he was bringing them out. He loved that Dave was willing to simply touch and feel. Sex was... expansive.

Sex was delicious and luscious now, something to linger over.

Dave found his nipples, fingers running back and forth across them, gentle and easy. The pressure made his toes curl. It built slowly, and soon he was shivering with each touch. He tried to answer the touches, but he was getting clumsy, his fingers jerking over Dave's skin.

Dave made happy noises, though, pushing into his touches as they continued to kiss, so he must not be so bad at it, right?

"Love your touch. So much."

He must not be bad at it at all.

"Thank you. You're making me dizzy."

"I'm glad I'm not the only one. I guess it's good we're in bed, eh?" Dave laughed softly, looking so happy.

"Yes." He had to chuckle. If they collapsed, they'd bounce.

Dave rubbed their noses together, fingers sliding over Kenn's body in random waves, but they kept returning to his nipples.

"You ever thought about rings for these?" Dave asked, stroking again and again.

"Shh." Of course not. Only in the darkest hours of night.

"You shushing me makes me think the answer is yes."

"I wouldn't." Never.

"You wouldn't ever even think about it? There's nothing shameful in thinking about things like that." Dave took his right nipple between two fingers and tugged gently.

His lips popped open, the tug so good, so lovely. It came again, and again, then Dave moved to do it to his left nipple too.

"Can you imagine it? A gold ring that I can grab anytime I want and tug, give you this sensation and more."

He shook his head, but he moaned too. He couldn't help it.

"No? You can't imagine it? I can. I can totally imagine the glint of metal shining and bisecting your nipples."

His head fell back, the image behind his eyes.

He felt Dave's breath on his right nipple, then soft lips closed over them, making him moan.

"If you had rings, I could play with them with my tongue when I do this." Dave closed his lips over Kenn's nipple again.

"Oh God." The pressure was sharp—not sharp enough, but enough to make him dizzy.

"Can you imagine it now?" Dave asked.

"Y-yes." He could.

"Good. Can you imagine going to get the piercings done? You sitting in the chair. I'll be holding your hand."

"What?" Oh God…. Oh, that was….

"Play with me, baby. I'd be right there with you."

He grabbed for Dave's free hand, the other still stroking his nipple.

Dave squeezed his hand and pinched his nipple. "It would only be a little pinch as the needle pierced your skin. Then an ache as the metal runs through it."

He shook his head, swallowing convulsively. Oh fuck.

"It would make you so hard, and the piercer would leave us alone after we got it done. Let me bring you off in privacy."

"They… they would?" He squeezed Dave's hand, then brought their joined hands to his cock.

"That's right, babe. They would." Dave wrapped their hands together around his cock and stroked. It was weird, but super neat at the same time.

Incredible.

He let himself imagine, let himself revel in the grip of Dave's hand and the fingers around his nipple.

"I know you can feel it now. You can imagine being there with me."

"I…." He could. He so could.

Dave breathed on his nipple, then flicked it with his tongue. He arched up, moaning deep in his chest. Dave continued to flick his nipple, working it, and that touch resonated all the way to his balls.

"M-more. More. Please."

Dave hummed around his nipple, then added suction, pulling steadily. Kenn's cock leaked, dripping as they stroked it together. Dave moved to his other nipple, sucking on it too.

He let himself fantasize, let himself rock and moan, begging softly. Dave sent him higher and higher, bringing him to the edge.

"Soon…," he whispered, caught in his own dreams. Soon.

"Do it. I want to smell you. I want to taste you." The words were muttered against his nipple, then Dave began sucking again, teeth and tongue working the hard nub of flesh.

"More," he begged. "Please. So close."

"If your nipples were pierced, I could tug and play with both at the same time. Twist the metal and make you ache and burn."

"Fuck...." He reached down, pinched his nipple firmly, and came so hard his bones rattled. His ass closed around the plug, squeezing it tight inside him as the come poured out of him.

Moaning, Dave held on to him, arms like bands keeping him close. He needed this. God, he needed Dave.

Dave gave each of his nipples a lick, then brought their mouths together. He slid his fingers through the come on their bellies and brought his hand up. Licking at his fingers, Dave watched him, making it seem so sexy and hot.

Kenn gasped, his world spinning like mad. Oh God.

Dave's smile was like that of the cat who'd gotten the cream. Well, he supposed Dave had, after all.

"You want a taste?" Dave asked, holding his index finger out, a bit of Kenn's own come making it glisten.

He shook his head but wrapped his lips around Dave's finger and sucked. The flavor was familiar, salty, but it was Dave's moan that he felt inside.

"Making me need, babe. Like, I can feel what you're doing in my balls. I love the way you suck. I love how you love it."

He did. It was a comfort, a joy, arousing and lovely.

Dave worked with Kenn, pushing his finger deeper, fingerfucking Kenn's mouth. He could feel Dave's eyes, too, gazing at him as he sucked.

He let himself go with it, rock with it. Moan like the needy man he was.

"You make me need." Dave's voice was thick, and Kenn could literally hear that need in it. "And leak. I'm so hard for you."

He nodded and slid down, lips parted, needing Dave's cock in him.

"Oh please, Kenn. Yes." Dave shifted slightly, giving him better access to the thick erection.

"Need you." He groaned, tongue sliding over the tip of Dave's cock.

"Uh-huh. Need you too. Please." Dave grabbed hold of his hair, then let go again, hands opening and closing.

He reached up, put Dave's hand on his head.

Groaning, Dave curled his fingers in Kenn's hair. "So good, Kenn. You're magic."

Magic? Was he? He opened up and took Dave in, sucking steadily, giving Dave what he needed. More groans and moans rained down on him, Dave's pleasure clear. Oh, this was… the best sort of pleasure, of gratitude for his orgasm.

Dave's hips began to move, small thrusts at first, sliding the thick cock along his tongue. He opened wide, accepting Dave in, encouraging him. More low moans sounded, Dave pushing deeper.

Kenn hummed and licked, tongue sliding on Dave's shaft.

"Don't stop. Oh God, please don't stop, Kenn. You're amazing. Feels so good."

No. No, he wouldn't. He swallowed gently, keeping Dave floating.

"I could let you do this forever." Dave petted his head.

He moaned softly, tongue swiping slowly, steadily. Dave's sounds grew increasingly needy, filling the air, and he encouraged each and every one.

Dave began to move faster, pumping into his mouth, the hand on his head holding him in place now.

He trembled, that casual power arousing, wonderful.

"Kenn. Soon." Dave pushed into his throat again and again, and he could feel the thick cock throbbing.

He swallowed hard, over and over, gulping around the swollen tip.

Dave moaned and thrust up, came down his throat. When the pulses ended, Dave collapsed back against the pillows with another groan.

He leaned down against Dave's stomach, resting. Dave ran his fingers through Kenn's hair, stroking and petting.

"Thank you, Kenn. That was wonderful."

"It was. God. What a lovely Friday."

"It's been the best, hasn't it?" Dave grinned, hand sliding along Kenn's spine all the way to his ass. It made him hyperaware of the plug inside him.

"Uh—uh-huh."

Dave chuckled lazily. "I like that I've made you incoherent."

"Shh." Butthead.

That had Dave's chuckles increasing before he asked, "You want to sleep with the plug in?"

"I can't, can I?" Was that possible?

"You totally can if you want to. Or we can take it out. It's not going anywhere. We can play with it a lot. I like how it makes you feel."

"I do too." He liked the pressure, the weight.

"So let's leave it in while we nap. Then you'll be ready for me if we wake up feeling needy in the middle of the night."

"I…. Okay? I can do that." He snuggled in with a happy sigh.

"Mmm. It'll be a wonderful night."

"A wonderful weekend," he whispered.

"Oh yeah." Dave slid down so he was lying with Kenn, arms wrapped around him. "A fantastic weekend."

"Our weekend." He sighed and melted into his lover. "Thank you."

"You're welcome. Thank you too. This is a two way street, eh?"

He nodded, eyelids heavy. Nap. Rest. Dream.

Chapter Twelve

Mimosas and a brunch buffet that included made-to-order omelets, hand-carved roast beef, and fresh pancakes and waffles. It was pure decadence.

Dave sat across from Kenn, feeling lazy and good deep into his skin. His body felt loose and easy, the last few days of lovemaking having left him happy, aching slightly in all the right ways.

"Thanks for introducing me to your favorite Sunday brunch place."

"You're welcome. I love it here. It's a luxury, but I do enjoy it." Kenn licked maple syrup off his fork.

Dave found himself caught in that act, eyes glued to Kenn's mouth. "Uh-huh."

"What do you like best?"

"The waffles with fresh fruit. Although the mimosas are pretty damn good too. What about you?"

"The eggs Benedict is lovely, but mostly it's the ritual of the whole thing. It's just the perfect way to start your week."

"I think any time with you is the perfect way to start the week. The day. Anything."

"Thank—" Kenn's words stopped like a faucet abruptly turned off. He looked like he'd seen a ghost.

"Babe? What's wrong?"

"Kenneth." A tall older man in an impeccable suit stood before them, staring down his nose at them. "I wouldn't have expected to see you here."

Dave didn't like way the guy was looking at Kenn. He stood up, putting himself on an even keel with him. "Can I help you?"

"I most seriously doubt it, Mr. Burgundy."

"Bram, please," Kenn said. "We're simply trying to enjoy our brunch, if you don't mind."

Oh, this was the evil ex. "I'm sure there are plenty of tables," Dave said. "You'll be able to choose one on the other side of the restaurant."

"You're not going to invite me to join you, Kenneth?"

"Seriously?" Kenn actually looked shocked.

"Hey, man. We're trying to have a quiet breakfast here. Why don't you just carry on to wherever your table is. Or, you know, you could just leave." Dave knew Kenn wouldn't want to make a scene, but he would do it if necessary. He wasn't scared of this asshole.

"Go away. I don't want you to join us. Leave me alone, or I will call the police."

Dave was so proud of Kenn. "I think that was clear enough, buddy."

Bram stared at Dave. "You know he's a—"

"I'm leaving. I'll pay at the door." Kenn stood and headed for the front, grabbing his coat on the way.

"A wonderful man. I am aware. And you are an asshole. Leave us alone, because if he doesn't call the cops—I will. I know what you did to him. I know that you are an abusive fuck. I'll stand by him if we have to take you to court to prove it." He stared the man down for a moment, then turned on his heel and went after Kenn.

Kenn had obviously paid and was heading out the door at a dead run toward home.

As soon as he was clear of the restaurant, Dave called out to him. "Kenn! Hold up!"

Kenn shook his head and hunched in his coat. Dave hated that. Kenn had nothing to be ashamed of. He put on some speed, jogging to catch up with him.

"Hey. I'm here."

"I'm sorry. I paid the bill." Kenn wouldn't look at him.

"I know you did." He touched Kenn's arm. "Stop for a minute. You didn't do anything wrong."

"I know. I mean, he never…. What is he doing here?"

"I don't know." He hugged Kenn tight and held on for a moment. "He had you followed by that private eye. Maybe he needed to see in person that you had moved on. Maybe he was trying to mess us up. I don't know." He slid his arm around Kenn's shoulders and continued walking with him.

"I'm going to go home and… maybe go to the pool or something."

"I know you're upset, and I can guess why, but I'd like you to talk to me about it. The pool sounds good—get some of that negative energy out through exercise."

"Right. Go and go." Kenn sighed. "There's nothing to talk about."

"No? You're obviously upset. I want to help make you feel better. I want to remind you that he doesn't get to judge you."

"I just... feel dirty."

"Because of him or because of the things we do together?"

"Because of him." That was immediate, quiet, but sure. And Dave was glad of that being the answer.

"Then let's go home and wash him off you."

Kenn looked at him, tears in the pretty eyes. "Yeah?"

It broke his heart to see those tears. "Yes, absolutely. We'll wash him away. Come on, we're almost there."

"That was my place, you know?"

"It still can be, if you want it." Kenn didn't have to let that man run him off the places he enjoyed being.

Kenn shook his head. "It was a luxury, that's all."

"There's nothing wrong with luxuries. We could find someplace that's ours. Yours and mine." He guided Kenn across the street to Kenn's place.

Kenn nodded, but Dave wasn't sure he was listening.

They went up the stairs and into Kenn's apartment, and Dave tugged Kenn in close, wrapping him in a hug. Kenn was stiff for a second, then he melted.

Dave kissed the top of Kenn's head. "I've got you. Hell, you've got you. You are strong and good and your own man. You stood right up to him. It was hot."

Kenn stiffened in his arms, then looked up at him. "It was?"

"Uh-huh. It totally was."

"I just... I didn't want him to hurt you."

"That you were so brave to keep me safe is even hotter, babe. I'm okay, thank you."

"Good. Shower? Please?"

"Yeah. Definitely." He began to strip Kenn down, beginning with Kenn's coat.

He was filled with a deep rage that the asshole had hurt his Kenn, scared him, but the fact that Kenn defended him? That was delicious.

"Do me while I do you, babe," he suggested.

"Yes. You're coming in with me." It wasn't a question.

"Absolutely." He began working on the buttons of Kenn's shirt, half shuffling them toward the bathroom as he undressed Kenn.

Kenn answered him, sliding his shirt down over his arms.

It didn't take them long to be standing naked together in Kenn's little bathroom, facing each other.

Kenn searched his eyes. "We're okay?"

"We're okay. I am firmly in camp Kenn. I don't care what he said or thinks. You know I believe in you."

"I know. God, my head hurts."

"How about a couple of aspirin before the shower?" He opened Kenn's medicine cabinet and located the pills.

"Thanks. I hate that he can still make me so freaked out."

"Yeah, me too…. But it didn't paralyze you. That's a big thing." He squeezed Kenn's shoulders. "Promise me you won't try to confront him or anything without me." He didn't trust the guy not to hurt Kenn.

"I don't want to confront the motherfucker. I want him to leave me alone."

"You want to call the police? We could do it right now. Tell them what happened."

"No. No, I just want a shower. I want my Sunday back." Kenn stared at him, eyes begging him for help, then turned away, heading for the shower.

As he followed, he grabbed the glass on the side of the sink and filled it with water. Then he offered Kenn the pills and the water. Once Kenn had taken the aspirin, Dave turned the shower on, adjusting the knobs until it was the right temperature. Kenn liked it fairly warm, but not too hot. Dave didn't talk; he simply focused on Kenn. On comfort.

One day this would be aftercare after a scene. One day.

They washed each other, Dave taking extra care to massage the tension in Kenn's back and shoulders. When the temperature began to cool, he turned the water off and helped Kenn out of the tub before wrapping him in a towel. Kenn leaned toward him, offering a sweet, soft kiss.

He hummed into the kiss, sliding one hand around Kenn's head, cradling it. He poured care and love—yes, love—into the kiss, offering Kenn all of himself. Kenn accepted him, opened to him.

He brought his other hand up, cupping both cheeks as he hummed over the flavor of Kenn's mouth.

"I hate being so… broken." Kenn's whisper brushed his lips.

"I don't think you're broken. Bruised, maybe. But you're strong. You left an abusive relationship. That's not easy to do."

"I did. And nothing will make me go back." A line of steel ran through Kenn's voice.

"That's what I like to hear. You don't need him. You don't need anyone, though I'm glad you keep me around."

"I am too. I'm glad you're around."

"So did you want to go swimming, or did you want to make love?" He thought either would be a good way to work off some energy, and he was willing to follow Kenn's lead.

"I want to get out of here, Dave. I want to just… go."

"Okay. Swimming or… I could borrow Annie's car and we could drive out of the city and go hiking?"

"Can we? Just drive out for the afternoon?"

"Let me double-check with Annie." He grabbed his phone and zipped through his contacts, finding Annie's name and pressing it.

"Hey, Davey. I thought you were deep in Kenn-town this weekend."

"Ha-ha. You think we could borrow your car? We're looking to go see the countryside."

"Sure thing. Just make sure you gas it up when you get back, eh?"

"You got it. Keys in the usual?"

"Yep. Have fun." He could hear her laughter as she cut off the call.

It had him grinning as he pocketed his phone. "We're on."

"Thank you. I just… I need to get out of my head."

"That totally makes sense. You need anything before we go?" He started getting dressed.

"No. I'll grab us a couple of waters and some apples."

"Sounds good. Did you want to stay here while I go get Annie's car, or do you want to come with me?"

"I'll come with you. It'll be a fun walk." Kenn hooked arms with him, bumped their shoulders together.

"Everything with you is fun." He loved being with Kenn. Loved it.

"Not everything, huh? But a lot."

"Even the not-fun parts are okay because I'm with you."

"Flattery will get you anywhere." Kenn was beginning to relax as they walked.

"Oh good. I was hoping so. Today I'd like it to get me to the Gatineaus. Maybe we'll find a place that serves ice cream or something."

"I can handle that. I love ice cream. All sorts."

"Have you got a favorite?" They rounded the corner and there was his place, Annie's car in the driveway.

"Oh, dulce de leche."

"Can you get that as ice cream? That's pretty cool. I'm a pistachio man myself. I just need to grab the keys from the front hall." He left Kenn by the car, zipping up the front walk. The keys were on the hooks in the front hall with an *A* on the keychain. He grabbed them and headed back to Kenn.

Kenn watched him, a warm gaze on his face. He took a moment to bask in that, in the way Kenn looked at him. How fucking lucky was he?

It hit him suddenly, almost like a physical punch. He loved this man. Not just cared for him or enjoyed spending time with him or wanted to do scenes with him. He loved Kenn.

He knew there was a pretty goofy smile on his face as he came to a stop in front of Kenn. "Hey."

"Hey. You look happy." Kenn touched his stomach.

"I am. I'm very happy. Thank you."

"Thank you for everything. Let's go play."

"I would love to. Love to." He chuckled. He loved Kenn. He unlocked the car and opened Kenn's door for him.

Kenn slid in, body language relaxed again, happy.

Dave got around the other side, started the car, and pulled into the street. "And we're off on our adventure."

Chapter Thirteen

Kenn stared at the new sets of pictures that came in the mail. Every one was taken from outside. Some showed them walking in the neighborhood or on campus. Some caught them through windows at home or in restaurants.

None were… explicit, but the promise was that they could be. Dammit.

There was even a photo of Dave's mail, the box with the plug in it. This was crazy. Insane. And scary as hell.

He texted Dave to cancel their date tonight. He needed to spend a few weeks alone to get Bram to calm down.

He'd barely hit Send when there was a knock at the door.

Kenn's breath caught in his chest, his eyes going wide, and he had to force himself to say, "Come in."

Dave entered and waved his phone at him. "Why are you trying to cancel our date?"

"I need to. I'm going to be busy for a bit, that's all."

"What's all this?" Dave asked, pointing to the pictures spread across his mattress.

He stepped closer to Dave, standing between him and the pictures. "Nothing. Please, I—"

"Kenn. Those were pictures of us. Is this more stuff from your ex?"

"He'll leave me alone. I just have to lay low a while."

"So as long as you stay hidden inside by yourself, he leaves you alone? That's crazy. Let's gather these up with the envelope they came in and go to the police." Dave started gathering the pictures in a pile.

"It's not illegal to take pictures."

"No, but sending them to you like this is a sign of harassment. They have a file, right? From when he beat you? So we take these down and get them put in your file. Build a case."

"They have a file, but I don't want to make it worse." He didn't want Dave in trouble.

"What do you mean you don't want to make it worse? Bram is the one making it worse. If he didn't want his file any uglier, he shouldn't be stalking you, sending you pictures of yourself."

"And you."

"Right. So he's stalking me now too. I could make sure that's on record with your stuff. More evidence against him in case he ever escalates. The fact that he showed up in person at the restaurant worries me. What if he corners you somewhere? We definitely need to have this documented with the police."

"I want to stay here and sleep for a little while." With the curtains drawn.

"I let it go last time, Kenn. I think you need to report Bram this time." Dave drew him in for a warm, strong hug. "I want you to be safe and happy, fulfilled without worrying about Bram."

"I do too." But what he wanted didn't matter. He'd learned that lesson well.

"Then let's go to the police station now, cite your file, and give them these photos. What Bram is doing is wrong. If we don't stand up to him, he's going to keep trying to make you unhappy. Or worse. Please, Kenneth. I think it's really important."

He nodded and stood up. His entire body was shivering, and he covered it with a hoodie. "Let's do it."

Then he'd come straight home and go to bed.

Dave grabbed his hand and squeezed tight. "I'm very proud of you, Kenn. I know this is hard."

He squeezed back, but he didn't answer. He just nodded and put the new photographs, along with the others, into an envelope.

"When we're done, we can come back here or go to mine, and I promise to make you forget everything else."

"Didn't I cancel our date?" Kenn managed a wink.

"This isn't a date. We're on an errand, and then we're going to make love. See? Not a date."

"Not a date? Are you sure?" He didn't want to be in a better mood, but he was.

"I'm pretty sure. Like I said, we're running an errand. We aren't going to go out to eat. Or see a movie."

"No. Going to the police isn't a date." He bumped their shoulders together.

"There you go." Dave took his hand as they got to the sidewalk, and they turned toward the police station. "It's going to be all right."

"I hope so." For Dave's sake.

"I'm not going to let him hurt you." Dave sounded so sure, so confident.

He knew better. The physical pain had been fleeting. The real pain never ended.

Dave looked at him, one eyebrow raised. "What?"

"Nothing. Nothing at all."

"You sure you're not holding anything back?"

"I'm fine, Dave." Perfectly fine.

"Okay." Dave squeezed his hand, and they turned up the walk to the police station.

A man was standing there as they entered, watching them. Watching him. Asshole.

Dave frowned and went up to the guy. "Excuse me. You got a problem?"

"Not at all." The guy snapped a picture of Dave with his phone.

"You son of a bitch. You leave us alone." Dave grabbed Kenn's hand and tugged him toward the officer at the front desk. "We'd like to report harassment."

"Please have a seat."

They went to perch on the hard seats. The envelope shook in Kenn's fingers. Dave covered his hand and squeezed gently.

"I'm sorry. I wanted to let him calm down."

"What you do should have nothing to do with Bram's behavior. He's his own man. You are your own person. Are we going to lay low and hide anytime he gets it in his head that you're somehow overstepping your bounds?"

Yes. Yes, he probably would.

"He needs to understand that he's not a part of your life."

"I'm sorry." He should never have let Dave in.

"Shh. You don't need to apologize to me. But you deserve better than you're getting." Dave jiggled Kenn's hand emphatically. "I'm going to make sure it happens."

The officer finally called them up, and a detective came over. "I'm Detective Simmons. My desk is over here."

Kenn sighed and stood. He introduced himself and the situation, starting out with "I have a restraining order."

"And the person you have it against hasn't been following it?" Simmons asked, pointing to a couple chairs in front of a desk.

"He's sent a private investigator."

"And you know this because…?"

Kenn passed over the photos. "He sent pictures the guy took. From different days and different times."

Simmons looked through the pictures. "Unfortunately, if he hasn't been following you himself, he hasn't broken the restraining order."

"He was at the restaurant on Sunday, Kenn. Remember?"

"Did he threaten you?"

"No. I left."

"Yeah, he didn't have a chance to. He said, 'I wouldn't have expected to see you here,' like Kenn didn't belong at the restaurant."

The detective sighed. "Next time, ask him to go, and if he doesn't, please call us."

"So we shouldn't have left—he should have?" Dave asked.

Simmons nodded. "He's been served. He knows if he sees you somewhere, he has to leave. Coming and talking to you is a violation."

"Good to know," Dave said. "What about the private detective and the pictures?"

"He's not doing anything illegal, sir. I'm sorry."

"And mailing them to Kenn isn't illegal either?"

"Not unless he includes an obvious threat."

"But you'll put these in the file, right?" Dave insisted.

Simmons took them and put them into a folder. "Absolutely."

"Thank you." Kenn didn't say "I told you so" because that would be bitchy. He wanted to, though.

"Should we not bother next time he sends pictures?" Dave asked. "Because there will be more—his private eye is in the lobby. He's already snapped several pictures of us here."

"He'll slip up eventually. He can't invade your privacy. You hear me?"

Kenn nodded, gave the policeman a smile. "I think I want to go home now."

"Thanks for coming in. I know it's frustrating, but you're going to have to continue to be proactive about this. Until he steps over that line, we can't actually do anything. So call next time he confronts you. Keep bringing this kind of thing in." Simmons stood and held out his hand. "Stay safe."

"Yes, sir." He shook Simmons's hand and then smiled at Dave. "You ready?"

Dave stood as well. He nodded at the detective and took Kenn's hand. "Let's go home."

"Sounds good." He didn't look around, pretended that there was no one on earth but them.

Dave kept hold of his hand as they left, seeming to be pretending right along with him. "Did you read that cozy mystery I suggested?" Dave asked as they walked.

"I did. It was clever. Made me laugh out loud a couple of times."

"Cool. I thought you'd like that one. We should go to the bookstore on Saturday after swimming."

"You're not going to let me go to bed for the weekend, are you?"

"No, I am not. We are not going to let your insane ex dictate our days." Dave nudged his shoulder. "So I have a question for you."

"A question? Shoot."

"You know what a safeword is, don't you?"

"What?" Of course he did. He read.

"I think you should pick one." Dave said it like he'd say the sky was blue.

"What? Me? I can't—" His heart started pounding.

"Of course you can. I think you need to. Because it means you have control, and I think you need that."

"I don't know." He ducked his head, making a beeline for the house.

Dave caught up to him easily. "Kenn. We both know you're into the stuff you looked up. I am too. I'm not him. I'm not going to hurt you."

"No. I know that." That deserved eye contact. "I know that."

Dave stopped him right on the sidewalk in front of his place and gave him a warm hug. "Good. Good. I want to explore things with you, Kenn. I want to turn you on and make you happy."

"Come inside, hmm?" Where it was safe.

"That's the plan, babe. You're going to pick a safeword, and we're going to explore these things that turn you on."

"Huxley," he whispered.

"Was that his last name?"

"No. No, Aldous Huxley. The writer. I would never bring him into... us."

A warm smile bloomed across Dave's face. "Oh. That's perfect."

"I want to go inside now."

"Of course." They went in and upstairs to his rooms. Dave locked the door once they got inside, and finally they were safe.

"I'm going to... take a nap."

"No, I don't think so. We're going to make love. We're going to play. We're not going to let him affect our love life."

"He already has." He closed the curtains tight.

Dave tilted his head. "How so?"

"He's made me scared to try."

"Well, I'm going to help you, okay? Help you get past being scared."

"Come sit for a minute. I'll turn on some music, and we can veg."

"We can talk about the things you want to explore. Now that you have a safeword, and we've started the discussion."

He didn't have anything in his head, not really.

Dave drew him down onto the bed. "Or we can make love and hold each other. I won't push tonight. Not after this last week. But I will push eventually. I will ferret out the things you hold so close to the vest."

Kenn snuggled in, not wanting anything but to remember how to breathe, to be held a minute.

Dave sat back and wrapped around him. "You're safe. I have you."

"And I have you." For what that was worth.

"I'm glad. Thank you." They lay together for a few minutes. "It's dark, and we're safe and together. We could talk."

"Okay. We can." It was easier, here in the darkness.

"Should I tell you about some of the things I think about? Some of the things I want to do? Or do you want to start?"

"Can you? Please?" He felt so... naive. Untried.

"I totally can. I know you've read a lot of stuff, but if you have any questions, feel free to interrupt and ask, okay?"

"Sure. Of course." God, was this real?

"Great." Dave kissed the top of his head. "So I'm a Dom. I knew that from early on. Thank you, internet. I mean, I don't know how people knew about BDSM before it. Not unless you knew someone who knew someone, etc. But I was able to explore early on through reading, and

I knew. I also knew where to go when I was ready to start interacting with people."

"Were you frightened?" He leaned in, breathing a little quickly.

"I was nervous and excited. It was new and amazing and, yeah, a little terrifying."

Kenn played with Dave's fingers. He couldn't imagine trying this in public. Seriously.

"I learned a lot at a club, watching Doms with their subs. Sometimes people let me help so I could understand how to play safely."

"It was quite formal, was it?"

"It was specifically a BDSM club, and safe, sane, and consensual were very important. That's where I learned that the safeword is key, and the sub has a lot of power. Even if it doesn't seem that way. That's also where I learned that there are as many different ways to have sex as there are people having sex, and as long as everyone is onboard, there is no 'bad' sex, no 'perverts.'" Dave kissed his temple. "There are pairs that never have sex—either in the club or in private. They only need the power exchange."

They were both quiet for a long moment, Dave letting Kenn digest everything he'd said.

"Your turn, Kenn?" Dave suggested.

"Well, I've read the literature for research. I've read a lot. I didn't expect how varied things could be."

"That's one of my favorite parts about it. That and how my kink is okay and your kink is okay, too, even if it's not my kink."

"Right. I found videos, images online. I was intrigued."

"Oh good. I was going to ask what interested you the most. What turned you on."

"I don't know how to answer that out loud." At least it was dark, right? "I watched a couple of videos over and over."

"So tell me about the videos."

What if he said things that disgusted Dave? He didn't know if he could handle that.

Dave hugged him tight. "Babe? You know you can tell me anything?"

"I'm scared that you'll think I'm nasty. I care so much about your thoughts."

"I watched a man tied to a St. Andrew's Cross being beaten with pine boughs, and the scent of pine will forever be a turn-on."

"What?" Oh, that was fair. That was fair. "I w-watched a video with a man chained up and taking a big cock as his legs and arms gave out."

"Mmm. Do you have that bookmarked? We could watch it together."

He didn't say anything, but he nodded.

"You said a couple of videos. What was the other one like?" Dave asked, voice husky.

"It's your turn." He would answer as long as Dave did too.

"You're right. I was invited to help a pair of Doms once with their sub. They needed someone to bring water, lube, towels, keep everyone hydrated, etcetera. They double penetrated him. I had never seen anything like it. I didn't know you could even do that, but they did, and the bliss on their sub's face was incredible."

"A pair? That sounds... hard."

"He was unbelievably happy when it was over. Fulfilled." Dave nudged him. "Your turn, babe."

"I've seen.... I have one with body piercings and chains and... and a plug in the guy's cock."

Dave's hand dropped down, fondling Kenn's cock through his slacks. "You would look so sexy with a plug in your penis, a little jewel at the top."

Oh, maybe they should have taken their clothes off.

Dave licked his earlobe, then asked softly, "You wanna get naked and watch your videos together?"

"Uh-huh...." His voice was tiny.

"I was hoping you'd say that." Dave pulled Kenn's shirt out of his waistband and began tugging it up. "I love this—exploring you. With you."

He shivered and raised his arms so Dave could pull the shirt right off. Dave tossed it aside, then touched his nipples. "So the one with the penis plug. The guy had his nipples pierced, didn't he? What else was pierced?"

"His cock. There were chains and things. His Master was teasing him."

"Mmm. Driving him crazy?" Dave pinched his nipples, both at the same time.

"Uh... uh-huh." He arched over the touch, whimpering softly.

"Can you imagine having those piercings?" Dave pinched his nipples again, then one hand headed south, fingers pushing beneath his waistband.

"I...." God yes. He gasped, trying not to shake apart.

Dave used his other hand to open the top button of Kenn's slacks and tug down the zipper, and then his other hand found his cock and wrapped around the head. Dave pressed against Kenn's slit with his thumb. "I know a place where we could get you pierced."

He shook his head, his cock jerking in Dave's fingers. God he was burning alive. "We can't."

"Why not?" Dave asked, pinching his cockhead.

"Be-because." He wanted his pants off, wanted to be bare with Dave.

"That's not an answer. I know a place that's clean, safe, and very discreet. Don't you want to know what a piercing here—" Dave pinched the edge of his cockhead this time. "—would feel like?"

He cried out, the sound wild, sharp. Needy.

"I want to do it. I want to watch you as the needle pierces your nipples, your cock." Dave let go of his cock, tugging at his slacks and his underwear, trying to get them off.

He helped, then he tugged at Dave's shirt. "You too."

"Uh-huh." Dave wriggled and shifted him and grunted but managed to get naked. When he was done, Dave pulled Kenn back against him, skin on skin, and Dave was so aroused, cock like a brand.

"H-hey." They breathed together, both of them panting.

"You have me so turned-on." Dave ran his hands up and down Kenn's body.

"Yes. Me too." He pushed into the touch.

"Let's watch your favorite of those two videos. I'll touch you the entire time we watch it." Dave nuzzled against his ear. "And then we'll find one of mine. Fair, babe?"

"Uh-huh. Fair." He was being as brave as he could as he grabbed his tablet and pulled up Bing.

Dave nuzzled his neck and petted his sides and legs as he brought up the video, the touches easy and exciting at the same time.

The first one that loaded was the submissive chained to the ceiling, feet on two stacks of books. There was a fat dildo attached to the ground and pointed at his ass and a man in leather wielding a flogger.

"Oh wow, that's already pretty damn hot." Dave slid his hand down to Kenn's cock and wrapped his fingers around it.

The blows weren't hard, but the pumps to the man's cock were rough. Every so often one of the books was removed.

Whenever the Master in the video yanked on the sub's cock, Dave would match the motion, giving Kenn a rough jerk.

The dildo slowly breached the sub, the huge cock spreading him wide.

Kenn couldn't hold back his moan, but it was matched by Dave's groan, letting him know he wasn't alone in this.

It became a dance—the blows, the dildo filling the sub up, the needy, leaking cock that was never allowed to come.

Dave's jacking of Kenn's cock stopped matching the action on the video and turned into smooth, quick motions, and Kenn could hear Dave's breathing in his ear, coming fast.

Finally the man was fucking himself on the fat cock, up and down, over and over.

"That's stunning, babe. So damn hot." Dave rocked behind him, rubbing himself off against Kenn's ass, even as the hand around his cock kept moving.

"Yes. He's taking everything for his Master."

"Do you want that? To take more than you even think you can because your Dom demands it?"

He cried out, his balls drawing up tight. "Dave!"

"I'd love to put you through your paces. To push you. To watch you fucking yourself like that." Dave's voice was thick with desire.

He rocked hard, rubbing his ass against Dave's cock.

"I want you to come for me. I want this to be enough to make you spew."

"Uh. Uh-huh. Please." Soon. Now.

"Yeah. Yeah, you're going to shoot for me when the sub gets to."

His eyes rolled. The sub's feet were on the floor now, the dildo buried to the hilt, the flogger landing on the tight nipples randomly as the leather-clad hand rubbed the now-red cock.

"You watch this and imagine that's you, don't you?"

He couldn't answer that. He couldn't. He hid in Dave a little deeper.

"I know the answer is yes, Kenn. And so do you." Dave bit at his shoulder, hand still moving hard on his cock.

"Oh God." He curled around Dave's hands, his eyes rolling. "Please."

"When that boy riding the cock gets to come. Not until then." Dave didn't stop stroking him, though.

"I can't...."

Dave tugged his balls, fingers circling the base, and Kenn wanted to scream with need.

"You will. And I know you know exactly how much longer you're going to have to wait." Dave chuckled softly. "I know you've watched this over and over."

He couldn't deny it.

"How much longer do you have to wait?" Dave asked, hips driving the thick cock along his ass and back.

"Two… two minutes." Two long minutes before the flogger landed on the man's cock.

"Oh, that's not going to be easy, is it?" Dave's chuckle was husky, and his hand moved harder, faster. Dave pinched the tip of his cock on every upstroke.

"No…." There was no way. None. He always came before the end.

Dave grabbed his balls again, twisting them and backing him off from the edge. "I know you can do it. I'll even give you a hand, make it a bit easier."

"Please." Help. God yes. Help.

Dave let go of his balls and began jacking him again. "Which part do you like best—the flogging, the chains, or the way he has to take the world's biggest dildo?"

He shook his head. God, he didn't know. He didn't know.

"We can try all of it. Separately, together. We can invent our own scene or imitate this one."

He looked away, nuzzling Dave's neck, overwhelmed.

"Mmm…. You're supposed to be watching."

"It's too much, love."

"How will you know when you're allowed to come if you aren't watching?"

He groaned softly and licked Dave's throat, trying to distract him.

"Kenn." Dave squeezed the head of his cock, pinching it. "Watch."

His eyes went wide, and he turned toward the screen.

"It's coming, and soon, you will be too."

"What… what about you?"

Soon. God.

"Uh-huh. I'm going to come too. Gonna shoot up your back." Dave's voice was thick with his need.

"Oh." His eyes rolled as the sub shot, Dave's hand unavoidable. As was Dave's thumb, pressing into his slit and sending him over the edge.

He shot hard, his entire body shuddering, trembling as his balls emptied. Heat poured up his back as Dave came too, body convulsing against his.

"Oh God." He was going to shake apart.

Dave reached around and closed his laptop, pushing it to the side before wrapping around him and keeping him close. "You can say that again."

He blinked into the darkness, shivering with reaction.

"I've got you." Dave squeezed him tight, then began to pet him. "Thank you for sharing that with me."

"Thank you," he whispered. "Stay?"

He needed Dave to stay with him.

"I'm not going anywhere, babe. I promise."

He brought Dave's hand up to his mouth and kissed his knuckle.

"Mmm." Dave kept touching him, gentle and soft. "We're going to have an amazing weekend, babe."

The words made him shudder, but it wasn't a bad thing. "I thought I cancelled our date," he teased.

"I think maybe we're beyond the dating phase. We're lovers now, wouldn't you say?"

"Lovers. I swore I wouldn't have one of those."

"What's wrong with being lovers?" Dave asked.

"I was a little heartbroken after the last one."

"Ah. Hopefully I've restored your faith. And hopefully you'll appreciate that I don't want to be lovers for long. I want to be your Dom."

"Are they separate?" That was an honest question.

"No, not at all. Dom and sub is… deeper than lovers. It touches us in places we need to be touched."

He didn't know what to say to that, so he didn't say anything. He didn't.

Dave held him tight, cradling him, and Kenn let him. He needed the connection.

"This is aftercare," Dave told him, fingers still sliding on his skin as Dave continued to hold him. "After a scene, there is loving, and caring and making sure you're okay. Answering any questions, reminding you how much I care."

It sounded like heaven. He would do anything to have that.

"This is my favorite part of a scene, which was what we just did. And that was good. But this is the prize."

"The prize." He hummed the words, his eyelids dropping at the sound of Dave's voice. He wasn't sleeping; he was relaxing.

How long had it been?

"Yeah. This is what we work for in the scenes. A time together where we've pushed and worked, and now we can be easy in our skin and hopefully quiet in our mind." Dave kissed the top of his head.

"You learned how to do this?" He could feel that kiss everywhere.

"I was very lucky to have a few Doms take me under their wings. Men generous with their time and their lives."

"Tell me about it?" He wanted to know everything.

"You mean the specifics of aftercare or the men who taught me how to be a Dom?"

"Yes." Everything.

Dave chuckled and kissed the top of his head again. "Janus and his sub Peotre let me live with them for nearly a year when I finished my bachelors. I learned so much from them."

"Wow. A year? Do they do it all the time?"

Dave chuckled softly. "They had jobs, just like we do, so no, not all the time. Most weekends, many evenings. They did live the lifestyle 24/7. Peotre served his Master always."

He shivered, hoping Dave didn't feel it. That would be something else.

"Does the idea appeal to you?"

"What idea? I don't have an answer to that."

"The idea of being a full-time submissive. I think it appeals to you."

"I don't… I don't even know that I can…."

"Shh." Dave nuzzled his neck and stroked his belly. "Easy, love. Just breathe, huh? This is easy. This is the safest place on earth."

"The safest place on earth. I like that."

"It's the truth. I know the things I talk about appeal to you, even if the questions I ask often worry you. But it's also the truth that you are your own person, and you can do anything you want. Nobody else gets to judge you for what you do privately."

"I don't want you to think I'm too needy."

"You shouldn't have to worry about what I might think either. Revel in who you are, because you are amazing. And for the record—I don't think you're too needy. Let me tell you the most important thing I observed while I lived with Janus and Peotre. I have never seen two men who were more balanced together, who were more in love. And Peotre had as much power as Janus in the relationship. Janus needed his sub as much as his sub needed him." Dave nuzzled his ear. "I need this. I crave it. I crave you and your submission."

The words made him tremble.

"I mean it, Kenn. And on top of that, I love you."

Tears fill Kenn's eyes, and he held on. Tight. Dave held him in turn, arms like warm bands around him.

"I don't want you to feel bad about the things you want and need, because I want them too. I need them too."

"That was… incredibly erotic. Earlier." Dave deserved that admission.

"Yeah, it was super hot. But mostly because I had you in my arms, writhing and needy, wanting."

"Because you were here with me."

"Yes, exactly." Dave sounded so pleased.

"I'm glad you didn't listen to my text."

"I was already at the door when I got it, but yeah, I'm glad I didn't listen to it either." Dave tilted his head and took a kiss, long and slow. Kenn turned in Dave's arms and pushed close, allowing himself to snuggle in.

"I love you," Dave said again, the words soft but so real against his lips.

"I love you." God help him, he did.

"Oh. I was hoping you did. Or would. I'm glad you do." Dave kissed him again.

"Yes." Kenn let them float. Together.

Chapter Fourteen

Dave hummed softly as he buttered the toast and added it to the little tray he was putting together for Kenn. His boy deserved breakfast in bed, though he was afraid he was going to have to wake Kenn up, or it would go cold. Honestly, he'd thought the smell of breakfast cooking would do the trick. On the other hand, he supposed Kenn had had a very big evening.

It had been rather glorious. Dave found himself grinning like a fool.

Kenn was melted, hidden in the sheet, tight little butt up in the air. It made him want to go over and spank it.

It was Saturday. They had all day today, tomorrow. He actually got a little weak in the knees.

He took the veggie bacon out of the pan and added it to the tray, then put eggs in the pan, scrambling them about.

"Mmm. Smells good." Kenn rolled out of bed and padded toward the bathroom. "Be back."

"Breakfast, and you're up just in time." He watched Kenn make his way to the bathroom, admiring. "You want coffee? Tea?"

"Coffee please."

He turned the button for the coffee machine, which he'd set up in case that was what Kenn wanted. He was back to humming as he got the mugs prepped.

Kenn came to him, robe on, face washed. "Morning."

He opened his arms and wrapped Kenn in a hug before taking a lazy morning kiss. "Hi."

Kenn leaned into him, offering him a sweet little smile. "Thank you for breakfast."

"You're very welcome. Though I should admit, I have an ulterior motive." He filled their coffee cups.

"You do? What do you need?" Kenn grabbed the creamer from the fridge.

"I need for you to have a good meal so that you've got a lot of energy."

"Do we have plans?" He loved that innocent blink.

"We do. Wonderful plans for exploration and enjoyment."

"Okay. Well, breakfast looks good. Do you want jam for your toast?"

"No, I'm going to eat it with my eggs, but if you want jam, go for it." He moved the food from the tray to the little table, making the decision not to have breakfast in bed.

Kenn kept touching him, stroking his arm, his hip.

He loved the touches, the connection. He put their coffees on the table with their food. "Okay, babe. Time to eat."

"Veggie bacon for the win!" Kenn had teased the hell out of him, but Dave had to admit, the man had been good about it.

"It tastes great with eggs." He didn't chow down on it like people tended to do with the real thing, but he liked the salty crunch it added. "And it's got texture."

"It makes a fine egg sandwich."

"Indeed." He loved that Kenn was more than happy to eat vegetarian with him.

Kenn ate, chatting with him, comfortable as they drank their coffee.

He loved how bright and easy Kenn was after their first scene together. It made him feel that he was definitely on the right path. Kenn truly got so much out of it.

"You're thinking hard today," Kenn said. "Do you have a lot of work to do?"

"No, a lot of pleasure. I was thinking about how well yesterday evening went and how I want to continue in that vein today. How that seems to suit you."

Kenn's cheeks went pink. "You think so?"

"I do. Look at how relaxed and happy you are this morning."

"I slept well. No dreams."

"That's great. I thought after we eat we could do some more toy shopping online. After seeing that video yesterday, I want to get a flogger and a much bigger plug. Maybe a nice-sized dildo too."

Kenn's eyes went wide. "What?"

"I think you heard what I said." He thought Kenn probably needed a moment to process. Maybe two.

"Oh. Oh dear." So prim. So proper.

He reached out to take Kenn's hand and wrapped his fingers around it. "This is a safe place to talk about these kind of things, Kenn. To explore them."

"It's easier to talk about it in the dark."

"How about we go talk about it in bed while we're cuddling?" He could give Kenn that much.

"I can live with that." Kenn's cheeks were bright red.

"Excellent." He was so pleased Kenn was always willing to try.

"I'll do the dishes. You cooked."

"That's fair. I'll refresh the bed and boot up the laptop. Find our favorite toy store."

Kenn turned on some music and cleaned up the kitchen, taking maybe a little too long.

He cleared his throat. "Don't rub the pattern off the dishes, babe."

"Huh? No. Just washing them." Kenn rinsed the last dish, then dried off his hands.

"Take off your robe and come to bed, babe. It's cold over here without you."

Kenn came to Dave, sliding the robe off his lean, fine body and sliding into the blankets. Dave put his hands on Kenn, his fingers seeming most happy whenever they were touching Kenn. Then he settled Kenn between his legs with his back against Dave's chest.

Kenn snuggled into him, settling hard. "You're warm."

"Gotta make sure my boy isn't cold."

He loved that blush. Loved it.

Kissing Kenn's cheek, he clicked on the link on the laptop, bringing up a picture of a huge dildo that was very reminiscent of the one in the video. "What do you think?"

Kenn jerked in his lap, hips pushing hard into the basket of his hips.

"Mmm. That feels like an 'oh my God, yes' to me."

"That's big." Kenn's whisper echoed in him.

"It is. Not as big as the one in that video, but it's close." He thought Kenn wanted to try it. "We'll have to work up to that size."

"I—shh."

"We will. You can't start with a great big one like that. I don't want to hurt you. I want to bring you intense pleasure." He leaned in and whispered softly, "I want to stretch your hole, boy. I want to be the one to push your boundaries."

"Dave!"

Yeah, like that. He knew simply talking about it was pushing Kenn's boundaries right now. But he also knew Kenn wanted so badly to be pushed past them and into the things he saw.

"Now for a bigger plug and a flogger. Maybe some leather cuffs." He added them to his cart.

Kenn squeaked but didn't say anything.

"You see anything you want me to add to our purchase today?"

"No. No, this is more than enough."

"We need at least one more dildo—in between my cock and the big dildo size. Maybe two." He clicked around the site, checking out dimensions. He ordered two of those and a soft flogger that would warm his boy's skin. He'd have to see how Kenn felt about pain. He knew the roughness and flogger had been part of the scene, but he also knew Kenn had no practical experience with it, so who knew which way it would go?

Who knew what excitements they could discover together?

He put in his credit card information and hit Purchase. "Ta-da! We are going to have so much fun exploring when this arrives."

"Listen to you."

"Um-hum." He loved having Kenn here at his mercy. "It's going to be so exciting, slowly opening you up. Getting you to the point where you can take the big dildo."

"I can't...."

Oh, Kenn could. Kenn so could.

"Of course you can. And if there's a problem, you safeword. It's going to be grand."

He began to stroke one nipple, nice and easy. He wanted to rev Kenn up gradually. He knew this would slowly drive Kenn out of his mind.

In a good way. In the best way.

He licked at Kenn's neck, and Kenn tilted for him, letting him in. Humming, he nuzzled further, using his lips and his tongue and breathing Kenn in. Kenn's eyelids went heavy as they breathed together.

"Can you feel that? How we're already more in sync after last night?"

"Is that real?" Kenn hummed deep in his chest.

"Can't you feel it? We're breathing together," he pointed out.

"I can. It's... comforting."

"It is. I think it feels amazing to be in sync."

"Yes." Kenn leaned into his chest.

"That's the goal of the Dom/sub relationship. To be better versions of ourselves. To be wonderful together."

Kenn's answer was a soft moan.

Dave bent his neck and brought their mouths together, touching his lips to Kenn's. Kenn opened up, hand touching his fingers on that sweet nipple. He loved how he had Kenn's full attention.

He didn't let Kenn pull him away, though. This was his call. He continued with a few more soft caresses, then pinched, knowing the sharper touch would be totally unexpected after the much gentler strokes.

"Uhn!" Kenn jerked, sat up tall. "Careful."

"I'm being very mindful of my touches." Incredibly, even. He wanted Kenn to be utterly aware of those nipples, the tip of his cock. All the places Dave intended to have pierced.

"Imagine my pinches are the end of a needle going into your skin as you're being pierced." Dave pinched again—one nipple and then the other, followed by the tip of Ken's cock.

"Shh. Stop that."

"No way. I know you enjoy hearing my plans." Got off on it was actually more accurate. Kenn loved to use that vast imagination. "I know you love thinking about what if you were the sub in the videos you watch."

"Dave, I don't know that we should talk about that."

"Oh, I disagree. We should most definitely talk about it. I love you. I want to hear what goes on in your mind. Especially what turns you on." He wasn't going to let Kenn hide; he didn't want Kenn to feel that he had to. There was nothing wrong with Kenn's desires. Nothing at all. They excited him, they excited Kenn. They were perfect.

"Talk to me, Kenn. Tell me what's on your mind."

"I don't know how. I never really talk about it as something to do with me."

"I think you should give it a try. Just tell me what you're thinking, honestly thinking about—not the 'oh, I shouldn't say' part, but the part beneath that."

"Last night was wild. Exciting."

"I liked it too. I'm so glad we can explore that kind of thing together."

Kenn leaned back, snuggling in deep. "You're making my nipple ache, Dave."

"Uh-huh. And you're loving it."

"We should stop. They're tender."

"Tomorrow, whenever your shirt brushes against them, they'll ache, and you'll remember the things we did—both yesterday and today." He nuzzled Kenn's ear. "And tomorrow."

Kenn cried out, pushing harder back into him.

"That's right. I'm going to spend the whole weekend working to make some of your fantasies come true. Or at the very least, find out what they are. Maybe we'll call a piercing studio. We could get nipples and cock done this afternoon, and I could spend the next day caring for you."

"We can't!" Kenn's protest came immediately and right on cue.

"Why not?"

"Because I... I'm a teacher!"

"I've seen what you wear to class, babe, and no one would be able to see the piercings. No one would know." He teased the flesh at the head of Kenn's cock, toying with it. "There will be a sweet heavy ring here, small ones in your nips."

He could feel Kenn's heartbeat against his chest, pounding away like it was running a race.

"We should call and see if we can get in. If we can't, then it's a sign." Dave was pretty sure they could.

Kenn's breathing was little more than soft gasps, and his hands curled on Dave's thighs.

"Can you imagine it? It would look amazing. It would feel amazing." He nibbled gently, tugging Kenn's earlobe. "I'd hold your hand the whole time. Then bring you home, fuck you until you didn't have a drop of seed left in you."

A shudder moved through Kenn's body, and Dave loved that he could make Kenn react like that with nothing but his words.

"Tell me we can call, boy. Tell me."

"Dave...." Kenn groaned softly, nodding.

"Thank you." He tilted Kenn's head and kissed him hard and deep, rewarding him for saying yes.

Kenn whimpered and leaned into him with a soft little cry. He cradled Kenn, deepening the kiss, letting it linger right there. Even while his mouth was busy, his brain was buzzing.

He needed to find a body piercer. He could actually give Janus a call. He would bet that his old friend would have some recommendations. Someone who would take his boy today, decorate nips and cock.

When their kisses ended, he reached for his phone and sent a text off to Janus.

give me 10 to make some calls.

He could totally do that. He knew how to spend those ten minutes too. "My friend is on it."

"You sure that's not cheating?"

"Absolutely not. I don't want to go to just anyone. This has to be a reputable piercer. One who works safe. One who is the best. No one else touches you."

Kenn's cheeks went a sweet pink. "If there's an opening today."

"That was our deal." And he was hoping like hell there was. The fact that Kenn had even considered the deal proved how much he really wanted it.

"Okay. Yes." Kenn snuggled into him.

"Mmm. Have you ever noticed how perfectly you fit?" He had a Kenn-shaped spot along his side.

"I have. It's amazing and so warm."

"You're amazing and warm." He rubbed their noses, then shifted, turning it into a kiss. Teasing Kenn's lips open, he slipped his tongue inside. He loved how Kenn tasted, and the wet warmth was delicious.

Kenn cuddled in farther, their legs tangling together. He grabbed hold of Kenn's thigh, tugging him even closer. The warmth they generated together was incredible, was just what they both needed.

"My boy. I can't wait to see the jewelry decorating you. Would you like to show me your other video?"

"Oh. I thought you'd forgotten about it."

Dave couldn't help but tease. "Thought or hoped?"

"Sort of both, I think. More thought than hoped."

"Good deal. So let's see it. I want to see this man with all the piercings that intrigued you so."

"Wh-what about you? You are supposed to share too."

"We'll figure something out for me to share later. I think this video would be a fun way to spend the ten or fifteen minutes it'll take Janus to give me a name."

He nuzzled Kenn's temple, encouraging his boy to relax, to share this with him. They'd enjoyed themselves last night, so much. He petted Kenn's belly and breathed slowly, loving that Kenn gradually matched his tempo.

That felt so right, so natural. So fucking real.

Dave nuzzled their cheeks together as Kenn pulled up the second video. "I'm excited," he whispered.

"Are you?" Kenn whispered back.

"I love finding out new things about you, like what turns you on. And I love being turned-on with you."

Kenn leaned harder, ass rocking against him.

"And I love how my talking to you turns you on, makes you need."

Kenn kissed his hand, hiding his face away.

"And I'm going to keep talking, keep turning you on."

"Incorrigible," Kenn teased. "This is the most…. I feel a little tipsy."

"Yeah? It feels good, huh?"

"A little out of control, but yes."

"You don't like being out of control. At all. I think that's why the BDSM excites you so much. It's very appealing to you to be made to give in to someone else's will. To be forced to be out of control."

Kenn shook his head but stayed close, moaning for him.

"Of course, that's why we have the safeword. In the end, you have ultimate control, even as it feels like you've ceded it all."

"Right. And no matter what, everything stops."

"That's right. No ifs, ands, or buts. Everything stops."

"And you won't be mad."

"I promise I will absolutely not be mad, ever. That's the most important part of BDSM."

Kenn nodded, pulled his tablet over. "One more video."

"The pierced-man one." Dave rubbed his hands together in anticipation.

"Yes. Then it's your turn." Kenn started the video, which showed a lovely man with heavy rings in his tits, in his cock. Chains ran through the rings, and a man in leather came up, a jeweled penis plug in his hand, a thick thing with three lumps.

"I'm going to fasten it in. It's in until I say it comes out, boy."

Kenn shivered, and Dave hummed. "I can give this to you, Kenn. I can make you glow with it."

"It's… that's so big." Kenn spread as Dave reached down and stroked the slit of his cock.

"And it's yours. Just because something is big doesn't mean you can't have it." Dave nuzzled his ear. "In fact, you deserve it."

Kenn arched into Dave's touch, moaning.

"Such a sweet boy. I'm going to give you everything."

The man in the video was chained, plugged, and desperately hard. Dave admired the Dom's imagination and command. He could see why Kenn gravitated toward this particular video. Control, beauty, a hint of pain, and an aching cock. It made Dave's mouth dry. He curled his hands around Kenn's upper leg, digging his fingers into Kenn's skin before stroking the soft flesh of Kenn's inner thighs.

He wanted that text to come in; he wanted to see those rings in Kenn's flesh. More, he wanted to be there to hold Kenn's hand while the needle slid through his flesh because Dave had asked.

Just because he'd asked.

His phone buzzed, and he grabbed it immediately to check.

2pm. Xeno. He'll come to you. Scene friendly.

You rock. He added Kenn's address to the text. *Thanks.*

"What did he say?"

"He said that Xeno will be here to do it privately at 2:00 p.m."

"What?"

"That gives us a few hours to get ready." Should he do a scene first, so Kenn was relaxed from being pushed, from orgasming? Or should he get Kenn all revved up so that the potential for him coming from being pierced was higher?

He tapped Kenn's cockhead idly, slowly.

"A few hours from now, I'll hold your hand while Xeno pierces your nipples and your cock." Dave hummed softly. "He's scene friendly, so I can hold you, naked, in my lap."

"What?"

"I'm going to hold you while he does it."

"But… you can't. But. Oh."

"But I can. And so can you." He tilted Kenn's face and kissed him. Kenn sobbed into the kiss, reaching up for him.

He deepened the kiss. He would make Kenn come, then build him back up again.

Chapter Fifteen

He was not going to do this.

Not. At. All.

Kenn cleaned the house, refusing to think about this whole stupid thing.

Dave was curled up on the bed, reading a book, relaxed, like this whole thing was normal.

He was just going to lock himself in the bathroom until the man left.

"Kenn. Come and sit with me, love."

"There's dusting to be done."

"The place is ten-foot square. I think it's pretty clean already. Come sit with me."

"But—"

"Boy."

The single word made him stop, eyes going wide.

Dave stared at him, silently waiting for him.

His nipples went tight from that look alone.

Then Dave held out a hand to him, palm up.

"I don't know about this, Dave." He went right to his lover.

He fit perfectly in Dave's arms, his ass snug up against Dave's crotch. "Tell me what's got you spooked."

"Besides the whole needles in my body part?"

"Yes. Because the needles are only in your body for a second or two." Dave rubbed his arms, warming him up immediately.

"The rings aren't, and someone will see me." And know that Dave was his Dom, and that was too exciting.

"The rings aren't needles, though. And so what if someone sees? There's nothing wrong with having piercings. Frankly, it's nobody's business but ours." Dave began to stroke his nipples again. "Would you like a blindfold, boy? I can arrange that."

Dave continued to touch him, making him ache as Dave waited patiently for his answer.

"I don't know." Would that make it easier?

"I think it would be hot if you watched right along with me, but it's your decision and you can make it at any point up until the piercing starts."

"Okay, this is so weird."

"By weird you mean out of your experience?" Dave asked.

"Yes. Absolutely. Outside of my comfort level too."

"I don't see that as a bad thing," Dave told him softly. "I think being out of your comfort zone is good for you. I also think on some level it excites you, makes you hard. It's my job to push, to keep you happy and fulfilled. Trust me. Trust me, boy."

Kenn flushed at the "boy." He didn't know if he could get used to that.

Dave's hand slid down his belly to fondle his cock, and he was almost surprised to find he was already hard. From Dave's words and the anticipation of what was coming alone.

"This is going to be a scene until he leaves, for sure, and we may decide to let it continue. Do you know your safeword?"

Kenn nodded. "Huxley."

"Perfect. Remember—you will not get in trouble for using it."

"Are you going to want me to call you Sir for this?" He didn't know why, but the idea that he had an out was soothing.

"I want you to call me Sir because I've earned it. So you'll decide when that happens."

He wanted to *know* when. He wanted to understand. Dammit.

Dave tilted his head. "I can see the gears turning behind your eyes. What? I can't read your mind, so if you have questions or anything, you have to let me know."

"I need to do some research. I feel… lost."

"About what, babe? Calling me Sir? I don't want to leave you floundering on that front, but I really feel like it would mean more if you choose to do it rather than are told to." Dave squeezed him. "I also feel some research is a great idea. Not furtively checking things out, but boldly searching out answers to your questions."

"Research is sort of what I do, right?"

"It totally is, which is why I think it would be a good thing. Plus, it would make me happy that you really knew I would never belittle you or punish you for anything you researched."

"Would you punish me?" What did that mean to Dave? What did it mean to him?

"Well… that would be something we'd have to discuss. Would we want to be in a place where I punished you, or do we want to do away with that? I think it's a very useful tool, for both of us."

He loved that Dave wanted to discuss these things with him—there was no shame, no censure.

"What does that mean? Exactly, that is." Kenn was beginning to relax, to breathe with Dave.

"Well, if we set up rules and punishments, you'll know exactly what happens if you break a given rule. That means if you want a particular punishment, you can deliberately break the corresponding rule."

Dave's words made him shiver. "Does that happen a lot, do you think?" He reached out, stroked Dave's thigh.

"I think it depends on the couple. It didn't happen very much with Janus and Peotre, although now and then Peotre would push to get what he needed without asking. Some couples that I've met, though, the sub was constantly breaking rules for the attention, for the punishment."

"That seems…. I don't know. I just don't know how that would work."

"It seems like a lot of game play. I hope that in time you'll be comfortable enough to tell me if you need something I'm not giving you." Dave said it like it was so easy to talk about this stuff. Funnily enough, with Dave it was becoming easier. "And there's the idea of having rules in scenes. Things to help you focus, hmm?"

"Like?"

"Like no swearing. No touching yourself."

"You've talked about that." He tried not to think, tried to will his cock to go down, but it wasn't working.

"And you like the sound of it." Dave wrapped one hand around his erection, jacking him easily.

"It… the time…." He groaned and leaned into Dave.

Dave looked over at his bedside clock. "We've got twenty minutes. Besides, I think I want you needy when Xeno gets here. I'm going to spread your legs over mine and spread them wide. I'm going to hold your hands."

He shook his head. "No."

"Yes. That way you're spread and open but supported and held at the same time."

"I don't want to think about this." He was hard still. Again.

"And yet, it's going to be happening very soon." Dave rubbed his thumb across the tip of Kenn's cock, back and forth across the slit.

"You'll never be able to do that again, after." He knew better, but….

"Of course I will. It will be different, but I'll still be able to." Then Dave pressed down on his slit.

Kenn arched and keened, his eyes crossing. Oh, no fair. No fair.

"There are these penis plugs that attach to a ring that's right here. So hot."

"Shh…." His nipples drew up tight.

"You wouldn't like it at all if I actually hushed. You like it when I talk dirty to you." Dave chuckled softly, nuzzled his ear. "My naughty professor."

He cried out and pushed back into Dave again.

"Yeah, you love it. And I love that you do."

Dave cupped Kenn's needy cock again, the touch hot as fire, and he arched. Dave slid his hand down to cup his balls, tugging on them and keeping his orgasm at bay.

"You're not going to come until the piercing."

"I'll never come again, after." He knew he was fussing, but it felt good to do it, to let himself worry.

"I promise that you will. In fact, I'd lay odds that the penis piercing is the one that's going to make you come like a gusher."

"Dave!" He started laughing, suddenly tickled.

Dave grinned down at him. "What? Coming like a gusher's a good thing."

"A little messy, and the visual is… whoa." He was rolling with laughter.

Dave chuckled and shook his head. "I'm not sure if I should be insulted or not." Dave was clearly not upset.

His chuckles faded along with his tension, and he cuddled into Dave's arms.

"Have I told you today that I love you?"

"Probably, but you can tell me again."

"I love you." Dave kissed him softly, lips sliding against his, making him tingle.

"I love you." They breathed together, nice and easy, almost floating.

"This is the feeling. This peace and togetherness. We're searching for this, only even deeper, when we do scenes."

"Do you think it will work?"

"Absolutely. We've already found some peace together. We've fallen in sync breathingwise. We're going to make so much magic together."

He liked that idea. Magic. Together.

The doorbell rang, and he tensed up. Dave stroked his back several times. "You should answer the door, boy."

"I don't want to." He did it, though, fully intending to tell the man to go.

"Hello, I'm Xeno." A beautiful man stood there with a warm smile, long hair the color of night, and shockingly blue eyes.

He took Kenn's breath away.

"Hello, Xeno. I'm Dave, and this is my boy." Dave came up behind him and slid his hand along Kenn's spine, warm through his shirt.

Tell him to go home. Tell him to just go.

"Hello, I'm so pleased to meet you both."

"Thank you for coming on such short notice. We really appreciate it."

"Of course. I'm in the lifestyle. I specialize in body mods in scenes—tattoos, piercings, brandings, cock pearls. I have a little shop in the Rosebud, but it's always best at home, isn't it?"

"It is. Cock pearls, eh? That sounds fascinating."

"It's very intense. I'm always honored to be a part of a scene. It's such a blessing."

Dave ushered Xeno in. "I thought we'd do it on the bed. We won't need to put a towel down, will we?"

"Oh, no. There will be a drop of blood, if that. You're wanting nipples, a PA, and a guiche?"

"We hadn't planned on a guiche, but it might be a great addition to the other three," Dave noted.

"I brought some different ring options—your boy is lovely, by the way. What feels right to you, gold or stainless?"

"Thank you. What do you think, Kenn? I believe gold will compliment your skin tone best."

"I...." He didn't know. He didn't.

Xeno waited, then pulled out a set of rings with a lovely luster, the beads on either end the same gold. "These are heavy, masculine, classy."

"Beautiful," murmured Dave. "You'll look stunning in those."

"Is he shaved behind the balls? I can do it, or you can, if not. It won't take but a second."

"Are you good with doing the guiche?" Dave asked him. "I know we only agreed to the nipples and cock, but it seems like the perfect time to get the guiche as well. I can just see you with a fine golden chain connecting all four rings."

"I'm going to die."

"Is that a no?"

"I…. It's not a no."

Dave beamed at him, looking so pleased, and the look went all the way through Kenn. He hid in Dave's arms, hearing a soft "oh."

"You can shave him—I'll be holding him open."

"No problem. I'll set up at the foot of the bed. I'll mark all the spots and then do the piercings. Do you have a preferred order?"

"Nipples and work our way down." Dave tilted his head and looked into Kenn's eyes. "You're never going to forget this."

"I'm going to die."

Xeno's chuckle was warm. "I don't think there's ever been a piercing-related death."

Dave's lips quirked up in a half smile. "There you go. I think you're safe." Dave moved him to the bed, undid the belt of his robe, and pushed the soft material off his shoulders.

His cheeks burned, his heart pounding hard and fast.

Dave kept their eyes locked, and he found he couldn't turn away. "I love you, and I'm so very proud of you."

"I'm scared," he whispered.

"And yet you're doing it. Do you know how brave that makes you?" Dave drew him down onto the bed, sitting behind him, hands sliding along his arms. "I'm right here."

Dave draped Kenn's legs over the top of Dave's longer ones, then spread him wide, holding his hands the entire time.

"I've got you," Dave said. "And I'm not letting you go."

"I need your safeword, please," Xeno asked.

"Hu-huxley."

"Huxley. Got it. Use if it you need to, okay?"

"Everything will stop if you do—no recriminations. No anger." Dave ran his fingers along the insides of Kenn's thighs, and it brought his attention to his body, to his cock, which was shockingly hard.

"I'll start by shaving. It's just one swipe."

This was insane.

Xeno's fingers were warm against his skin, but it wasn't sexual in any way. The swipe-swipe on his perineum was quick, shocking.

"I'm right here, boy. And you are doing so well. Breathe with me, and be aware of every moment. You're going to want to remember each one." Dave's voice was quiet and confident.

He felt soft touches to the sensitive skin behind his balls, then to the tip of his cock.

"Okay. I'm going to hold up a mirror and then ease your balls out of the way so your Master can look."

His Master. The word felt... like a warm blanket.

"You can look too, Kenn. If you want. Make sure you're happy with the placement."

"I trust him." He couldn't look. No way.

Dave kissed the top of his head. "Thank you, boy."

"Well, then. Do they meet your approval?"

Xeno's fingers lifted his balls, and Dave made a pleased sound. "Oh yes. They're perfect."

"Okay, I'll mark the nipples next. Such a pretty pink."

"Yeah. My Kenn is beautiful. The piercings are going to bring that to the next level." Dave sounded so proud of him.

"Absolutely."

The touch of the Sharpie to his nipple was even bigger than to his cock, and he gasped. Dave massaged his thighs, and a soft kiss landed on the side of his neck, Dave easing him without saying a word.

Xeno held the mirror up, and Dave hummed. "You're good."

"I try."

"Okay, boy. Are you ready for Xeno to start?"

"No. No, this is a bad idea."

Dave met his eyes. "I know you need to say that. And I know you know what to say if you have to have this stopped." Dave kissed him gently, then turned to Xeno. "We're ready to begin."

"Excellent. You say Huxley, everything stops, right?"

Kenn stared at Xeno, the man's face a little watery. "R-right."

"Take a deep breath in," Xeno told him. When he did, Xeno drew the needle through his flesh, the ring following in one smooth motion. A burn lingered behind, a dull throbbing.

"Well done!" Xeno didn't give him any time to think before doing his other nipple just as quickly and efficiently.

Dave was hard as nails behind him. "Perfect. God, boy. You make me ache."

He felt sexy and lovely, thanks to Dave.

"PA or guiche next?" Xeno's voice was soft, unobtrusive.

"Guiche first." Dave spoke softly, and he gently rubbed Kenn's perineum.

Kenn's eyes rolled involuntarily, and he shook his head, his toes curling tight. Dave stroked his legs, petting him.

"Easy. Easy, boy. Let it happen."

Dave took in a deep breath, and when he took in another, Kenn matched him.

"Little pinch," Xeno warned, and then it happened—a pinch and a burn, and he cried out.

"I've got you," Dave said again.

"Oh, that's lovely," Xeno murmured. "Would you like to see?"

Kenn shook his head, but Dave had a different idea. "I do, please. It's okay if you don't look, Kenn. You'll be able to see it later."

"I'm going to touch your sac again, so your Master can see."

Dave kissed his neck, lips lingering, giving him something else to feel, to concentrate on. Then Xeno touched him, and Dave gasped.

"Beautiful." Dave hugged him. "You're stunning, boy. Absolutely stunning."

"I—"

"Almost over. One left."

"You're doing great, Kenn. Keep breathing." Dave nibbled on his earlobe, then whispered, "You're allowed to come when he does this one."

"No...." Please no. He would die of embarrassment.

"I didn't say you had to, only that you could."

"This'll be quick, I promise," Xeno told him. "It's the easiest one."

"How can it be?" Kenn didn't understand.

"The pleasure and pain nerve centers are very close," murmured Dave.

"And the flesh is thin here, and soft. It'll be over before you know it." Xeno had such a kind voice.

"Okay. I'm going to close my eyes." That was the best he had.

"It'll be over before you know it," Xeno promised.

"I'm so proud of you," Dave told him softly.

"I'm scared," he whispered.

"You're hard, boy."

He just shook his head.

"You are. This turns you on as much as it scares you. Do you know how hot that is? How much you turn me on?" Dave's fingers danced on his thighs, gentle, but leaving warm tingles. "My brave boy. We're going to find you chains, decorate you. Maybe a couple of tattoos. One at the tip of your prick."

"That would be beautiful," Xeno noted. "My partner does tattoos and can make house calls like I do."

"I've got your number," Dave noted. "I'm sure we'll use it."

"Please do. My Master is... amazing."

Xeno's partner was his Master? That made him a submissive—oh! A sharp sting made Kenn cried out. Then came a tug he felt deep.

"There you go. You're done."

Dave groaned, fingers digging into Kenn's thighs. "So beautiful."

"Yes. I'll invoice you." Xeno spoke in a low voice, easily ignored.

"Thank you, Xeno. We really appreciate it."

"You're so welcome. I'll see myself out."

The click of the door shutting seemed loud because it meant they were alone.

Kenn didn't know what to do, what to think, so he sat, perfectly still, barely even breathing.

"You're all right," Dave told him softly. "You need to remember to breathe."

"I just...." No, he didn't even think. He couldn't even think.

"You should look, boy." Dave cupped his balls, making everything shift.

"Don't touch," he begged, his eyes squeezed tight.

"I'm not touching your piercings. I'm not actually touching your cock, either." Dave's voice was as gentle as his hands.

"You're making things move, though."

"I am. And I'm going to keep making things move until you look. Until you come. Until you're a pile of goo."

He shook his head, refusing to look, refusing to make it real. Not yet.

Dave began to lick at his neck, tongue dragging along his skin, teeth threatening. It made him shiver.

"Be nice, Dave. You let someone poke me."

"I paid for someone to poke you. And I am being exceptionally nice." Dave hummed. "You look so lovely, boy. It turns me on so much, seeing you decorated for me."

Dave let go of his balls in favor of running the strong hands over Kenn's body once again.

He sighed and relaxed back, his muscles shaking from being so tense.

"That's it, boy. Just relax. You need to take deep breaths and enjoy this. Can you feel the places you were pierced throbbing?"

"Shh...." God yes. God, he could.

"Has shushing me ever worked?" Dave asked him.

"I have faith."

Dave laughed, the sound happy. "God, I love you."

"I can't believe we did this." He was never going to move again. Never.

"I can. You're amazing, and I knew you could do this. Just like I know you're going to love the piercings." Dave nuzzled his ear. "You were so hard, the whole time. And you're still hard. Proving how much you want this. So fucking hot, boy."

"Please. Can we...? I want to stay like this."

"That sounds good to me. Easy access." Dave wrapped his hand around Kenn's cock and began to stroke, the movements slow and easy, each one culminating in Dave's fingers barely missing the new ring in the tip of his cock.

"Don't...." Don't what? Don't stop? Don't touch?

"I won't stop." Dave had clearly decided what he'd meant, even if he didn't know.

"Okay. Thank you. God, I ache."

"It's good, hmm?" Dave kept moving his hand, sliding it along Kenn's heavy flesh.

"Uh-huh. Good. Hmm." He stayed where he was, spread wide, aching, hard.

Dave slid his free hand up toward his nipples, moving slowly, inching along and full of promise.

"No… no, you can't."

"But I am." Dave touched the very tip of his right nipple, pressing against it.

He arched, his eyes flying open. The ache was deep and so, so right.

Dave slid his fingers across to Kenn's other nipple, pressed on it as well. Then he touched the ring.

He needed to get up. Get away. Get more. God, he didn't know. He didn't know what he needed.

"You're so hot like this. So special. I want to touch you all over for the rest of your life." Dave took his hand, holding it, then bringing it down and pressing it behind his balls. "Feel yourself, boy. Feel the ring inside your skin."

"Oh God." His hand shook, part of him wanting to explore, part wanting him to jerk away.

"Breathe, Kenn. Just breathe. This is part of you now—you should touch it, explore it, feel it."

"I—It's overwhelming, you know? Seriously overwhelming."

"You can handle it. I believe in you, in your strength."

"You're the only one."

"The only person you need to believe in you is you. I'm just a bonus."

He knew that. He'd managed fine on his own.

"Now touch yourself."

"What?" The command surprised him, and his cock jerked.

"Touch yourself, boy. I want you to feel the ring behind your balls, the ones in your nipples and finally, the one in your cock. Do it."

He shook his head, but he did it, the damn thing seeming so fucking big in his fingertips. Dave's hand was right there with his.

"It's going to be amazing when we can play with it. Turn it in your skin and twist it." Dave moaned softly. "Attach your PA to it with a chain. Lead you by a leash."

Kenn was going to die.

"Baby, we're going to have so much fun. I promise you that."

Even Dave's breath across his skin was turning him on.

Dave arched underneath him and made him moan. He shivered at the hot slide of Dave's hard cock against his spine. It was echoed by Dave's free hand moving up his torso.

"I want you to submit to the pleasure and the need and come for me."

"I'm aching for you." His cock was aching, throbbing, but it was the soft voice in his ear that made him dizzy.

"Then give it up to me. Shoot for me." Dave continued stroking his cock, moving a little faster now, pushing him toward an orgasm.

He thought the ring inside would hold it back, hold him back. He could feel it building, though, feel his balls get fuller. If anything could make him come, it was Dave.

"I want to feel your come splashing against my skin. I want to smell it. It's so hot. You're so hot."

"I need you." He arched, his toes curling with his need.

"You want to ride me?" Dave asked. "All we have to do is turn you in my lap and slick you up. Then you can ride, rubbing your cock between us. That ring will catch, make you burn."

"Oh fuck…." He tensed, his entire body shuddering. "Please. Please, yes. Love. I need you."

"You've got me, boy. I am your Master and your lover and your Dave, and I will always be here for you." Dave grabbed his waist and lifted him, helped him get himself turned around so they were facing each other. Once he was settled, Dave smiled, the look slow and easy and steaming. "Hey."

"H-hey." He leaned forward and took a kiss, slow and easy and perfect.

"Love you." The words were spoken against his lips, Dave's hands on his ass, fingers digging in as Dave squeezed.

Then Dave let go and leaned slightly, grabbing the lube off the side table. Kenn nodded and stared, needing Dave more than he needed his next breath.

"Want you to fill me up."

"I will. You fit so perfectly around me." Dave pressed kisses over his face, and then came the sweet pressure of Dave's fingers, breaching his hole and pushing into him.

He rolled his hips, begging silently for more, harder, deeper.

"Such an eager little bottom, aren't you? I am the luckiest man in the world." Dave pushed another finger into him, stretching him wider.

"Eager. Yes." He couldn't argue with that at all. "Goodness yes."

"And it's a good thing, hmm? For both of us." Dave pushed those fingers into him over and over, filling him and making his body sing.

He could feel the piercings throbbing every time Dave thrust those two fingers into his body.

"Yes. More, please. Please, I need to fly."

"I'm gonna send you far into the sky. Send you so high." Dave pushed another finger in, spreading him so good. The stretch burned, and when Dave hit his gland, his entire body lit up.

He arched, his aching cock sliding on Dave's belly, making him want to scream. The ring caught and tugged, not a lot, but enough to feel.

Dave pegged his gland again and again, giving him no quarter, no time to recover, to calm himself, between the dings.

He didn't want it to be over. He wanted to fly and fly, not crash back to the ground.

Eventually, Dave pulled his fingers away, leaving Kenn empty. He whimpered, but Dave patted his hip. "Easy, boy. Easy. I'm getting my cock slick so I can be inside you." Dave smiled, the look naughty as hell. "Imagine that after that I'm going to plug my seed inside of you."

Kenn grabbed the base of his prick and squeezed.

"No touching," Dave reminded him. Then he leaned over and searched through his bag, coming up with a plug in a plastic baggie. "It's clean. Ready to use."

"Oh God. Love. Master, please. Please, I need you." He was going to lose his mind.

"I'm right here, boy." Dave met his eyes, the look in them hot and full of love. Dave cared for him, adored him. He could read it in Dave's face.

He rose up to his knees, Dave helping him, guiding him down until the thick cock pressed against his hole. Then Dave pushed up, cock breaching him.

Kenn whimpered, shooting as soon as Dave brushed his gland, his orgasm rocking him.

"Oh fuck. So tight." Dave groaned and rested their foreheads together. He didn't move, only breathed with Kenn.

Kenn arched a little, rocking gently on Dave's cock. His prick was still achingly hot. And hard. He wondered if he was ever going to go soft with that ring embedded in his flesh.

Dave began to move, carefully circling his hips, then pushing up, moving the cock inside him so he could feel it all over.

"Can you feel the ring down there?" Kenn whispered.

"Uh-huh. Against my pubic bone. So fucking good. You are amazing." Dave kept moving, pushing into him over and over.

He closed his eyes, and that made his world spin faster. Dave's hum filled his ears, filled him. It was like Dave had pushed into all his spaces and made them his.

"Let go, boy. Let me in everywhere."

"How do you know?"

"This is what it means to be connected as Dom and sub. Your sub space is wonderful."

"Yes." This was wonderful.

Dave kept the pace fairly deliberate, giving him time to feel everything as they stared into each other's eyes. "You are amazing. Tight and hot and so good."

Kenn nodded. He did. He did feel amazing. He was soaring.

Dave wrapped his hands around Kenn's hips, digging his fingers into Kenn's flesh. It made everything even better. Like that little spark of ache increased the pleasure. He tensed, his entire body clenching, gripping around Dave's prick.

Dave's nostrils flared. "Kenn!" His eyes rolled back, and his fingers dug in harder, bringing Kenn down with more force.

The little sting burned his ass, and he clenched over and over. Dave made wonderful noises for him, pleasure clear.

He needed more. Wanted more. He wanted it all. Dave seemed determined to give it to him, thrusting up harder and harder. Kenn ached, his entire body on fire as they ground together.

Then Dave touched the ring in his prick.

The world went white-hot, and he screamed, his balls emptying. Dave thrust one more time, filling him with heat. He hung there, leaning hard, his universe broken.

Dave was right there with him, though, holding on and keeping him from falling apart.

Chapter Sixteen

Dave sat across from Kenn, smiling at his lover. God, happy was a good look on Kenn. Dave could easily sit across from him and simply be for ages. That they had mimosas and plates full of delicious brunch items was a bonus. The waffles were especially good, and he'd slathered his with butter and a dulce de leche caramel that had him honestly moaning it was so good.

Kenn's gaze flew to his. "Dave!"

He shook his head—he was not taking flack for this. "Have you tasted this sauce? It's the kind of thing you want to slather all over your lover and lick off."

Kenn's cheeks heated, but he didn't look upset; in fact he laughed softly. "The way your brain works…."

"You love it," Dave suggested.

"I can't deny that."

Dave beamed. He was glad Kenn was beginning to sink into these things, accept them and, he thought, revel in them.

Kenn ate the last bite of his omelet and smiled. "I swore I wouldn't come back here, but I'm glad I did. I do love this routine."

"Sunday mornings are a lot more fun with mimosas." He tilted his in Kenn's direction, then drank the last mouthful. He loved how the champagne made the orange juice fizz in his mouth.

"This is true. Sunday mornings are fun with you," Kenn offered, gaze holding his, eyes sparkling.

"Not just Sunday mornings either." He waggled his eyebrows. They had had a wonderful weekend. Wonderful.

"Shh…." Kenn laughed, though, didn't he? A huge, happy sound that filled the air.

Dave fell in love all over again. This man did it for him. "Did you try your waffles yet?" Kenn had a huge appetite this morning, taking not only the omelet, but waffles, bacon, and fruit. Dave knew it came from spending the weekend making love and playing. Sex built up an appetite.

"I did. They are crispy and sweet. Perfect." Kenn nudged his leg.

Oh, Kenn was playing with him. Out in public. His boy was so brave. Or maybe he was simply growing the confidence he needed to be himself. Either way, Dave loved it.

"Sexy boy." He dragged his eyes up and down Kenn's fine body—as much of it as he could, anyway—making sure that Kenn could feel his admiration.

Kenn's cheeks went a darker pink, and he ducked his head. He looked pleased, though, and Dave rubbed Kenn's leg beneath the table, running his foot from ankle to almost knee.

"Be nice, now. I don't need to get hard here."

Dave didn't point out that Kenn had started the game of footsie they were playing. "I am being nice. And it wouldn't be the worst thing if you got hard, would it?" He thought Kenn looked hot when he was turned on and squirming in public. And it wasn't something that Kenn hated anymore either.

"Not the worst thing," Kenn allowed.

Dave had to laugh softly at the bare concession.

He could see Kenn trying hard not to match his laughter. "Maybe even not a *bad* bad thing."

"Dare we go for not a bad thing at all?" Dave rubbed Kenn's leg again, demonstrating how not bad the touches were.

"Maybe not a bad thing at all," Kenn admitted. "At all."

He beamed at Kenn for that, but before he could say anything in reply, a shadow fell over them.

Kenn glanced up and tensed immediately, his mouth going tight. "Dammit."

"You always did have a filthy mouth on you." Kenn's ex Bram stared down his nose at Kenn. He looked like he was smelling a skunk or something.

Dave couldn't believe it. The guy had a fucking restraining order against him, and here he was—again—harassing Kenn. Dave stood and grabbed his phone to document this. That way it wouldn't be their word against Bram's.

"Call 911," he told Kenn as he began to take pictures, proving that Bram was breaking the law because there he was, right next to Kenn.

Kenn pulled out his phone without any hesitation, making Dave want to cheer. This was so much stronger a response than running away had been. This was telling Bram he wasn't going to be able to get away with trying to intimidate Kenn anymore.

"Don't you dare, Kenneth." Bram's words were little more than a snarl, the threat behind them clear.

Dave flipped his phone to video and started taping. If this asshole threatened Kenneth again, he was getting it on tape. That was more than just breaking the restraining order.

"The cops will be here five minutes after Kenn makes the call," Dave said. "I think you should leave before this gets any uglier." He nodded at his lover. "Make the call, Kenn."

"I'm on it." Kenn hit 9-1-1 on his phone and put it to his ear. "Go away, Bram. You're not welcome here."

"I have more right than you to be here. You're a filthy, dirty boy who doesn't deserve to be sitting in a nice restaurant like this."

Oh, Dave was going to beat Bram until he begged for mercy. This guy didn't care for Kenn. Not for a second. He wondered if Bram ever had. He'd used Kenn during their marriage, taking what he needed without thought. And when Kenn hadn't lived up to his expectations in the bedroom, had gone off the script, Bran had turned on him. Well, no more. No more.

"Hello, yes. I have a restraining order on my ex-husband, and he's in the restaurant threatening me." Kenn's voice didn't even shake.

Dave was so proud of Kenn. So proud.

"You little asshole! How dare you!" The snarl was gone; this was full-blown yelling. Hell, Bram was almost spitting.

Dave growled, "Get out of here," because he was ready to do something he was going to regret later, the anger riding him. The need to protect Kenn, even from nasty words, was so damn strong. Of course, hitting Bram would only get him in trouble, because he was sure Bram would press charges.

Kenn stood up, grabbed a glass, and flung its contents in Bram's face. "Leave. Me. Alone."

"You tell him, Kenn." Dave didn't have to protect Kenn—Kenn was clearly more than capable of protecting himself. So fucking proud. He wanted to cheer and clap his hands but figured that would only add fuel to the fire.

"You piece of trash!" Bram reached for Kenn, face twisted with anger, but Kenn stepped back out of the way.

The manager came up to them along with their server, and Dave moved to stand next to Kenn, offering his lover all his support.

The manager turned to Bram. "I'm sorry, sir, but you're going to have to go."

"Me? This is the filthy low-life you should be kicking out." Bram pointed aggressively at Kenn.

The manager seemed unfazed. "Please, sir. You're disrupting our guests, and if you don't go, we'll be forced to call the police."

"Already done," Kenn said, voice cold. Dave put his hand on Kenn's shoulder and squeezed.

"Then you can wait in the lobby. Dr. Brannigan is a regular here." The manager made shooing motions.

Bram's nostrils flared, and for a moment Dave thought he was going to hit the manager. Bram didn't, though. Instead, he spat at Kenn's feet and turned, heading toward the exit just as two uniformed officers came in the door.

Kenn sat hard, his face bright red, tears in his eyes. Dave stepped behind him and put his hands on Kenn's shoulders, squeezing. He offered his support, but he knew Kenn was strong enough to deal with this. And now Kenn knew it too.

The next few moments were a flurry of police and people and questions, and Dave was relieved and pleased when the handcuffs finally went around Bram's wrists. The man was being arrested for violating his restraining order. Dave knew it was a hollow victory. Unless Bram actually hurt Kenn, this would be a slap on the wrists, and he'd be out in the morning. Still, this was the first time Kenn had not only stood up to Bram, but there had been follow-through. Dave was totally taking it as a victory for Kenn.

The manager came up to them after Bram was taken away, the restaurant finally calming again. "Would you like another mimosa, Dr. Brannigan?"

"Please. Thank you." Kenn hadn't even needed to clear his throat.

Dave pulled his chair over so he could sit closer to Kenn. He took his lover's hand. "You are the strongest man I know." He was proud and impressed and so pleased Kenn was facing his demons, having them arrested.

Kenn met his gaze. "I'm trying. I'm trying to be strong enough to be yours."

"I think you've got it backward, babe. I think I need to be strong enough to have you." He wasn't blowing smoke up Kenn's ass, either. He truly meant it. Kenn was already amazing. Him knowing his own strength, his courage, and his confidence was only increasing that.

Kenn leaned over and kissed him. "You think so?"

"I do." He held Kenn's gaze so Kenn could read how serious he was.

A man cleared his throat, and he and Kenn turned together to find Detective Simmons standing there.

"I'm sorry to interrupt, but when you're finished here, I'll need you to come down to the station and give us a statement. I know he's violated the order in the past, but as this is the first time you've reported it while he's still in violation, it's important we get it all in the file."

Dave squeezed Kenn's hand. "We can do that. And I've got pictures and video on my phone of what happened."

"If you can send that to me, that would be great." Simmons handed Dave his card. "Email is on there."

Kenn spoke up before Dave could reply. "Of course. Yes. Right now we want to make sure this man is kept away from my partner."

There was his boy, looking out for *him*. Kenn was something special. Very special. Not that this was news to Dave, but Kenn kept proving it.

"He'll be spending the day in jail, Mr. Brannigan."

"Doctor," Kenn corrected.

"I beg your pardon?"

"It's Dr. Brannigan." Listen to his boy—listen to that confidence, that happiness.

Simmons responded to it too. "I'm sorry, of course. I'll see you shortly at the station."

With Simmons's departure, the last of the hullabaloo finally died down, and the manager brought them each another mimosa.

"Your brunch is on the house today," he told them—told Kenn, really.

Dave thought that was generous, considering that it hadn't been the restaurant's fault Kenn's ex had shown up and caused a scene.

"Oh. Oh, that's awfully kind." Kenn stood and shook the manager's hand. "Honestly."

The manager held Kenn's hand and patted it for a moment. "We hope you'll continue to come in on Sundays, Dr. Brannigan. We enjoy serving you."

"This is my favorite place to brunch. You'll have our business every Sunday," Kenn promised.

"That's wonderful to hear. Please stay as long as you like, and we'll see you again next week." The manager let go of Kenn's hand and headed off.

"That was nice of him," Dave noted. Then he smiled. "You have that effect on a lot of people."

"Thank you." Kenn leaned over and kissed him, the touch gentle as hell.

"It's because you're amazing. I'm so proud of how you handled the ex. That was… stunning, watching you stand up for yourself instead of fleeing."

"I'm tired of his shit." Kenn waved his hand dismissively. "I have more important things to worry about."

"Damn right." Dave thought maybe coming into his own sexually was translating in regular life, too, giving Kenn confidence in himself. He thought they went hand in hand. Or maybe Kenn had needed someone else to fight for. Someone to love. He supposed it didn't matter because no matter what the reason, Kenn was thriving.

"Do you want anything else to eat?" Dave asked. He was more than happy to enjoy a little more time relaxing with Kenn before they had to go to the police station and give their statements.

"I think I want to finish my mimosa and some of these berries. I wish we had some for the house…."

That was an easy wish to grant. "We can stop at the grocery store on our way home." He'd buy Kenn whatever berries he wanted. Hell, they could have a lot of fun with berries. His eyes went to Kenn's nipples, imagining he could see them through the blue dress shirt. They'd look neat, stained with berry juice, the golden rings shining. He'd have to make sure to clean them really well afterward, of course, but the image stayed in his mind.

Kenn stopped, his hand halfway to his mouth with a strawberry in it. "Dave…."

"What?" He didn't think stopping at the grocery store on the way home for berries was outrageous.

"You're making me hard, the way you're looking at me."

That was the best answer ever.

"My thoughts must be showing, then." He licked his lips. "I want you and berries and metal."

"No touching." Kenn licked the tip of the strawberry. Little tease. Dave loved it.

He groaned. "You're cheating, though."

"Uh-uh. Having a berry."

Was Kenn playing with him? Deliberately teasing him? He knew Kenn was. And he definitely loved it.

"You mean you're fellating that berry," he countered.

"I would never do that. Never." Those white teeth sank in, juice coloring Kenn's lips.

Dave had to groan again, his jeans becoming uncomfortably tight. Kenn was not the only one getting hard.

"I should take you home and turn your pretty ass the same color as your lips." He could play with Kenn for the rest of the day, make sure they both went to class Monday morning feeling easy in their skins and happy in their minds.

Kenn's mouth dropped open, and his cheeks went a pretty pink. "Dave!"

He smiled and nodded. Oh yeah. It was a plan.

"You need to be good," Kenn murmured. "We're having berries."

"And as I said, you fellated those berries. Now we have to stop on our way home and get more, because I have sexy ideas for them. And you. Combined."

"I was just eating them. Nom, nom, nom."

Dave laughed softly. "Tease." He downed the last of his mimosa.

"Are you ready to go home now?" Kenn sounded eager.

"Yeah. We need to stop off at the police station, then the grocery store, but yeah. I'm so ready. I have plans." He waggled his eyebrows. Kenn wasn't wearing the plug at the moment—he'd known his boy wasn't ready to go out in public with it yet—but while they were home, he was going to make Kenn wear that thing all the time. God, it was going to be sexy as hell. Soon, though, he would put the plug in on a Sunday morning, and they would come to have brunch. And he'd know, but nobody else would. They'd all just think Kenn had a sexy walk.

"Good plans?" Kenn left the waitstaff a twenty.

"Oh, the best plans." He let his thoughts come to the surface and hoped they showed in his face.

Kenn's nostrils flared. He'd definitely noticed. "Do we have to do the police? That seems like a shitty way to spend a Sunday."

"We just need to give them our statements, and then it's over. Do you really want it hanging over us for Monday?"

"No. No, although I hate losing our time."

"We will tell them that we don't have a lot of time, that we have plans." It would be a short detour. They could make sure of that. His pictures and video told the story. Which reminded him.... He grabbed the detective's card and emailed off both the pics and the video.

Kenn nodded. "Sounds good." Then Kenn hooked one arm in his, holding on.

It was going to be a wonderful afternoon, despite Kenn's ex. Maybe even because of him. Now that they both knew Kenn wasn't afraid of the man anymore, the sky was the limit.

Chapter Seventeen

Kenn headed across campus, Tim following along with him despite the fact that he was moving quickly.

"So seriously? You're like… kinky?" Tim asked.

"Shut up, Tim."

"I can't believe you hid it from me. I'm your best bud." Tim was bouncing, joyous. Evil man.

"It's not public knowledge." God, he knew better than to have showed Tim the nipple rings.

"Can I see them again?" Tim asked, looking like it wasn't a joke.

"No!"

"I'm so jealous. Are they hot?"

"Shut up!" He couldn't believe Tim was talking about this in public.

They turned the corner, their house coming into view, and Dave was there, lounging on the porch in one of the Adirondack chairs. Dave looked amazing. Handsome and wonderful. Happy. His.

Tim hurried past him, making a beeline for Kenn's lover. "Dave! O. M. G! You are amazing. Tell me you have friends!"

Kenn rolled his eyes and groaned.

One of Dave's eyebrows rose, and he turned to look at Kenn, then back at Tim. "Thank you?"

"I caught Kenn playing with his nipple ring. So hot." Tim was not going to let this go.

"It itched. Shut up, Tim."

Dave's quizzical expression cleared, leaving behind a wicked grin. "It *itched*?"

"Yes." Kenn headed inside without another word. Buttheads.

Dave and Tim followed him, and Tim was not shutting up. "I was serious, Dave. Do you have friends?"

"Of course I have friends."

"No, no, I mean, you know, kinky friends," Tim said, following him inside along with Dave. Three was a lot of people for such a small space, especially when he hadn't seen Dave since last night.

"Shut up. I'm going to take a shower. You're both fuckers." He couldn't stop laughing, though.

"Why am I getting lumped in with Tim?" Dave asked. "And I'm joining you." Dave turned back to his best friend. "Tim, we'll see you later, yeah?"

"No fair! I should get to see them again!" Tim insisted.

"No. I shouldn't have shown you in the first place." He should have let Tim wonder. Although he knew Tim, and that would have resulted in a different sort of bugging him until he finally gave in and showed them. "Now go away so I can shower, please."

Tim pouted exaggeratedly, making him laugh some more. Only then did Tim head back to his apartment, closing the door behind him, leaving them on their own.

"Asshole. How was your day?" He really couldn't be too mad at Tim, right? The man was incorrigible. And his best friend. And wouldn't hurt him for the world.

"It was good. The students in today's class are really into it, and we had a great discussion." Dave went into the bathroom with Kenn. "You look like you had a good day."

"I did. It wasn't bad at all." In fact, it had been pretty damn good.

"I like to hear that." Dave tilted his head. "No photos from the ex?"

"Nope. Nothing all week." Which was a little surprising, as he'd thought getting Bram arrested might have had him stepping up the stalkerish behavior, but maybe it had had the opposite effect, making Bram back off.

"Let's hope that continues to be the case."

Kenn shrugged. "That'd be great, but if he starts up again, that's his problem. I'm done letting his actions affect me one way or the other. I don't want to waste another second of our time with you giving him a single thought."

"That's the ticket—good for you." Dave held his hands out, eyes warm as they looked at him. And just like that, Bram disappeared from his thoughts, and it was simply him and Dave.

Kenn went right to Dave, pushing in close. "Hey."

"Hey." Dave dropped down, bringing their mouths together, the kiss soft but thorough. Kenn let himself melt into Dave, low cries buzzing between them. Dave pulled him close, his chest and his nipple rings rubbing on Dave's shirt. God, they ached. Itched. He needed to touch them again, stroke them.

What the hell? Why was he so damned horny today?

Dave hummed, fingers sliding between them to tug gently at the rings. Fuck. Fuck, they ached.

"Please... I'm going crazy." He couldn't think, so he offered it to Dave.

"You need to come, boy? Have the piercings got you all hot and bothered?" Dave asked, like he knew.

"Yes. This is your fault. You have me needing all the time." He wasn't even sure it was a bad thing. Actually, he was pretty sure it wasn't.

"I'll take the blame for that, and I don't think it's a bad thing." It was like Dave had read his thoughts. Dave pressed kisses across his face. It was tender and sweet, but with a promise of something further. "Are you going to beg me for more?"

"Jewelry? No."

"You sound so sure. A ladder here would be endlessly fascinating." Dave slid a finger along the backside of his cock.

"No...." He shook his head, the thought making him dizzy. He couldn't bear it.

"We'll talk about it again," Dave promised. "After the existing ones are all healed." Dave began to strip him down, bare him like it was Dave's right. "I can't wait until they're healed enough to play rough, to use chains with them. God, you're so fucking stunning you make me ache. We're going to play tonight, boy. We're going to make ourselves fly."

The things Dave said always excited him so. The fact that Dave followed his words with actions made him soar.

"In the shower. We'll clean you up, and then we'll play."

He loved the happy note in Dave's voice. "What about supper, Dave?" Love.

"I'll feed you. Once you're boneless and entirely relaxed." The look on Dave's face was wicked.

Kenn was so ready for this. He'd been ready for Friday since Monday morning. He felt like a bit of an addict, but he couldn't see that it was wrong. He and Dave weren't hurting anyone. And he'd never been so happy.

Dave pointed to the shower, and he went, stepping into the spray that was the perfect temperature for him. Dave always paid attention to the little details. It made him feel special. Loved. Like he was important.

Dave stripped quickly, Kenn watching every movement, every bit of flesh as it was revealed, and stepped in behind him, warm and solid. Slow touches moved along his arms, Dave sliding his fingers on Kenn's skin.

Kenn snuggled back in, a happy sigh escaping him.

"God, I love that," Dave murmured.

"What?" Kenn asked.

"Your relaxation. Your happiness. They're the best things." Dave traced his abs.

"You make me happy." It was that simple, really.

"And you make me happy." Dave laughed softly. "We're sappy, boy."

"Is that so bad? Really?"

"No, it isn't bad at all." Dave kissed the top of Kenn's head, then turned him and covered his face with little touches of Dave's lips.

"Good. I want to…." He took his courage in his hands and said it like it was. "I want to be yours, you know?"

"Ditto. I have you, and you have me. Which is corny as hell, but wonderful and amazing."

"Um-hum." He licked a line around Dave's ear. He wanted to make Dave as crazy as he was.

"Oh, that's nice." Dave tilted his head, giving Kenn more room, offering him more skin.

Good. He licked and nuzzled, daring to nibble a little, gently scraping his teeth along Dave's skin.

"You're hungry," Dave noted.

"All day." He'd admitted the same.

"I love being the object of your hunger."

"Can we… play this weekend?" he asked, going for broke.

A wonderful smile bloomed across Dave's face. "I would love that. And I love that you asked. That makes me happy."

Oh. Oh thank goodness. He had to beam, because he was so pleased, so honored.

Dave soaped up his hands and ran them over Kenn's body, slick and easy. "You have any requests or desires? Anything specific you want to do?"

"I want to know what it's like to let you have your way, Dave." That was the point, right? To give up control?

Dave licked his lips and hummed softly. "I have so many ideas, boy. So very many."

"We have two nights, two days." Weekends had always been good, now they were going to be bright jewels in his week.

"I know. I'll pick one or two things and save the rest for another time. And the time after that, and the time after that. Ad infinitum."

"That sounds amazing.... Sir." He leaned in for another kiss.

Dave moaned into his mouth, filling him with that sound of pleasure. He whimpered deep in his chest, allowing himself to lean into Dave, trust in him.

Dave slid his hands over Kenn, helping to rinse the soap from his skin. Every touch was electric.

"What happens next, love?" He wanted to learn everything.

"When we're finished in the shower, I'm going to bind your hands to the headboard and your feet to the baseboard. And I'm going to have my wicked way with you."

That sounded erotic as hell. "Are you?" he asked, looking up at Dave through his eyelashes, flirting.

"I am. I'm going to make us both fly, make you feel amazing. We're both going to feel amazing."

He thought he could manage amazing. "Yes, please. I'm all in."

"Yeah? You like the idea of amazing, huh?" Dave hugged him tight.

"I do. I like the idea of... letting go." It was suiting him so far.

"You know, the first day I saw you, I thought that might be exactly what you needed."

"Why? Did I look odd?" Had he been projecting? He'd thought he was sick, that there was something wrong with him.

"No, not at all. You looked like you needed, though. And I remember thinking I could turn you upside down and inside out." Dave cupped his ass, squeezed hard.

That made him ache, and he liked it.

"Bed, boy. Let's go." Dave swatted his ass gently.

"Pushy, pushy," he teased. He loved it, though, the need that showed through Dave's words and his actions.

"Yeah, it's kind of in the job description."

"Good to know." He cupped Dave's jaw. "I like it."

Dave turned his head, lips sliding along Kenn's palm. Dave licked him, tickling and turning him on all at the same time. There was a look in Dave's eyes, hot and masterful. Like Dave was going to give him exactly what he needed. Kenn could admit that he more than liked it. He was pretty sure he craved it.

He turned off the water, and Dave grabbed the towels, wrapping them close together.

"You know what I've always thought would be neat?" Dave asked as he began patting Kenn's back with the towel. "To have an air dryer in the bathroom. Something where you just stand there and it blows hot air on you. Gently, you know."

"Oh, wouldn't that be wonderful? I'm thinking about buying a towel warmer." Because that would make this even better.

"That would be the second-best thing. We should put it on a list. Our dream house and the things we'd like in it. Full-body air dryer."

He chuckled softly, but nodded, willing to play along. The idea of them having a house together felt intoxicating. "A puppy."

"You're a dog person—I can see that. What kind?" Dave rubbed his front gently with the softest of the towels he had.

"One that needs a home, hmm?" He groaned when Dave stroked his nipples.

"I like your style. We'll go to the pound together and find our dog." Dave ran the towel back across his nipples again.

"Don't. They ache." It was so good. He'd never felt anything like it.

"I imagine it'll take a while before you need a good hard tug to make them ache. For now, just the rings being there is enough, isn't it? That's why you were touching earlier—you couldn't resist." Dave was reading his mind again.

"They itched." And he wanted. So badly. He couldn't wait for Dave to touch them, skin on skin.

"Uh-huh. I'll put some antibiotic cream on them once I've played for a while." Dave leaned down and blew against his ringed flesh.

"A-after?" He arched up, his hips trying to drive his ringed cock against Dave's body.

"Yeah, after I drive you crazy." Dave held him away, fingers wrapped tight around his waist. "I'm driving this bus, boy."

Oh sweet fuck. "Yes, Sir."

Dave hummed and nodded, rubbing circles with his thumbs along Kenn's hips. "I do love the way that sounds. I'm the luckiest man in the world to have you be mine."

There didn't seem to be any reason to pretend he didn't know what they were doing. Especially as he not only wanted it, he'd admitted as much. To Dave, to himself.

Dave continued to dry him, touching his PA and the guiche, but with the towel, so they were simply gentle brushes with the terrycloth. Enough to stimulate, but not to really give him what he needed, which was Dave's actual touch. The sensation of the terrycloth against his skin was almost too rough, too intense. Like Dave's gaze, which never left him. It made him feel like the center of the universe.

It made him feel like he could ask for what he needed. "Bed? Please, Sir? Now?"

"My eager boy." Dave put the towels over the rack, then turned and picked him up, hands beneath his ass as his feet left the ground. Dave carried him out to the bed.

"Dave!" He cracked up, the world spinning around them.

"God, I love that sound." Dave spun around in place a time or two, then put him down on the bed and moved his arms and legs so that they were spread out. Kenn felt exposed, vulnerable, and his cock was hard as nails.

Dave stared down at him for a long time, his cock pointing at Kenn as Dave took him all in. All of him. There wasn't a part of him that didn't feel that virtual touch. His nipples throbbed like they were trying to get Dave's attention. It seemed to take forever, though, Dave watching him, looking at him, but not putting hands on him. At the same time, it seemed like Dave was fucking him with his eyes.

"What do you want me to do?" He felt weird lying there, spread open, exposed.

"I've brought some rope, and I'm going to tie you to the bed, spread eagle like that. You'll be able to squirm and pull and fight the ropes as much as you want. As much as you need to."

"You keep bringing pieces over, you'll be living here soon."

"I like the way that sounds." Dave went over to his bag and pulled out some lengths of rope. They were red. Dave put them on Kenn's belly, and they were softer than he'd expected and so dark against his skin.

"I do too." Maybe they could join forces, get the larger apartment here. They'd fit nicely in the bigger place, and the current tenants were moving out at the end of the month.

Dave picked up one of the ropes and wrapped it around Kenn's right wrist, then tied the other end of the rope to the headboard. "The beginning of a new semester seems like a good time to move."

"Does… does it?" He watched Dave's hands, excitement building from what Dave was doing, and from what they were talking about. "There's a bigger apartment here, you know? It'll be vacant soon. We could rent it."

Dave stilled, then grabbed another rope and began to tie his other wrist up. "A place that's ours. I really like the sound of that."

"I do too. Our home. Together." It felt so right.

"Let's do it. I want to come home to you every day."

"Okay. I'll call the landlord. Later." Much later. Possibly Monday.

"Put it on your mental to-do list because at the moment you're otherwise occupied." Dave finished tying his other wrist to the headboard, then grabbed the remaining two ropes from his belly and headed to the foot of the bed.

"Mental to-do list…." His belly rippled as he tugged his hands, more focused on that now than their conversation.

"Uh-huh. And now you forget all about to-do lists. The only thing you need to be focused on is us." Dave slapped the ropes against his right foot.

Kenn pulled his foot away, knee drawing up. Dave reached up and grabbed his foot, tugged it back down. After wrapping the rope around his ankle, Dave bound his left foot to the corresponding bedpost.

"Oh." Oh, that was nothing like he'd ever felt before. Then his right foot was tied in the same manner.

"How does it feel, boy?"

"Strange. Exciting."

"Those are good words for an exploration." Dave ran his fingers along Kenn's sole.

Kenn's toes curled tight-tight, and he tried to pull away, but he couldn't.

Dave's grin was wicked as hell and slightly smug. "See? You can squirm and pull as much as you want. You're stuck right where you are."

"It's a little unnerving, huh?" A little scary.

"That's part of the appeal, isn't it? Having your boundaries pushed and feeling a little uncomfortable, but trusting me to see you through it."

"I don't know. I guess so. I do trust you." He wanted to trust Dave.

"And you have your safeword. It's going to be wonderful, I promise." Dave took his big toe between two fingers and pinched. It wasn't a hard pinch, but it was unexpected, making him gasp. Dave smiled and bent to kiss it before running his cheek along the curve of his arch. He groaned softly, the sensation so different, so interesting.

Dave continued to kiss his foot. Soft and light, occasionally kneading harder with his fingers. It was erotic as hell, and all Dave had done was play with his feet!

Kenn melted, moaning softly as Dave touched him.

"Has anyone ever loved on your feet?" Dave asked, him, fingers continuing to slide along his feet.

"No. I told you, things before were strictly blow jobs and missionary. Once a week."

"Thank God we found each other—you were meant to be loved on, to be pushed and made to feel like the center of the universe. I am going to love on every inch of your body before I untie you."

"Every inch?" Kenn laughed softly. "And it's only Friday."

"Every inch. Because I have something else planned for tomorrow." Dave looked happy and wicked and full of love.

"Oh...." His head spun from the rush.

"Look at you." Dave reached up and ran a single finger along the length of his cock, tapping his slit and nudging the ring at the end of the motion.

Kenn's lips dropped open, and he bucked hard. That was wild, bright. "Fuck!"

"I love that. I love your filthy mouth."

No one had ever said that to him before. In fact, Bram had given him the silent treatment more than once for swearing. There was freedom in Dave's words.

"Fuck me," he tried.

Dave grinned. "Still love that filthy mouth, but that doesn't mean you're setting the agenda here. Touching you everywhere, remember?"

"Everywhere." His hole was somewhere, surely.

"Yep. I'm starting at your extremities." Dave tickled the soles of his feet, stretching his arms wide to reach them both at the same time. "And working my way inward."

"No tickling!" He laughed, head tossing.

"There should absolutely be tickling! Your laughter is joy made sound, and I'm not going to deprive either of us of it." Dave tickled once more.

"So mean to me!" He rolled, then gasped as Dave covered him with that sweet, strong body. Dave pressed into him and rolled, sliding their hard cocks together.

"I should always be this mean, shouldn't I?"

"Yes, love. Oh, you feel so good."

"So do you." Dave continued to roll them together. "You want to know what one of the best things about being your Dom is?"

"Yes." He wanted to know everything. Always.

"I can change my mind halfway through." Dave pressed a kiss on him. "Because I am totally making love to you right now."

"You can touch me everywhere after." He grabbed the ropes and began to rock.

"I totally can. After I feed you. You ever been fed while you were tied up?" Dave asked, meeting his motions, their bodies gliding and bumping.

"Never been tied up, Sir."

"That's what I figured. I wanted to put the idea in your head, though." Dave kissed each side of his mouth, then the middle. "And to make sure you know that I am going to take care of you. That I will make sure you get what you need."

A long caress against his side made him shiver.

"You make me dizzy."

"Then it's a good thing you're lying down." Dave reached over to the side table, and the next thing Kenn knew, two slippery fingers pushed into his body.

He tried to move, but there was only so far he could go.

"You have to let me have control." Dave rubbed a cheek against his left nipple, pressing and moving the ring inside his flesh. "All you can do is lie back and take it."

"I'm trying." He hadn't thought it would be hard, but it was, even though he trusted Dave.

"I know. The fight is a part of it, you know? Which is why it's nice for you to be able to pull and tug and try to move without getting anywhere." Dave rubbed his cheek along Kenn's other nipple.

He cried out, bucking as best he could. Dave hummed and pushed his fingers deeper, hitting Kenn's gland. He bucked again, twisting and trying to get more sensation. Dave kept working him at his own pace, though, and Kenn had to take it. He did.

Dave continued to work him, opening him up before sliding the thick cock into him, joining them at the root. All the while Dave held his gaze, keeping them connected there too.

He kept trying to reach for Dave, to wrap his lover in his arms, but the ropes stopped him, holding him spread wide and open for Dave. Finally, he relaxed back into the ropes, letting them hold him as Dave fucked him.

Kissing him deeply, Dave filled him with breath, with heat, with the essence of Dave. Whimpering, he kissed Dave back, their tongues sliding together. Dave sucked on the tip of his tongue, then bit gently, and he arched, his entire body going stiff as he came. Dave filled him with heat and collapsed on top of him.

They lay there, the ropes supporting him, his body cradling Dave's. He couldn't ask for anything more.

"Love you," Dave whispered.

"I love you too." He did. And he couldn't wait for what Dave taught him next about his desires.

Epilogue

"Kenneth? Kenn? Dr. Brannigan!"

Kenn stopped and turned, grinning at his best friend, Tim. His mind had been on Dave and the puppy, who were waiting for him to get home to go for a nice long wander.

"Your head is always in the clouds. At least you weren't texting this time."

"I don't text and walk—I read and walk. It's much safer."

Tim laughed, and they fell into step together.

"Are you and Dave coming to the Rainbow Mixer tonight?"

"Of course." It was where he and Dave had met, after all. He couldn't believe it had been a year already. A year filled with wonders and new things. A year filled with love.

"Did you tell Dave he has to bring a bunch of his kinky friends so I can have someone to go home with?"

"I didn't." Kenn knew that Tim would find someone. He was a good guy.

"Damn. I guess I'm going to have to do it the old-fashioned way, huh?"

"Yep." He laughed as he saw Dave and Rope, their huge mutt of a puppy, coming toward them, Rope's ears flopping as he loped along. God, he loved them.

Everything else faded away as the world narrowed to Dave. This was his life, and everything else was simply details.

Often referred to as "Space Cowboy" and "Gangsta of Love" while still striving for the moniker of "Maurice," SEAN MICHAEL spends his days surfing, smutting, organizing his immense gourd collection and fantasizing about one day retiring on a small secluded island peopled entirely by horseshoe crabs. While collecting vast amounts of vintage gay pulp novels and mood rings, Sean whiles away the hours between dropping the f-bomb and pursuing the *Kama Sutra* by channeling the long-lost spirit of John Wayne and singing along with the soundtrack to *Chicago*.

A longtime writer of complicated haiku, currently Sean is attempting to learn the advanced arts of plate spinning and soap carving sex toys. Barring any of that? He'll stick with writing his stories, thanks, and rubbing pretty bodies together to see if they spark.

Website: www.seanmichaelwrites.com
Blog: seanmichaelwrites.blogspot.ca
Facebook: www.facebook.com/SeanMichaelWrites
Twitter: @seanmichael09

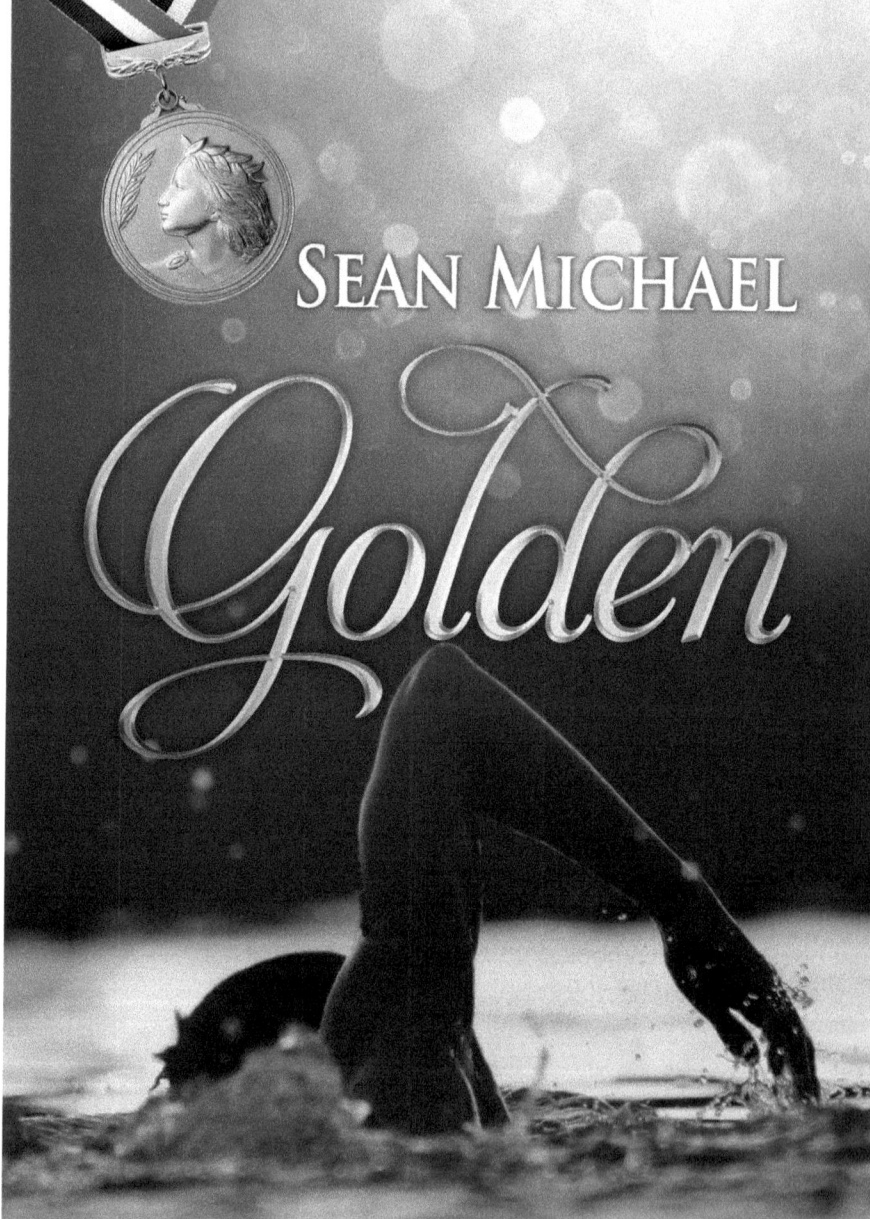

After winning Olympic gold four years ago, Justin retired from swimming, and he's been floundering ever since. The Fourth of July finds him contemplating doing something stupid, so Justin calls up his former coach, Chris Jarvis. To his surprise, Coach answers.

When Justin retired, Chris cut all ties with the swimmer he'd fallen in love with. He never wanted Justin to love him just because it was easy. But he's been waiting for Justin to reach out, and he'll gladly take Justin back into his life.

When he finds out Justin is drowning in a pool of self-doubt and the belief that his happy years are behind him, Chris realizes he made a mistake letting go so suddenly, and that Justin needs structure and a firm, dominant hand to keep him on the right track. It's time to remedy that error—as long as he can convince Justin that it's really love.

www.dreamspinnerpress.com

Just the Right Notes

SEAN MICHAEL

Elliot is an up-and-coming architect who just opened his own firm—which is a lot more work and pressure than he expected. His partner, Graham, is a respected composer and conductor. They share their love and lives in a beautiful house designed by Elliot, and whenever things get too hard to handle, they retreat to their cabin getaway where Elliot becomes Dom to Graham's needy little sub.

When things at Elliot's firm begin to crumble, Graham needs to be the tough one, the one to suggest the cabin and the games they play there, knowing Elliot's role as Dom will give him strength and that their games will recharge his lover. Together, they keep working to find that precarious balance in their lives—until an accident threatens to change everything. Elliot and Graham's love faces its greatest challenge yet, and only the resilience they draw from each other can see them through hardship and keep the music in their lives.

www.dreamspinnerpress.com

An Iron Eagle Gym Novel

Lance Packet just got a contract to shoot an erotic BDSM deck of cards; the only problem is finding models. So far everyone he's interviewed thinks he's looking for sex for hire. Then in walk three perfect examples of men: Tide and his friends, Tyrone and Bran.

Tide Germaine is a model and a Dom. He and his best friend Tyrone opened The Iron Eagle Gym as a place for gay men in the lifestyle to work out, do scenes, and congregate with like-minded men. The modeling is just another job for Tide, but it soon turns into a grand seduction as Tide falls for the shy, self-conscious photographer. The problem is Lance doesn't believe he's in Tide's league, and he's not at all sure about the Dom and sub thing.

It's not going to be easy, but Tide's going to have to convince Lance he belongs at Tide's side as both lover and sub.

www.dreamspinnerpress.com

Sequel to *The New Boy*
An Iron Eagle Gym Novel

While new couple Tide and Lance spend time deepening their relationship and further introducing Lance to the joys and vagaries of being a sub, established couple Tyrone and Bran discover that they still have a thing or two to learn as well.

A new job finds Bran run off his feet, and a visit to the eye doctor leads to the discovery of a brain tumor. Bran is terrified. He strives to be the perfect sub for his beautiful master and sees the tumor as a personal failing as he tries to handle every last phone call, e-mail, and text that comes in, no matter how early or late. When Tyrone finally finds out about the tumor Bran's been keeping a secret, he realizes he's been taking his sub for granted, and he works to rediscover his boy and their relationship. Of course, that's easier said than done given that Bran's job is taking up all his time and he would rather pretend the tumor just doesn't exist than actually deal with it.

It's going to take all of Tyrone's prowess as a master to help guide Bran through these troubled waters.

www.dreamspinnerpress.com

An Iron Eagle Gym Novel

When Master Damien Richardson (Day to his friends) takes over the front desk manager job at the Iron Eagle Gym, he knows he's going to need an assistant. But finding the right person for the job is harder than he thought it would be. When he meets Saw, he thinks he's found the solution to all his problems, and maybe something more.

Sawyer Whitehead lost his master to a tragic car accident some years ago, and since then one opportunity after another has gone sour on him. Thoroughly convinced he's cursed and a jinx to everything and everyone he touches, he refuses to officially become Day's assistant because he knows that as soon as he does, something terrible will happen. He's even more determined not to get involved with Day, despite his attraction, because it would kill him to be responsible for tragedy befalling the lovely man.

Day must convince Saw that he's not cursed and that together, they can face any challenge that comes their way—in both their professional and personal partnerships.

www.dreamspinnerpress.com

 FOR **MORE** OF THE **BEST GAY ROMANCE**

dreamspinnerpress.com

CPSIA information can be obtained
at www.ICGtesting.com
Printed in the USA
FSHW010237030419
56900FS

9 781640 808973